He was bent in the middle, his body half in, half out of a ceramic water trough. Naked. His head wasn't visible but I imagined it bobbing under the inky, semi-frozen water. His mottled skin held patches of dark colors I couldn't make out in the eerie illumination.

I noticed, oh my God, a wet path of blood—what else could it be?—tracing his last movements from an oil-black puddle to the container. Shocked into listlessness, I let snowflakes as large as cotton balls hit my nose and melt. In spite of the wind, I heard them land on my face, muffled pops. Lying on this vast, flat land, had he listened to similar flakes hiss as they struck his steaming blood?

"A beguiling new voice in mystery."
—Deborah Donnelly, author of *May the Best Man Die*

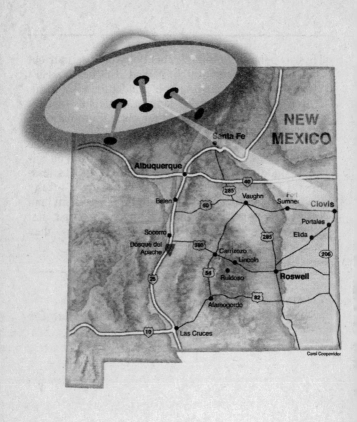

Carol Cooperrider

THE CLOVIS INCIDENT

PARI NOSKIN TAICHERT

W🌐RLDWIDE®

TORONTO • NEW YORK • LONDON
AMSTERDAM • PARIS • SYDNEY • HAMBURG
STOCKHOLM • ATHENS • TOKYO • MILAN
MADRID • WARSAW • BUDAPEST • AUCKLAND

THE CLOVIS INCIDENT

A Worldwide Mystery/July 2005

First published by University of New Mexico Press.

ISBN 0-373-26535-2

Printed in U.S.A.

To Marva, Paul, Al & Jack
Thank you.

ONE

I SHOULD'VE STAYED in bed.

Instead, at nine a.m. on a sunny Sunday morning, I went to work. By ten o'clock, I'd been fired. Meet yours truly, Sasha Solomon, *former* director of PR for "TrueHealth: *Your Alternative HMO.*"

Things didn't get better.

First, there was the stress. Other people get heartburn and take antacids. I get hallucinations. And yes, my therapist knows. In the year since reality began doing the mambo, I've been poked and prodded, my molecules knocked hither and yon. No one has an explanation for the visions. As long as I'm not too stressed out, they only show up as dopey conversations with my cat.

Which brings me back to my story.

I drove home from my erstwhile place of employment. Tears blurred my view of defunct volcanoes to the west and sacred Mount Taylor past them, as I headed into Albuquerque's once lush—but now drought-dry—valley. On Fourth Street my little Tercel zipped past a used appliance store with some of its wares on the sidewalk. Then beyond a French pastry shop in a crappy strip mall, and a razor-sharp wire fence encircling an adobe church, before turning onto Aztec. From there, it was a quick left into Cuidado Street— my duly named neck o' the woods. As I bounced up the dirt driveway to my little *casita,* I prepared for an all-out moan and groan.

Leo da Cat was at the door, tail high, claws ready, smart-aleck comment dangling from his thin black lips. His left ear bent with an old injury, giving him a cocky air of insouciance.

"You look like someone stole all your catnip," he said, his voice a dead ringer for a cabbie from the Bronx.

"Ha, ha." I fumbled for my keys.

"I mean it. You smell wrong, too. Upset." He pulled his back leg forward, prepared to lick. "Wanna talk?"

"Leo, please. Not right now."

You get the picture.

Actually, *I* knew the origin of my hallucinations but the neurologists and radiologists would never believe it. True-Health was Albuquerque's only holistic HMO. Its practitioners were the groovy set: spirit healers, energy manipulators, psychic seers. During my first week on the job, I'd visited a shaman, an acupuncturist, a pyramid healer, and a Reiki master. They'd done their voodoo-hoodoo on me and had detonated a metaphysical meltdown. The healers had their own take on my nuttiness. They said I was opening to my higher self. Yeah, right.

My gig at TrueHealth had had another lousy side effect. During the year I'd been there, I'd let all my old clients slip away. It's amazing what a regular paycheck and health insurance will do to the entrepreneurial spirit. Well, that was going to have to change, pronto.

But first, I needed to think.

After feeding Leo, I took a walk along the irrigation ditch near my house. The cottonwood trees dripped red catkins, which looked like long frilly caterpillars against the dirt and new green growth of spring. I kicked a couple of them, but didn't feel better. My swollen eyes hurt from too much crying for a job I'd planned to leave anyway. It was the firing that stung. That, and the timing.

With sore legs, I went home. Mae King had left a message

on the machine. I planned to stay at her place for the few days I'd be bidding on the Clovis Chamber of Commerce project. Mae sounded...well, a little "off," but she was crusty by nature. I returned her call and began another round of telephone tag in our years-long friendship.

Shortly before noon, I threw cold water on my face, tossed my suitcase into the car, and headed toward St. Kate's for a dreaded weekly obligation. Mom. The drive left me plenty of time to wonder what on earth to do about money. My upcoming Clovis trip had transformed from a lark—a professional adventure—to an absolute necessity.

The St. Kate's parking lot scattered the midday sun off a hundred cars. Inside the rehab hospital, Mom languished, waiting for a miracle. Room 133, at the farthest end of the brain-injury wing, lay quiet when I stopped to listen at the door.

A nurse whizzed by, then returned to say, "Your mom's in the cafeteria."

I retraced my steps through the double doors and cut across the lobby to the dining room.

No salt, no sugar, no fat. No wonder Mom's expression was sour when I walked up to the table. Paul Katz, her boyfriend, stood to welcome me and pulled out a chair. Gilda, a long-time bridge companion, also rose to say hello. Mom transferred her frown from me back to her food.

"Hannah, try a little more," said Paul when we sat down. "You can do it."

This was one of Mom's bad days. Her latest stroke ruled her, cruel and silent. She gripped the fork in a two-year-old's fist, her green beans falling off as she brought them to her mouth. Angry, Mom put the utensil down and grabbed her tuna melt. Her vise-like hands clasped it with such ferocity the contents spewed out the sides. She grunted with frustration.

"I think I'll have some lunch, too," I said, springing away from the misery.

Sandwiched between two wheelchairs in the cafeteria line, my ability to walk flaunted my wholeness, television-commercial loud. I felt uncomfortable, certain people resented me.

"Come on, I don't have all day," croaked a voice at my side.

I looked down into the eyes of Mary Stanford, another of Mom's bridge friends.

"What are you doing here?" I said.

"You look like a startled lamb, Sasha. What's gotten into you?" Mary laughed. "Your mama didn't tell you I was in here?"

"No," I said.

"Funniest thing. One morning I woke up and my legs didn't." She rolled forward a half-turn of the wheel. "Doctors don't know why. So, I got into Gimps-r-Us as fast as I could."

"Doesn't this place depress you?"

"Misery loves company," she said.

I snorted, then handed money to the cashier, who met my eyes with a glare.

"No, really," Mary said, ignoring the cashier's rudeness. "What would I do at home? Feel sorry for myself? No. This place is full of people with real troubles. It keeps me grateful."

We made our way back to Mom's table. Mary joined us without an explicit invitation.

Mother scowled at her friend and said, "Hello, Miss It-Could-Be-Worse."

"And a fine hello to you, Miss I'll-Be-as-Ornery-as-They-Let-Me," said Mary.

Five people at the table and not a peep from anyone. I resuscitated the conversation with details about the trip I'd be taking later that afternoon.

"What if something happens to me?" Mom asked plaintively.

"Why Clovis?" said Gilda.

"What if something happens to me?" Mom again.

"Friend of mine says Clovis is the only city that makes Lubbock look good," said Mary. She took a bite of enchilada.

"I know a woman who grew up there. Left thirty years ago and swears she wouldn't go back for three million dollars."

"Oh, it's not that bad. Have you ever actually been there?" I said.

"Sure. My daughter Connie lives there. Her husband works at the air force base. I'll give you her number. She'll be glad to talk to someone about something besides airplanes, cows, and Jesus."

"Why are you going, Sasha?" Mom's little-girl voice made me want to bolt from the table. "What if something happens to me?"

Oh, how I hated her strokes. Each one pulled my once fiery mother farther toward feebleness of mind and body. And even though our relationship had always had more fury than fun, I missed the intelligent, independent person she'd been. Being near her now caused me such discomfort I perpetually wanted to flee and felt doubly guilty for my response.

If I were a *good* Jew, I'd stay with Mom, comfort her, *do* for her. Taking care of the infirm was a *mitzvah*—a commandment, a good deed. And though I'd been raised nominally Jewish—Albuquerque doesn't have much of a Borscht Belt—Mom had hammered hard on the mitzvah idea. Especially when it came to doing good deeds for *her*.

After all the years she'd sacrificed for my sister and me—and never let us forget it—she now expected payback.

But I couldn't do it. Not the way she wanted.

I left as quickly as was politic, and tried Mae again from the parking lot. No answer. Well, I'd be in Clovis by eight o'clock. Whatever she wanted could wait a few hours, couldn't it?

TWO

BEFORE HITTING I-40 east out of town, I bought two sixes of Guinness—bottles, not cans—to be consumed with my hostess or left as a present. On an impulse, I veered south onto I-25, heading toward Socorro—and Mexico beyond. I had scads of time and this route was prettier than the traditional one.

Sure, if I'd gone the regular way, there'd have been the drive through the Sandias—our glorious Albuquerque-embracing mountains. But then, the landscape would have deteriorated into a giant tan matzo with only short scrubby juniper and blue-gray chamisa to punctuate the horizon. Since I figured Clovis itself would be the New Mexico version of the Texas panhandle, I wasn't in any hurry to be bored with panoramic nothingness.

On the road I felt lighter, relieved. My sense of adventure bubbled past the worries about money, the future, what I'd do for health insurance. Instead of turning off at San Antonio, I headed farther south to the *Bosque del Apache* to spend an hour looking at birds.

I parked in the nearly empty lot. Earlier in the year the *bosque* would have been bursting with Sandhill cranes, Canadian geese, rare whoopers. Today, a meager flock of bluebirds skittered, a great blue heron fished. Two pelicans stood baffled, searching for the ocean they'd lost in transit.

A single goose honked.

I turned at the sound and noticed something that didn't belong in the landscape. The image sharpened and I became aware of my heart tightening with each beat. A shape sprawled prostrate in one of the fields. I stared, disbelieving. Then squinted for a better view.

It was a small man. And with the topsy-turvy logic of a vision, he floated toward me.

Ignore it. Ignore it. Ignore it.

My mantra dissolved as he approached. Holes swelled from his stomach, crimson marks against his brown skin. The air crackled. I ran to the car, opening my purse as I tried to put distance between us. Once inside, my legs goosebumped when they touched the cold seat. My key wouldn't go into the ignition. I couldn't remember how to start the Toyota. I looked up and he hung in front of me, his face etched with confused pain.

"Help me. Please," he implored, his accented voice a whisper. He banged his fists on the windshield.

I closed my eyes against the sickening thump-thumping.

"Leave me alone. Please, please go away. Please," I said.

The thudding continued, but different now, a knocking sound with more substance.

"Ma'am, are you all right?" A uniformed park ranger peered at me, curious, analytical.

I looked past her, searching for the man. The bright sun dazzled the hills in blue and pink. Wide-eyed, I gazed at the steering wheel.

"Ma'am, are you okay? Are you able to get out of the car?"

I rolled down the window, flashed a confident smile that receded before it reached my lips.

"There's no need. I'm fine," I said.

"Please step out of the car."

I got out and blathered, "Geez, I don't know what happened. That was really weird."

The ranger stood back from me, assessing.

I shut up.

Eyes narrowed, she observed me for a few minutes, neither one of us moving other than to blink or scratch an elbow.

"Well, you look all right," she said. "Do you want to tell me what happened?"

In PR, lying is just about the most idiotic thing anyone can do. So, I don't. But telling this ranger about my hallucination would have been even worse.

"Okay. Here's what happened," I said, gritting my teeth in the half-truth. "I've been under a lot of stress lately and it's been affecting my sleep. I guess I must have conked out for a few minutes, had a bad dream." It was a small lie, but a lie nonetheless. I didn't like myself very much for doing it. "Would you mind if I went in and splashed some water on my face? I'm sure that'd help."

"Okay." She turned to escort me into the visitor center. "You want a cup of coffee or something?"

"No, thanks."

My therapist had been teaching me stress-reduction techniques. They worked when I remembered to use them. I took a couple of deep breaths.

In the bathroom, the cold water felt good, sobering. I evaluated my reflection in the scratched-up mirror. I didn't look any crazier than usual.

The ranger knocked at the door. "You okay in there?"

I opened it. "Thanks. I feel better." A quick glance at my watch. "I ought to get going."

"You sure you're okay?"

"Yeah, I'm fine."

She walked me to the car. "You know, if that was a nightmare, I sure wouldn't want to go to sleep."

"Believe me, sleep is not my friend," I said.

We waved as I pulled out of the lot. I watched her watching me until she was a speck in my rearview mirror.

No more leisurely driving. That gruesome vision was

worse than anything I'd had in half a year. I needed to get to Mae's, do some deep breathing. I needed to calm down.

But due to my impulse to see some birds, I was stuck with a longer drive—onto state road 380 to Carrizozo, north onto 54—argh! I didn't want mountains and beauty now; I wanted to be in Clovis. I wanted to drink a Guinness, to erase that poor man from my memory.

More than an hour later, I chugged into Vaughn and found highway 64 with little trouble. From there it was a straight shot east through Billy the Kid country to Fort Sumner.

Next stop, Clovis.

THREE

"NO LUCK, HUH?" The young cashier saw me punch the power button and jam the cell phone into my purse.

I shook my head.

Buzzing fluorescent lights in the Pump-n-Snak combined with the five-hour drive to further jangle my nerves—a caffeine buzz without the coffee. I'd waited close to an hour already. Mae and I had agreed to meet here when we'd last talked. Where was she?

Closing the register, the girl held out another candy bar. "This one's on me."

Across the street, trains roared in and out of town, rumbling and shaking the windows. I opened her gift, doffing it to my forehead as if toasting champagne.

She smiled. "You ever been to Clovis before?"

"Nope. Tell me about it." I wiped a dab of caramel off my lower lip. "What do you like best about living here?"

"The people are real friendly."

"I can see that."

She batted off the compliment and continued, "And everywhere you look, it's horizon."

"That's a beautiful thing to say."

"Yeah, well. The local joke here is," she imitated an old farmer with a twang, "Yep, my dog ran away last week. I watched him go for three days."

We both chuckled. Then Mae walked in. The frigid night air smacked the store's warm interior and I blinked, half-expecting to see a mini-thunderstorm right there. She was decked out in denim. I felt comforted, as always, by her presence.

Greeting me with a hug, Mae smelled of high-range dust, sage, cedar, and the coming snow. Her thick gray braid hung down her back, fastened by the kind of rubber bands newspaper carriers use.

My five-foot-four struggled to reach her shoulders. My girth, normal according to actuarial tables, transformed to flab in her shadow. On the savanna, I'd be the wildebeest, plump and juicy. Mae would be the panther, lithe and lean.

She held me at arms' length. Her strong voice quivered, "You look tired."

"Well, you look worse."

"Really?" Her green eyes flashed quick surprise. She tugged my scraggly brown ponytail but there was no mirth in the playful gesture.

Before I could ask the right question, she patted my shoulder and said, "Come on. I need to eat."

"I've already had dinner." I waved the candy wrapper, then raised a can of whipped cream, popped the lid and filled my mouth. "And dessert."

She rolled her eyes at the cashier, then walked out the door to the orange-lit parking lot. Thick clouds rushed across the broad sky, propelled by wind roaring over the plains. A heavy moistness blended with the icy air, threatening snow. Mae strode over to the biggest pickup truck I'd ever seen.

"You making a statement?" I pointed my chin toward the monster.

"You ever tried hauling a calf in a compact?" Her grin wasn't right; off by millimeters. Blasts of chilly air fought her rubber bands, freeing strands of long hair to lash against her face. She grabbed one, and holding it, said, "Follow me, if you can, in that pipsqueak car of yours."

Mae drove down Prince Street for a few minutes, then turned into a parking lot. I pulled in behind her.

The Cotton Patch featured the kind of food cardiologists wish didn't exist. I ordered chicken fried steak, fried okra, mashed potatoes, and biscuits and gravy. Mae got the two-inch-thick pork chops with applesauce, buttered broccoli on the side. Her manner was guarded, a complete turnabout from the friend I knew.

"What's going on, Mae?" I stabbed a piece of okra.

"What're you talking about?" She stared at her brimming plate, then looked up. Irritation pulled at her lips, creating a row of fine wrinkles. "Sasha, why didn't you call me back?"

"I did. I left two messages."

"When?"

"Before and after lunch," I said. "What's going on?"

"What do you mean 'what's going on?'"

"Hey, Mae. Remember me?" I pointed at myself. "Your drinking buddy?"

"I'm sorry," she said. "This is a really bad time for me."

"Can I help?"

Mae shook her head and cut into one of her chops.

Food and booze had accompanied our friendship for more than sixteen years. We'd met at a professional writers' conference. Our whispered comments at the rubber-chicken awards dinner garnered glances from the other diners at our table. The bar beckoned and we succumbed. Our war stories weaved through shots of scotch. Mine were about clients. Hers centered on the editors she worked for as a journalist in Jal, Roswell, and finally, Clovis.

A fall-spring friendship bloomed; Mae had thirty years on me. Our lives were a study in differences. She'd been married, had kids, lived in the middle of nowhere, hung out with cows. I relished my singleness, eschewed children, lived in a big city—by New Mexican standards—and knew less than nothing about livestock.

Across from me now, Mae cut each piece of meat with a precision born of royalty. I watched her hands, freckled with age and sun damage, her fingers slender but strong.

"Well," she said. "Excuse me a sec, will you?"

I followed her with my eyes, thinking about how sixteen years could pass in a sigh. At first, Mae hadn't opened up about her personal life. It took a few years before I learned her husband, Damon, owned one of the biggest dairy farms in the state. When he died four years ago, Mae had inherited a multimillion-dollar concern and didn't know squat about the business. She fell hard in her grief, then got up, dusted off her jeans and started milking those cows.

My memories vanished with the sound of a dropped dish nearby. I resumed gobbling my artery-clogging dinner, savoring the sodium and butter. Around me, families, young mothers, and grandparents, laughed and ate. The place vibrated with wholesomeness; I'd entered a time warp, a 1950s twilight zone where people knew their neighbors, kids minded their parents, and the U.S. reigned as the mightiest country in the world.

I opened *Clovis Magazine,* a propaganda piece I'd picked up at the restaurant's entrance. On page two was a four-color ad for a Baptist church. Next page, another church. And another. No doubt about it. I was in Bible Belt country.

A man clapped his hands to get everyone's attention. I stopped my reading to watch the action.

"See this pretty little gal here?" he said. A teenager dressed in green turned fuchsia as he spoke. "Well, she's kind of shy. But today's her birthday. How about we all sing her a song? Her name's Kaylee."

The poor thing withered with embarrassment but we sang anyway. Her family clapped. We all clapped. And if she ever left Clovis, she'd be in therapy for years.

Mae returned to the table, muttering. "I got you a room at the Roadrunner Motel," she said. "It's clean."

"You still haven't told me what's wrong. Maybe I can help."

She gave me the kind of frown I associate with tough women, a no-nonsense turn of the lips, a flintiness to the eyes hinting at so much they'll never reveal.

"Kiddo, if I could tell you, believe me I would," Mae said. "Let's finish dinner, I've got a fifth in the truck."

We left the restaurant and headed for the motel.

A smoky cigarette fog hung in the small lobby, out-hazing a Parisian café. I requested a no-smoking room. The night clerk reached for a key, oblivious to the befouled air enshrouding her. I escaped into the frosty night, gasping for breath and thankful for train fumes and the faint odor of cows.

Sure enough, my room was clean, the bed comfortable. Mae entered with a bottle of Glenlivet and a bag of potato chips.

"Not bad," I said, unwrapping a plastic cup. "Do we need ice?"

"Why ruin a good thing?" She poured generous shots, stopped, and poured some more. "Sasha, can you promise to keep a secret?"

"You know me well enough for that," I said. "Of course I can."

"Even if it puts you on the wrong side of the law?"

Uh-oh. I drank.

FOUR

THE SKY WAS a dirty brown mess, ugly as raw wool from a newly sheared sheep. Far from city lights the night glowed with a bitter storm up high. Snow came down in spurts, not sticking anywhere. The luxurious truck glided warm and smooth though we'd long abandoned paved roads. We stopped.

Mae got out, walking mannequin stiff, unnatural as hell. I wondered why she'd left her door open, the lights on. I got out, too. My feet crunched on pieces of something. What were peanut shells doing in the middle of nowhere?

Big shapes huddled on the ground beyond the glare of the brilliant beams. Cows.

My friend's green eyes phosphoresced as they found mine, daring me to speak. I hugged myself against the wide-open cold and searched for whatever she needed me to see. Then found it. I turned away, my moving but silent lips beseeching her for answers. She shook her head.

I swayed, trying to avoid what I couldn't deny. Ignoble death had flung a small-framed man into this rough, dark night. The car lights stabbed the dark like moonbeams. He was bent in the middle, his body half in, half out of a ceramic water trough. Naked. His head wasn't visible but I imagined it bobbing under the inky, semi-frozen water. His mottled skin held patches of dark colors I couldn't make out in the eerie illumination.

I noticed, oh my God, a wet path of blood—what else could it be?—tracing his last movements from an oil-black puddle to the container. Shocked into listlessness, I let snowflakes as large as cotton balls hit my nose and melt. In spite of the wind, I heard them land on my face, muffled pops. Lying on this vast, flat land, had he listened to similar flakes hiss as they struck his steaming blood?

My legs buckled. I sank to the ground. Sharp rocks pressed into my flesh but couldn't distract me enough.

"How did this happen? What—" I said.

"I don't know," said Mae, her voice hard. "I've got a dead man on my property, Sasha. I don't know who he is. Where he came from. Nothing. Not a damn thing."

"I can't believe the police left him here like this," I said.

She didn't answer, just shook her head again.

Wrong side of the law.

"The police don't know? You didn't call them? What on earth are you thinking?" I tried to stand, to confront her, but couldn't move.

"Look at what he's holding." She pointed.

I refused to go closer to him.

"Go on," she said. "Look."

"Mae, I can't." I inched backward on my butt, held my knees close to my chest, and sought to cradle myself against the ghastliness a few feet away. "You've got to call the police."

"The man's clutching one of my nightgowns. He's got my latest diary in his other hand. How the hell did he get them?" She spat. "I've never seen this man in my life."

"You can't leave him here, Mae. You've got to call the police." I rose with the effort of true shock and staggered back to her pickup truck, shivering.

Mae got there first and started the heater, doors wide open. I hoisted myself into its huge cabin, using a knee to reach the step. I sat for a moment, closed the door, then opened it again to throw up.

We drove back to the hotel without speaking. My shakes

wouldn't go away. Once back in the warm, impersonal room, Mae got our plastic glasses and filled them with scotch. She shoved one into my trembling hand. I gulped it down hoping the booze would erase the image of the dead man.

"How's the job?" Mae's voice punctured the uneasy silence. She twisted the plain gold band on her third finger, unwilling to make eye contact.

"I got fired." The answer was automatic, no thought involved.

"Really? How come?"

"My boss thought I wasn't, quote, 'giving it my all.' He had some stupid idea that I was angry about something and it was affecting my attitude. I—" I realized what she was doing. "Mae, you know you've got to call the police."

She rubbed her eyes, looking old to me for the first time in all the years I'd known her.

"I'll call them tomorrow. I need time to think about it, that's all." She took a slug of the amber liquid. "I've been a reporter long enough to know that when I make that call, my life's gonna change."

"Why?" I knelt before her, forcing her to look at me. "You can't think the police are going to blame you. How could they?"

"I said I'd call them. Let's talk about something else."

"You think they're stupid?" I said. "So what? He has some of your stuff. That doesn't mean you're a suspect. Let the pros figure it out. It's not up to you."

"Sasha, let it drop."

"I can't, Mae." I grabbed a handful of potato chips, sucked the whipped cream nipple like a baby. "When did you find him?"

"This morning."

"That's hours ago. The police are going to have a fit."

"Sasha, I'm warning you."

"What's that supposed to mean?" I said. "Mae, if you're not going to look after yourself, I will."

I went to my purse, pulled out the cell phone. Mae lunged

and knocked it out of my hand. The little phone flew across the room, hit a wall, and the plastic cover cracked. The case opened, leaking batteries and wires. The pathetic piece of machinery was broken for good this time.

"Great move, Mae. Really smart," I said.

Then she did something I'd never seen before. She cried. Not noisy tears for show, but quiet ones, copious and horrible to behold. I went to her.

"It's gonna be okay," I said, hugging her wiry body. "I promise."

"You don't know what you're talking about," she said without rancor.

"I've worked with the police before. They're out to get the bad guys, Mae. You've done nothing wrong." My second lie. The police would be plenty pissed about her not calling them.

"A dead man on my property is only the tip of the iceberg, Sasha. I've got bigger problems than that."

I sat back on my haunches to take all of her in, to see her face, body movements. I wanted to get a clue about what she was talking about.

"You asked me what was the matter at the restaurant," she said.

I waited.

She squeezed her cup until it snapped. We watched it fall out of her hands and land on the floor with a single bounce.

"Mae, are you having financial troubles?"

"Honestly, you worried about my finances, that rates right up there with a hawk worried about humane hunting." She guffawed, the edge of hysteria too loud for the small room. It wasn't that funny, but she snorted again, face red.

"Okay, I'm way off base. So, what is it?" I said.

"Honey, you wouldn't understand."

"Try me."

"You know those people down in Roswell?" She got another cup, filled it halfway from the bottle. "The ones who spout that crap about space aliens?"

"What does that have to do with anything?"

"Humor me," she said. "Do you believe there's life on other planets?"

"I don't know what I think. Given my delightful hallucinations, I—" *The man at the bosque, the man in the cattle trough. Oh no.* I drank my liquor like it was medicine, then poured myself more.

Mae didn't notice my consternation at the dawning realization. She was humming. At first I didn't recognize the melody but after a second I pinned it as the first few notes from the *X-Files*.

I shook my head back and forth, back and forth, trying to pry loose the suspicion that I'd seen the dead man in my hallucination and what that meant.

"Mae, why are you singing that?"

She wore an almost-smile, her eyes intent, willing me to understand, to get the hint.

"You've got to be kidding," I said.

We studied each other. During the last few minutes, she'd become more solid, as if she was ready for me to try to push her down and had centered her stance.

"You can't be serious. You?" This was all too much. I wanted her gone. I wanted to call the police, let them take care of things. I wanted to do some to-my-toes deep breathing.

"Yep. And you'd better keep this quiet." Mae wiped her nose with the back of her hand, rolled her shoulders to release tension. "During the last couple of months, they've taken me for at least five rides in their saucer. Bumpy as all get-out, cold, brighter than the Second Coming." She tossed back the last of her drink. "Either I'm going crazy or Carl Sagan—God rest his soul—has some real explaining to do."

FIVE

I WAITED FOR MAE to leave. Instead she passed out from the booze. Minutes later, I did the same, though shock had more to do with my grogginess.

Waking up well before dawn to her irregular, loud, and disturbing snores, I winced with the thought of ever spending more sleep time in her company. Her deviated septum almost drowned out the constant reverberations of the trains across Mabry Avenue. I tried to focus on my wristwatch, rubbed my eyes and tried again. It was four a.m., too early to do anything but mope.

Then everything surged back in confusion and ugliness.

I tiptoed into the bathroom and sought a way to call the police without waking Mae. What would I say? I had no idea where she'd driven me. And what about the whole alien thing?

Mae was the most practical, grounded person I'd ever known. If real people were called "salt of the earth," Mae King was the ore. For her to believe she'd been swooshed off by space aliens stretched my image of her to new and unpleasant places. Fact was, my friend was a trained observer with a fine mind residing inside her turtle-shell exterior. Otherwise, I'd have dismissed her story in a second.

The wind yowled like a coyote. It would have been spooky, but Mae's snores and the trains overpowered it. I heard footsteps grinding on gravel outside my door. Scotch-induced imaginings, no doubt. Only a complete idiot would be out on a night like this. The doorknob shook, then stilled. Rattling windows, whistling wind, staccato snores. Nothing had prepared me for Clovis.

The cheap lamp bolted to the table next to the bed cast a pale, grating light. The telephone, its cord too short to reach the privacy of the bathroom, sat like a dare. I knew I was in trouble with the police, too. They'd want to know why I'd waited to call.

The wind shoved the doorknob again. There was a thump on the window, as if a small animal had been swept up in the storm and had slammed against it.

Stress pried through my fragile composure. I sat down on the chair nearest the telephone, one hand on the receiver, and made frantic attempts at healing breaths. Time stretched and warped. The noise outside pounded. I squeezed the arm of the chair and the receiver in my hand, braced for the hallucination, feeling it roil within.

The man stood before me, Asian, small, sad. His eyes beseeched me, his lips moving. No sound in the room but Mae's persistent snores. *He looked down at the holes in his stomach, then at me, still speaking without volume.*

"What can I do to help you?" Tension from pent-up tears pushed behind my eyes. I would have cried if I could have. Instead, I said, "What do you want? How can I help you?"

I had to call the police, let them begin the investigation. This ghost needed to be set free.

He reached for my hand, something long and metallic in his.

"What? What is it?" I said. My neck hurt. I'd tucked my head as far back as possible, away from this horrid vision, from his obvious confusion and pain. I wanted him to disappear.

"Sasha!" Mae shook me, her concern palpable.

I tried to orient myself, my vision skewed, the room unfamiliar. I closed my eyes and in that darkness experienced the full wobbliness of a morning drunk.

"Sasha, what're you doing?" she said. "What's wrong?"

I dug the fingers of my free hand into my face, wanting to crush the hallucination into nothingness.

"Why's your hand on the phone, Sasha? Were you planning to sneak in a call before I woke up?" she said, a hiss slithering along the tip of her words.

I loosened my grip on the receiver and shrugged.

She stared at me a long, long time. Without another word, she grabbed her worn purse, tossed me a frown, and left.

I looked at my hands again, white from lack of cream, the scars from past cuts more noticeable in this moment.

Sighing, I picked up the phone and dialed 911.

SIX

THE POLICEMEN DIDN'T CARE that I was tired, hung over, perplexed. They crowded the hotel room like a murder of crows, and asked short and disbelieving questions. I couldn't help much. Not really. I didn't know where Mae had taken me. I couldn't give clear details about the man because I didn't know what part of my memory stemmed from hallucination and what part from reality. After more than an hour, they beamed their frustration with terse tones and tightened lips, then left.

I showered, dressed haphazardly. My appetite swerved into consciousness at about seven a.m., demanding satisfaction. Eating would be something to do besides worrying about Mae and what my call to the police might do to our friendship.

The parking lot overflowed at Brunchy's, an all-you-can-eat buffet. Inside, stations of food, beneath red-striped tents, checkered the large floor. Crispy bacon, ripe cantaloupe, fist-sized cinnamon rolls, dripping sausages, seedless grapes, omelets to order, and fresh pineapple. I filled my plate with mountains of grits and hills of sticky pecan buns. My coffee mug steamed. When the light hit it right, I could see the oily residue on its surface.

After breakfast I lollygagged at the hotel, trying to act casual for a nonexistent audience. The world intruded with thoughts of Mae, Mom, work, my sort-of squeeze Bob. I picked up the phone to call him, put it down, unsure what to say.

Surveying myself in the mirror, I made a gruesome face at

my reflection. Drinking too much scotch, eating too much food, and snitching on my friend hadn't done my self-image any good.

The interview with the chamber of commerce wasn't for another two hours. I decided to take a drive, force the fogginess out of my brain. I wanted to reframe my attitude to sell, sell, sell myself to my prospective employer. And I had to get the job or I'd be hitting the pavement in Albuquerque, not something to relish in the increasingly competitive PR market.

I emerged into a postcard day, sun shining in a cloudless sky, trees pulsing with hinted foliage. Because Clovis perched on the high eastern plains, its weather often manifested with more severity—tornadoes rampaging and baseball-sized hailstones pummeling—than in Albuquerque. Maybe that's why spring seemed to come later here, but it was coming, no doubt about it. Thoughts of Mae and the dead man fluttered in my head like gypsy moths. I batted them out of my consciousness.

The small city lay in a grid, most of its streets straight and long, except for the unexpected park plopped down willy-nilly, as if some mighty being had sneezed without a handkerchief.

Getting into the car, I headed for the abandoned Clovis Hotel smack dab in the center of town. Fading murals encircled its base, heralding Clovis's short but stereotypic New Mexican history. Horsemen rode, stagecoaches lurched, Indians died, and of course, trains steamed. However, its wall held no likeness of the young girl—a train official's daughter—who, in 1907 or so, supposedly named the town after the first French Christian king, *Clovis*. Who says kids don't have power? Ah, well. The once graceful hotel made me think of things unused, of death. I felt an urge toward life but didn't know where to find the balm I needed.

I could head out of town and go to the Black Water Draw Museum, visit Clovis Man. That wouldn't work; it was too early. And Clovis Man was dead, anyway.

Instead, I drove over a bridge, turned onto a small road, and parked under what will remain one of my favorite billboards ever: *Clovis By-Products—Your Used Cow Dealer.*

I pulled out the rolled-up *Clovis Magazine* from my purse and planned the day. Starbucks hadn't made it to the high plains, but an ad for the Coffee Connection enticed. I'd hit it either right before or right after chatting with the Clovis marketing folks. Lunch would be at the Guadalajara Café, then back to the hotel, call Mae and Bob, watch the Cartoon Channel, and go to the Cotton Patch again for dinner. I needed a new cell phone, too.

Someone knocked on the driver's side window. I snapped up and stared into sunglasses reflecting my face in silver. My vision traveled down the clean-shaven chin to a policeman's black uniform, shiny badge. I looked to the front and saw a squad car. A glance in the rearview mirror yielded the same result. I rolled down the window a tad, nervous though I'd done nothing wrong.

"Can I help you, officer?"

"I was going to ask you the same question, ma'am," he said. "May I see your license, vehicle registration, and insurance, please?"

Too polite.

"Is there a problem?"

I didn't like this. Not one bit.

"Your license, please."

He tensed his jaw so it bulged out, nice and big for me to see.

I opened the glove compartment, got the documents, pulled the license out of my overstuffed wallet, and handed it to him. He took everything back to his car. My mind went into overdrive, creating problems where there were none. There was a good explanation for this. After all, I'd done the right thing. I'd called the police. This was just a blip.

But then, my little Toyota was a used car. What if, after all this time, it was actually a stolen one? Or what if they ran my license and the records were wrong and they thought I was some kind of criminal?

"Ms. Solomon, do you know a Mrs. Damon King?" he said when he returned.

I stopped for a minute, took a deep breath. "Yes. Yes, I do."

"Would you mind coming down to the station? Detective LaSalle has some questions for you. It shouldn't take long." He handed my papers back, waited for me to agree.

"But I already spoke to the police. This morning. Early," I said.

Fantasyland: *Lead-footed, I press the gas pedal, ram the squad car in front, forcing it out of my way. The second one follows, but I'm too fast. My Tercel morphs into a Formula One racecar. A mile past Cannon Air Force Base, they give up. Free and clear, I zoom into the sunset.*

Okay, trying to elude two squad cars verged on major stupidity. Why be paranoid? I wasn't in trouble; a detective just wanted to ask me a couple of questions. I looked down at my gas pedal, a second away from insanity.

The policeman watched me, my thoughts so loud I knew he could hear them.

"Sure." I sighed. "Do you want me to follow you?"

"That'd be a good idea."

He nodded to his buddy in front, who started his car in response. Like majorettes, we lined up straight, moved on the downbeat, and made a nice little parade back into town.

SEVEN

"TELL ME ABOUT last night." Detective Henry LaSalle was compact, spring-triggered and radiated energy so intense I yearned for air.

"Do you mean when I saw the dead man?"

"How did you know he was dead?" he snapped, a turtle ready to take my hand off.

"He was lying there. Not moving. His skin looked wrong— um, like he'd already been there for a while. And his head wasn't visible. I didn't get close enough to see if it was in the water or, um, gone." A couple more "ums" and I'd sound even more moronic.

"How did you get there in the first place?"

"I already told the officer last night."

"I want to hear it for myself," he said.

"Mae drove me there," I said.

"Why did she do that?"

"Because she didn't know what else to do."

"So, instead of calling the police and possibly getting some advice, your friend took you out for a good time to see a dead man." His sarcasm made Mae's actions seem despicable.

"It wasn't like that," I said. "She was worried you all would get the wrong idea."

"Really?"

I sucked both lips in and bit on them. This was the kind of interview an investigative reporter might put one of my clients through. Adversarial, fast and leading, with the intention to ferret out dirt for the television cameras. Or if the reporter used newspapers as a medium, he'd be fishing, the hook set deep enough that my client would ramble, get distracted, speculate, and provide a good juicy quote for the article's lede.

"Ms. Solomon, I'm waiting," he said.

"I know."

"Are you going to answer any time soon?"

I had to regroup. This was serious stuff. I could get Mae in real trouble. I was sure she'd broken some kind of law by not calling immediately after she discovered the dead man.

"You know what? I really need to visit the little girls' room," I said. "Would you mind?"

He scowled in disbelief, mouth pressed as if he'd eaten a salty plum, eyes squinty.

"It's down the hall," he said.

I stood up.

"Ms. Solomon?"

"Yes?"

"Don't get lost."

The bathroom smelled of fear and disinfectant. I sat on the toilet, thinking. Mae had been a reporter for years. She'd seen corrupt police officers as well as honest ones. She'd seen how things could turn sour in a second. I understood her fear though I didn't agree with her decision not to call. How could I turn this into a win-win situation?

I washed my hands and splashed cold water on my face. I was doing a lot of that—splashing water. I'd have to mention it to my therapist.

The walk back to LaSalle's office took less time than I would have liked.

Still unprepared, I sat down and said, "Where were we?"

"I was asking why Mae thought we'd get the wrong idea. You know. About her finding a dead man on her property."

"I think she panicked," I said. "It wasn't rational. She saw the dead guy and got the heck out of there."

"Okay, but think about it a minute. What would you have done?"

"I don't know," I said. "I'd like to think I would've called the police. But who knows?"

"I see." His smile was almost real.

He wrote on a pad for a few minutes, leaving me to stew. Then he passed a hand over his buzzed hair, as if it was a new cut.

"Okay. But what about you?" he said. "Why didn't you call us right away?"

"I told you. Mae asked for some time."

"You've gotta know you're supposed to report crimes right away," he said. "You could be looking at a felony, Ms. Solomon. I need a good explanation here."

"It's not like she said, 'Hey, let's go look at a dead man,'" I said. "I didn't bring my cell phone with me. I didn't even take my purse."

"Okay. But what about when you got back to the hotel?"

"Look. I don't know why I waited. Probably because I respect Mae and figured the man wasn't going anywhere anyway. And I did try to call when we got back."

He'd been focused on his notes, but lifted his head to watch me.

"What time was that?" he said.

"Right when we got back to the hotel. I don't know. Midnight, one-ish."

"You called and no one answered?" he said, sarcastic.

I didn't want to get Mae in more trouble; I didn't want to get me in more trouble either.

"Look, Mae was distraught," I said. "We both were. I told her if she wasn't going to help herself, then I would."

"And?"

"And I dropped my phone and it broke."

"Try again," he said.

"We'd been drinking. Mae grabbed for my phone." I wiped sweat off my brow with an index finger. "It flew out of my hand and hit the wall and broke. Before you ask why I didn't use the hotel phone, I'll tell you. We both passed out right after the cell phone incident. When I woke up, I called. End of story."

I looked around LaSalle's office to avoid his eyes. A Navajo rug hung on the wall behind his desk. The room had a studied coziness complete with neat piles of paper, family photos, and kid art. Instead of snug, I felt cold. I hugged myself, knowing I'd screwed up royally.

He did the hair thing again.

"I believe you," he said.

"Am I really looking at a felony?"

"You could be. Technically, you contaminated a crime scene. If I was really mad I'd go for tampering with evidence, too."

"Are you really mad?"

"I haven't decided yet."

"Do I need a lawyer?"

"Probably not." LaSalle pushed back his chair. "You're not under arrest, yet."

"Yet?"

"Depends on how mad I get," he said.

I crossed, then uncrossed my legs. Leaned forward and back again. I resented being played with, the cat-and-mouse of this conversation.

"I know I should've called immediately," I said. "But this isn't about me. It's about Mae. And Mae King is as honest and honorable as they come. Period." I jutted my chin, pointed at the pad he'd been using. "You can write that down."

"It must be nice to be that sure of someone," he said.

I caught his gaze and held it until one of his eyes started to twitch.

"It is," I said.

EIGHT

To GET THE FLAVOR of the Coffee Connection, you need to think of a sweet Laura Ashley kind of kitchen, all small flower prints on the tablecloth and white wicker furniture, knick-knacks and doodads and dried braided wheat stalks hanging in wreaths. Then, imagine this place serving a decent cup of espresso.

I called Mae on the pay phone to tell her about my conversation with LaSalle. The telephone tag continued. Drowning my sorrows, I ate more pastries than I should have and drank enough coffee to regret its impact before I'd left the café. Irritated and hyper, I entered the Clovis Chamber's lobby.

"Well, hello there. May I help you?" The woman was in her late fifties, graying hair shellacked into place, a smile evoking summers spent canning strawberry jam.

"I'm here for an interview with Jan Cisneros," I said.

"Well, welcome to Clovis. You having a nice time? Can I get you a cup of coffee?" She came out from behind a small counter. "Why don't you have a seat? I'll tell Jan you're here. And does a cup of coffee sound good?"

"No, thank you."

The disappointment stopped her monologue for a split-second, then she rallied.

"How about some tea? A pop? Water?"

"Water would be nice," I said, not wanting it.

A homey couch with matching beige chairs occupied an alcove off the main entrance. I picked up a copy of an article about Buddy Holly and was halfway down the page when the receptionist reappeared with ice water in a tall glass. I thanked her and continued reading. Turns out Norman Petty, a man from Clovis, helped launch rock and roll. That fact didn't fit in with my image of the town.

The receptionist cleared her throat. I realized she'd been standing by my side watching me read. I looked up. She smiled again.

"Jan will be with you in just a minute," she said.

"Thanks," I said.

"My name's Sandra, by the way. Have you ever been to Clovis before?"

I always tell my clients to be nice to the seeming underlings—the secretaries and personal assistants—because they often have a direct line to people of power. I put down the article, smiled right back at her.

"Nope. This is my first time," I said.

"Do you plan to stay long?"

"I'm not sure yet."

"Oh, well, you've just got to," she said. "Did you get to see the zoo?"

"Not yet."

"Oh, you've got to. We've got a Bengal Tiger. He retired here from Las Vegas. And have you gone to the Black Water Draw Museum?"

"Not yet."

"Well, if you've got the time, you really should. Hold on. I'll get you some information." She went over to a rack of brochures.

I didn't mention I already had a zillion of them.

Sandra returned laden with literature.

"Some of our parks are just lovely. We've got a few little lakes—ponds actually—right in the middle of town. And our community college is something else. I can get you a pass to the gym. It's wonderful." She stopped to take a breath.

I sipped the water and prayed my bladder wouldn't betray me. Heels clicked down the formica hallway. A handsome woman in her forties walked up to me, hand extended.

"Ms. Solomon?" she said.

"Yes," I said, getting up.

"I'm Jan Cisneros. It's nice to meet you in person. Would you like some coffee?"

"No, thank you."

"Okay. Well, let's get this show on the road."

She led me to a conference room filled with several people. I sat in the point seat and prepared myself mentally for the ride. Rapid-fire introductions left no time to put names to faces.

First round, typical questions: How long have you been working in public relations? What is your experience with crisis communications? Do you have national media experience?

Second round, a little more creative: Describe your most challenging project. Describe your biggest success. What do you think of space aliens? *Huh?* I skidded off autopilot, bumped down the runway and back into focused attention.

"Excuse me. Could you repeat the question?" I said.

"What do you think of space aliens?" My interrogator was a puffy, chubby Anglo man. The sapphire ring glistening on his little finger echoed the blue of eyes set in too much face.

"Well, I think that's an interesting subject. I'm fascinated by the concept." I lobbed the innocuous answer back at him.

"Do you think they exist? That they visit us?"

As one they leaned forward, elbows on the table, breathing suspended. This wasn't an interview; it was a cobra, tense and ready to strike. Mae came to mind, her claimed abductions. The group waited. The energy in the room popped fiery red with flecks of orange.

I blinked my eyes to shut down the hallucination.

"Aliens," I said, pulling myself back. "Honestly, I don't

know. But until someone proves they don't exist, I'll keep an open mind."

The group relaxed. Jan Cisneros raised her head then lowered it again, as if gathering inner strength before she could proceed. Then she nodded to herself, a decision made.

"Ms. Solomon, the competition for this project is between you and another highly qualified individual," she said. "What I'm about to say must remain absolutely confidential."

"You've got my word," I said, pleased there were only two of us in the bidding.

"Before Roswell ever dreamed of space aliens, Clovis had its own encounters," she said. "One of the main crash sites is near where Clovis Man was discovered. Some people around here question whether that find is even of human origin."

"Are you telling me you want to go head-to-head with Roswell?"

"Not exactly. We're thinking more of a high plains UFO/space alien corridor. You know, put Clovis on the UFO map. Bring some of those dollars from Roswell up this way."

Repressing my glee, I said, "Tell me more."

The interview took nearly two hours, my excitement tempered by a glitch. They wanted me to come up with a full communications and marketing plan—with no guarantees they'd pay me for it. And they wanted it by five p.m. on Friday.

"Sure, no problem. I'll hand-deliver it," I said. "Just one question."

"Of course. Anything," said Jan Cisneros.

"Do I have your assurance you won't use my plan and hire someone else for the job?"

"Of course you have our assurance," she said.

"Absolutely," said someone else.

"No question," said number three.

Why didn't I believe them?

NINE

NONE TOO PLEASED, I decided to take Sandra's advice and check out the zoo, a snug place about the size of a thumbnail. Actually it would fit well into a football stadium, with room for bleachers and a couple of concession stands. Communing with the animals felt more possible here than in a bigger place with fancier enclosures and moats around customized ecosystems. I stood before two cages watching lynxes taunt a cougar and felt as low and ornery as his growls. Every inch of my being wanted to leave this vertically-challenged town, to get back to my mountains, my normal life in Albuquerque. Countering the flight response was the little question of money and needing it really, really badly.

I wouldn't have been in this position if I hadn't gotten so comfortable at TrueHealth. But no, like a dope, I'd let my business slide. I'd gotten lazy and had lost the hunger I'd nourished for more than twenty years as a consultant.

The cougar growled again, a rumbling, threatening sound.

"Yeah. No kidding," I said.

I walked over to the Bengal tiger. He looked as bored as I'd been before my demise at TrueHealth. I'd loved my job in the beginning, just as I'd loved others before. Alas, yours truly was a PR thrill seeker. The start of projects, the strategizing and scheming, the developing promo materials and tracking media hits—that was the stuff of creativity. Once the work devolved into routine, I wanted out. *Sasha Solomon: great consultant, lousy employee.*

Once I knew I wanted to quit TrueHealth, I'd dreamed up a new PR consulting scheme—my master plan. *Have PR, will travel.* My business cards would sport that tag line—right under the cool graphic for my brainchild, Bad Girls Press. I'd take my show on the road. Sniff out interesting jobs in smaller cities throughout my glorious New Mexico. Mountains, mesas, resorts, casinos—I could pick the locale, tour the state, and write off expenses. I'd also avoid a new problem in Albuquerque: a bumper crop of pimple-faced college grads who'd work for one-eighth the pay and do one-sixteenth the job I could do.

"See you later," I said to the tiger and left the zoo, underimpressed and overwrought about the work that lay before me. Work for which I might not earn a cent.

Although I'm good at self-pity, this wasn't the time to wallow. Survival had me changing gears before I reached the car. Hand on the door, I resolved to do the best job the Clovis Chamber of Commerce had ever seen. One so interesting and complex they'd never find local talent to implement it.

It was time for research. The PR pro's secret weapon.

First on tap, find out about the town. What would bring tourists to this unknown place? What would make them spend oodles of hard-earned cash? And talk about it to their friends? What would stimulate those friends to bring others and spend scads of money, too?

I drove down Norris, a big, straight street, and turned into a development called Sandzen. I wanted to get a feel for Clovis, for what made it tick.

With that spin of the wheel, I'd entered a different world. The houses, at least five thousand square feet apiece, nestled in elaborate grounds hinting at swimming pools and marble fountains beyond view. Lawns screamed for tractors and special fertilizers. Gazebos graced street intersections.

Not a soul in sight. And souls were at issue here. I noticed

the white squares, planted like for-sale signs in front yards—
one, two, three houses, then another—before registering what
they said. I stopped the car, crinkled my nose to see better.

Thou shalt not kill.

Ohmigod! The Ten Commandments, printed in navy blue,
sprouted like faithful fungi everywhere I turned. Well, we
had one definite audience for sure. The challenge: How to interest Bible Belters in UFOs?

Pondering this formidable question, I left the subdivision.

The red message light on my motel phone glistened like a
sore. Only two people knew where I was: Mae King and
Henry LaSalle. I wasn't ready to talk with either one. Instead
I dialed Bob's direct line, got his voice mail, and hung up.
Then I dialed the front desk.

"Room one forty-seven. Yes, you have two messages," the
clerk said.

She put the receiver down, coughed up a hairball, cleared
her throat. When she spoke again she'd transformed from a
soprano to a second alto.

"Here it is. Charlene Simpson left this number," she said.

I wrote it down.

"And Detective LaSalle asked you to call him back. Oh,
and did your husband find you? He said you'd forgotten to tell
him the room you were in. Did you find each other yet?"

"My husband?"

"Yes, Ma'am. He told me he was going to surprise you. I
couldn't give him the key though. Hotel policy. I hope he's
not mad." She hacked up another one and said, "Oh, darn, I
shouldn't have told you. I'm sorry. Don't let him know, okay?"

"All right," I said.

My husband? Had Bob decided to surprise me? Unlikely.
We were still in the whiff-reading stage. The period before
you're a couple. When you enchant each other with wit and
avoid family histories like they were poison. No intimacy

yet, either. I'd been burned, oh, going on four thousand times in my short forty years. I wanted to take this relationship—if that's what it was—slow. Bob didn't seem to mind.

If not Bob, then who? Was it someone's idea of a joke? The air sizzled. I took a long, deep breath, unnatural to anyone but a yoga master. There had to be an easy explanation. Another breath. I went to the door and locked the deadbolt.

I flipped on the TV and dialed Mae's number. The phone rang, then rang some more.

"King Enterprises," a woman said.

"Hi, this is Sasha Solomon. Is Charlene there?"

"Speaking."

We waited.

I watched Rocky save Bullwinkle.

We waited.

I heard her inhale, then breathe out forcefully.

"Mom wanted me to tell you that—oh, how did she put it?—that she was sorry for bringing you into this mess and that she'd be in touch," said Charlene.

"Can I talk to her?" I said.

"I'm afraid that's not possible."

"Is she okay?"

"No. She's not okay."

"What's wrong?" I said, alarmed.

"Oh, come on," said Charlene.

"What? The police didn't give her a hard time, did they?"

Stupid question. Of course they did. If LaSalle's behavior with me was the baseline, I suspected he'd been Attila the Hun with Mae.

"The police were okay," she said, sounding less raw.

"Good. Can I talk to her?"

"No."

"Why not?"

"I don't think it's a good idea," she said.

"Why?"

"You've already gotten her into enough trouble."

"What? Because I called the police?" I said. "I thought you said they were okay."

"You really don't get it, do you?"

"No, Ms. Simpson, I really don't."

"What I'd like to know, what I'd really like to know, is why you told Mom not to call the police," she said. "What were you thinking?"

"Wait a minute. It was the other way around," I said. "Your mother asked me not to call the police. She said she wanted time to think before she dealt with them."

"And you expect me to believe that?"

"Yes, I do," I said. "It's the truth."

"From what I understand, you PR people don't know the truth from your butt."

Her unwarranted venom startled me.

"Look. Let's start over," I said. "I'm sorry if you think I've done something wrong—"

"That's not even a real apology! You people twist everything," she said.

"Look, I know you're upset. Can I talk to your mom, please?"

"No."

"Okay, I'll call back later."

"I don't think that's a good idea," she said. "Mom's under a lot of strain."

"Don't you think she could use a little friendly support?"

"She has all the support she needs." With that, Charlene hung up.

I went into the bathroom, filled a glass with water, and gulped it down. I tried to see life from Charlene's point of view. It made sense she was upset; I'd be, too. But why did she blame me? Had Mae really said I'd forced her not to call?

If Mae claimed that lie, she'd probably said the same thing to the police. No wonder LaSalle grilled me. I drank more water.

Sitting on the bed once more, I decided Charlene needed a little TLC. I dialed Mae's number again. Surprise, surprise, she answered. Despite her curt manner, I invited her and Charlene to dinner. Outside, the sun lost its power as the afternoon wore on, the clock nearing 4:30. We agreed to meet at the Cotton Patch in an hour.

Dinner with two upset women. I could hardly wait.

TEN

"EXCUSE ME?" I SAID, not sure I'd heard right.

"Never mind her," said Mae. "Charly didn't mean anything by it."

"No. I want her to say it again," I said, wondering if she'd really called me a *kike*.

Charlene's pout must have been there since she popped out of the womb. A stick-thin woman with long hair, long legs, and an oval face, she blushed and mumbled something.

"I'm sorry?" I said. "What did you say?"

"Sasha, leave her alone. Haven't you done enough already?" This from Mae.

When I raised my eyebrows, Mae sawed at her roast beef. You'd think it was well done instead of pink.

Charlene reached for a roll.

"You don't need those," Mae said, pushing the basket out of her daughter's reach.

"But, Mom."

"No 'buts',"

"I want a damn roll," said Charlene.

"No," said Mae.

I think my jaw dropped open; I know I had to close it. Here was Charlene, thirty-five, maybe older, and Mae swatted her down like she was a snotty-nosed toddler.

"You always do this," Charlene hissed.

This was embarrassing.

"Charlene, behave." Mae's whisper sparkled with threat.

"No, Mom. You behave," she said, then threw her napkin on her untouched food. "I've had enough of this crap." She stood up, kicked her chair back into place, and left.

Mae watched her go, then said, "Never mind her."

I watched Mae for a minute, then concentrated on my baked potato. Alas, the mother-daughter love-fest had extinguished my appetite. Steak blood congealed in butter ponds from the broccoli on my plate. I used a salad fork to create designs in the waxy substance.

"Is she always this charming?" I said.

"Never mind her," Mae said, the refrain old already. "She's always been hyper."

"Mae, she called me a kike."

"She didn't mean it."

"Oh, come on. It's an ugly word and she didn't have a problem saying it."

My friend rubbed her temples before speaking again. "About the only thing I didn't love about Damon was his close-mindedness."

"He didn't approve of Jews?"

"Sasha, he didn't approve of anyone who wasn't a white, Christian male." She sighed. "He couldn't abide by Jews, Blacks, Hispanics. And he had a special hatred for anyone from the Far East."

"Why?"

"He was on the Bataan Death March in World War II." She picked up a pack of crackers loitering on the table and mashed them with her forefinger as she spoke. "He saw thousands of American soldiers murdered by the Japanese. And thousands more perish because of their cruelty. He could never forgive that."

"And your kids followed suit?"

"I tried, Sasha."

"I'm sorry," I said, knowing Charly had more problems than Mae would ever admit.

Most people don't know I was trained as a therapist. Although my MSW comes in handy when I deal with clients, it's not something I talk about. The last thing I want is for someone to think I'm analyzing her—even though it's probably true.

"Charly's under a lot of stress with this whole thing," said Mae.

"What about you? I'd imagine you're under even more."

Mae dismissed my comment, blowing air out of her mouth in a pfff. "I've been through worse."

"So, you're not mad at me?"

"Nah," she said.

"So, why—" I stopped, picked up a piece of broccoli with my fingers and ate it.

"Why, what?"

"Why did you tell Charlene I made you wait to call the police?" I said.

"Did she say that?"

I blinked in affirmation.

"Crazy girl. Sometimes I think she's missing a few marbles."

"You didn't tell her that?"

"Of course not."

"Why'd she say it?" I said.

"She's got this unpredictable side to her, you know? She could've heard me wrong."

A country pixie of a waitress came to our table, all bounce and health and rosy cheeks. She smelled like a vanilla bean. We ordered cherry pie à la mode and coffee. The discomfort between us grew. I wanted to know everything—how Mae's interview with the police had gone, what they'd said, what was going to happen next.

Mae chewed on the inside of her lower lip.

"How long you planning on staying?" she said.

"Probably the week. The people at the Chamber want me to come up with a plan and it doesn't make sense to go home."

"You might want to stay in a nicer hotel."

"Money's an issue. Remember?"

"Not if I pay for it," she said.

"That's silly. How about I stay with you instead?"

"It's not a good time, Sasha. I already told you that," she said. "Look, I feel bad that I can't have you over. You go to the Holiday Inn and I'll pay for it. They know me there."

"Mae, if it's about the police, you know it'll blow over," I said. "Wouldn't it be cheaper to have me stay like we'd planned?"

"I don't have any room. My boys are coming to town. Theo wants to be there when I talk to the lawyer. And Josh." She frowned. "Josh thinks I need his moral support."

"You don't?"

Mae shrugged her shoulders. "Don't get me wrong, Sasha. My kids are great kids."

"But?"

"No *buts*. They're great kids."

"Mae, why won't you talk to me?"

"I am," she said.

"You were going to say something about your kids."

"No, I wasn't. They're great kids."

The waitress brought our dessert.

Mae wasn't going to let me in, no matter how I tried. Her miserly communication made me wonder what could have wounded our friendship in less than a day. When I brought up Charlene again, Mae hushed me with an icy look that shoved more questions back down my throat. I swallowed hard and choked on the ice cream. Wrapped in her own drama, Mae didn't notice.

Before we left, Mae called the new hotel and reserved a room in my name for the next morning. The question of payment made me uneasy, but she was determined to be my hostess in one way or another.

We didn't hug when we said goodbye.

I stopped by the Pump-n-Snak for more whipped cream, a couple of candy bars. The new cashier held no smile for me, and less, when I pointed out the mistake he'd made giving me change. Flustered, I left the store, forgetting the forty cents I'd insisted he return.

The bristling sensation of hair rising on my neck presaged a potential hallucination. Deep breathing helped; the hairs settled. I reached my room, surging through the door like it was a safe house, and noticed the message light.

A call to the front office. A different voice, same smoky resonance.

One message: Detective LaSalle was coming for a chat at eight.

ELEVEN

ASK NOT FOR WHOM the detective knocks; he knocks for you.

At two minutes before eight, my own private Hardy Boy tapped at the door. I grabbed the whipped cream and took a long, mouth-expanding draught to calm my nerves.

"I'll be right there," I yelled, sitting on the bed. If he was going to make my night miserable, he could wait to do it. I took another hit, went to the sink and stalled, scrutinizing my iffy complexion.

Five minutes passed. He knocked again.

Opening the door with ill will, I frowned and motioned for him to enter.

"Why, Ms. Solomon, I almost think you're avoiding me." He reminded me of the Cheshire cat with a grudge. Dressed in khakis and a sweater, he leaned against the door.

"Sorry to make you wait," I said.

"I'm sure you are."

He wasn't in the room yet and he already annoyed me.

"Detective, what do you want?"

"Well, I called earlier and you didn't call me back. I figured we started off on the wrong foot," he said. "I was feeling sort of sad about that and came to see if you'd like to go for a cup of coffee."

"Are we talking on or off the record?" His ah-shucks manners didn't fool me.

"You must be confusing me with that cute fellow on channel twelve. Can't a guy take a pretty girl out without being suspected of something?"

"You're not just any guy, you're a detective. What do you want?"

He shrugged. "A cup of coffee. Come on."

Not much happens in Clovis at night. The local action was at the Denny's, a two-minute drive from the motel. A lone man sat in a booth reading the paper, tanking up on java. At a corner table, five teens ate burgers; their whispers stopped when I looked their way.

LaSalle headed for a booth, greeted the waitress by name, and ordered for both of us. Two coffees, two banana splits. His grin gave me the creeps.

"I saw the can of whipped cream. Figured you had a sweet tooth," he said.

Oh, no. What did the detective think I was doing with a can of whipped cream in my hotel room? I winced.

"It's medicinal," I said.

His laugh ricocheted against the restaurant walls. Massaging his closed eyes, he said, "That's about the funniest thing I've heard all day."

Caught off guard, LaSalle was handsome in a military sort of way. If Clovis was stuck in the 1950s, he could have been on the football team—one of the smaller guys, a kicker—popular with the girls, and the first one to volunteer for active duty. A wedding band had once adorned his finger, replaced now by a thick, faded line.

The b-splits arrived along with the coffee. He spooned ice cream into his drink. "So. If Mae didn't kill the man, who did?"

"What happened to foreplay?" I said.

"I'm a sixty-minute man."

My turn to chuckle. "Detective, I have—"

"Henry." There was whipped cream on his chin. I wanted to tell him but didn't dare.

"Sasha," I said.

He nodded.

"Henry. I have no idea."

"Well, we're in the same boat." He pierced half a banana and nibbled at it, alternating ends. "What I don't understand is why someone would go to the trouble to frame Mae King. That's what it feels like to me. Some kind of frame-up."

"Mae's got a lot of money, a lot of land. Maybe someone was trying to blackmail her and she didn't bite."

"You got anything to base that on?"

"No," I said.

"There's something else to confuse things."

"What?" My throat constricted, shrink-wrap tight.

"He wasn't killed at the scene."

"Ohmigod," I said. "Someone killed him and then deliberately put him in that cattle trough?"

"I wasn't aware that you were a religious woman, Sasha."

"Huh?"

"Taking the Lord's name in vain."

"Excuse me?"

"The 'Oh my God'," he said. The creepy grin was back.

"I'm not." I didn't get the joke. "This isn't funny."

"No, it's not."

We observed each other, waiting for body language to betray our thoughts. It took time, this careful watching. My ice cream softened enough that one of the cherries fell off its perch and landed on the table.

"Is Mae under arrest?" I said.

"Not yet. But it looks bad. Too many coincidences, no good alibi," he said. "She's strong enough she could have dragged him. She has enough employees, someone could've helped her."

"No way. Mae wouldn't kill anyone."

He considered it. Scratched his head, spooned up more of his dessert.

"I just can't figure a motive for it," he said. Taking my errant cherry, he dangled it above his mouth, his chin upturned, then bit it with an audible snap. "And, I've got a crummy feeling about the dead guy."

"Dead guys do that to me, too."

"Ha, ha."

Abashed, I said, "You mean he was a criminal or something?"

"Just the opposite. I'm pretty sure he's one of the pilots from Singapore over at Cannon."

"Singapore?"

"I guess you don't know about the four-twenty-eighth fighter squadron," he said.

I sure didn't.

"They're here for training. Great group of guys," LaSalle said. "If he turns out to be one of 'em, the whole city's gonna be up in arms. And it'd be bad PR, what with the president's latest push to close more bases." He mooshed another cherry into a gob of ice cream. "It could give him the ammunition to move our fighters somewhere else. And that would be economic disaster for Clovis." He ate the cherry. "All of this is going to confuse the investigation."

"You're full of good news," I said.

"Yep," he said. "A whole crew of people will get involved, a city of investigators, all looking for a scapegoat—don't repeat that."

"What can I do? How can I help?" I pushed my dish away.

"Can you tell me anything else? Do you know of anyone who'd be out to hurt her? Anything? Anything at all?"

"I can't think of a thing," I said. "God, I wish I could."

"God has nothing to do with this," said LaSalle.

TWELVE

SOULLESS ALMOND EYES, white faces stare at me. I hear a click. Feel the jolt before the blast registers. Bent over, I see one, two—no—five red pits in my stomach, my body smaller than I remember. Smaller, harder, and dripping blood as I fall to the frigid, unforgiving ground.

I lurched toward the bedside lamp, disoriented. The dream clung to my consciousness. Voices mumbled. Shadows flickered. Overwhelmed, I concentrated on my breathing and braced for a hallucination. Minutes passed, nothing happened. The oscillating light came not from a vision, but the television. Bad idea, falling asleep with it on. I stumbled out of bed to turn it off.

Aliens. I'd been dreaming about aliens, obsessing about work before even starting. I tittered, bird-nervous, and it sounded too loud. I yawned, stretched, rolled my head in a circle to release tension. Aliens. Was it true? Had Mae really been abducted?

In spite of great concern and caring for each other, I realized my friend had rarely confided in me. Our long-distance camaraderie was easy, but now it seemed impoverished. There were whole truckloads I didn't know about the woman. Take her relationship with her kids. I'd have thought she'd be a great mom, loving, supportive, like she'd been with me over the years. The dinner with Charlene bespoke tensions of which I'd never been aware.

Mae was from the old school, the one where personal prob-

lems were as private as underwear. But did her reticence stem
from more?

If I've learned anything in all my years in PR, it's this:
everyone has secrets, and everyone has a story that deserves
to be known. I realized I didn't know as much of Mae's story
as I needed in order to be a true friend. LaSalle's dire predic-
tions about the murder investigation didn't bode well. Mae
would need more than superficialities to survive this bad turn.

I dozed off for an hour or two, then woke to trains rumbling and the doorknob jiggling. I peeked out the window. The
sky, a midnight blue, held the beginning of light at its edges.
A hooded someone, big and wearing a bulky dark coat, stood
outside my door, gloved hand on the knob. Another rattle, then
he walked away, his footsteps silenced by the freight cars lum-
bering across the street.

The incident didn't upset me; I'd worked out an explanation. The man, a drunk, had been trying every door, looking
for a place to crash. I shook my head, glad to be switching
hotels in the morning.

On automatic, I showered, got dressed, packed, then went
in search of breakfast. Spring had almost sprung outside, the
air cool and fresh. The bright morning sun foisted skin cancer on all with equal zest. Dry sausage, hard eggs, and water
masquerading as coffee propelled my mood downward.

"Don't you need oxygen?" I said to the befogged clerk
while checking out.

"Excuse me?"

"Nothing."

The Holiday Inn stood less than five minutes away, but its
amenities were light years ahead of my former domicile. An
indoor swimming pool—too bad I didn't have my suit—a
sauna, Jacuzzi, exercise room, restaurant, and, praise the Lord,
a bar. Though it was too early to slug down a scotch, I liked
having the option a mere stroll away.

With nothing planned, loads of work to do, and too many questions about Mae and what was going to happen to her, I plugged in the laptop and got to work.

Space aliens, here I come.

THIRTEEN

HERE'S A TRICK OF THE TRADE. I call it the D.A.: slam your
fingers on the keyboard and don't look up until you've splurted
out all of your initial ideas with no regard to grammar, idea
idiocy, or practicality. *D.A.*...get it? Diarrhea Approach.

When I slowed down, the screen displayed page 22. Not a
bad start. Later, after some java, I'd see if any of it made sense.
In the writing, I'd realized a couple of things. I had to get down
to Roswell to check out the UFO Museum. And, in order to
make my plan sing—and it'd better be downright operatic to
secure the money I now needed—I'd have to interview people in and around Clovis who'd had UFO or space alien experiences. Authenticity, *baby*.

By ten, I sat in the Coffee Connection jolting my creativity to new heights with a double espresso. Sipping the sludge,
yours truly eavesdropped on whispered comments both
breathy and sorrowful.

"He wasn't even here for a month," said a woman at the
table next to me.

"Shot five times," said another.

"I heard they're bringing in the big guns," added one of
the workers when she delivered frothy drinks to a group near
the door.

"FBI, CIA, DEA," said the first woman.

A creaky voice to my left said, "I don't like to gossip, but
Terry says his wife is rude, rude, rude."

"Amen to that," someone responded.

I ordered a double latte to go and asked where I could buy a paper.

"I'm done with mine," said the woman who'd sat near me. She urged the crumpled mass of newsprint on me. "Here, take it."

Hey, fifty cents was fifty cents. With a thank-you, I threw it into the car and headed back to the hotel. My phone was ringing when I unlocked the door. Hands full, I dove onto the bed to reach the receiver, grasped it midair, hit the second mattress with a bounce, and slid to the floor.

The phone fell on top of me. Coffee leaked onto the paper and my leg.

"Ouch!" I said.

"Is this Ms. Solomon?" A girl's reedy high voice cracked, as if her vocal chords stretched an inch too far.

"Yes, it is." I stood up, rubbed my elbow, blotted my leg with a tissue. I'd broken a nail down to the quick and it was bleeding. "Oh, brother."

"Excuse me?"

"Hold on a minute, will you?"

I wrapped part of another tissue around the fingertip to staunch the blood and applied pressure to cut the pain. Then I sat down.

"I'm sorry. Who is this?" I said.

"Sue Carter." Pause, an intake of air with a wheeze. Poor kid had asthma. "Are you really Ms. Solomon?"

"Yes, I really am."

"Um."

My tush hurt. I wanted a cold washcloth, some ice.

What I didn't want was to coax conversation out of someone who'd called me. I dropped the receiver, on purpose this time, then fumbled with it for a second.

"Excuse me, Ms. Carter?" I said. "I think I missed that. What did you say?"

"Ms. Solomon, I heard you're interested in aliens. You know, the ones that land here." A breath, a whistle, another breath. "And I—I know some of them. If you'd like to meet them."

"You can introduce me to aliens?" My finger hurt like the dickens. I bit it.

"Yes. Well, sort of."

"Tell me more."

"Well, I can show you where they like to land. Let you look at our cows. You know, that kind of stuff."

"They land on your property?"

"Sure do." Her voice gained confidence. "And sometimes they come out of their ship and talk to me. Well, it's not exactly talking, but they sort of think at me and I pick it up."

Insane kid or cosmic gift? And how did she know I was looking for aliens in the first place? I thought the deal with the Chamber was supposed to be confidential. Someone had warned me about gossip in small towns. Maybe this was an example of it.

"Ms. Solomon?"

"I'm here, Sue."

"Do you want to meet them?"

"The aliens? They're there?"

"Yeah," she said. "I can see 'em from my kitchen window."

"Tell me how to get to your house."

Her place was due east of the city, on the straight road to Lubbock. More horizon with nothing to stop it but boredom. Though the air was sweet, I hardly noticed it. My mind whirled with anticipation. Holy cow! I was actually going to meet aliens. I couldn't believe my luck.

A train paralleled my progress, then prohibited me from crossing the road for five minutes. I honked in frustration.

An unpaved road led to a farmhouse, the wood grayed through rough weather and excessive wind. Tree branches dug

into the ground at intermittent intervals and buoyed the wire
fence encircling the property. An air of disuse, misuse even,
colored the buildings and land like an old woman who'd
worked too hard and sacrificed too much. Each structure vied
with the other for decrepitude.

I parked the car in the dirt driveway and approached the
main house. The front door was open, its screen torn on the
bottom. An orange tabby jumped out to greet me.

"Hello, beautiful." I said. He rubbed against my legs, pur-
ring. "You're such a friendly one."

He let me scratch underneath his chin, then rolled onto his
back. I bent to wiggle my fingers on the soft exposed fur. What
a pleasure to pet a cat who didn't talk back.

"Ms. Solomon?"

I straightened to see a short, *zaftig* woman. No more than
four-and-a-half feet tall. Sue reminded me of a munchkin.
Thick lenses set in pearl-pink cat glasses magnified her brown
eyes. She wore her hair in a small bun ringed by a purple elastic scrunchie. Her flowered, faded dress lacked the two last
buttons. And her wide grandmother's chest was bedecked
with several ropes of beads. The plastic gemstones sparkled
in the sunlight.

"I'm sorry," she said, taking my hand after opening the
door. "They didn't stay."

"Why not?"

"They had to go."

"Didn't you tell them I was coming?" I sounded ridiculous.

"I don't talk to them. I think at them and they think back."
Her eyes filled with tears.

"I'm sorry. I didn't mean to upset you."

She nodded, held the door ajar for me to enter. We couldn't
have been quiet for more than a couple of seconds but the time
felt stretchy, ropy like hot taffy.

"I can show you the cows," she said.

I didn't want to see any stupid cows.

"They get coated with alien ectoplasm. I always have to clean it up after they come," she said, passing through the kitchen to a back door.

I followed, ready for anything.

Sue led me to a paddock. Three brown cows watched our approach. Covered in clear goop, they chewed their cud. I stopped. The stuff looked like Vaseline.

"The ectoplasm?" I said.

"Yes. It's such a mess. I wish they'd leave my cows alone."

"What do they do to them?"

Instead of answering, she bustled past me into one of the outbuildings.

While I waited for her to return, I talked to the cows. "What did you see, girls? Was it really aliens?"

One of them came toward me. She had beautiful, long black eyelashes. I'd never looked closely at a cow before. She stuck her head through the wooden fence, nudged my hand with her nose. It was instantaneous; I liked her. She nudged me again and some of the goop got on my wrist. I sniffed it. No scent. I touched it. Vaseline. Or if not the name brand, another kind of petroleum jelly.

I stroked her above those gorgeous eyes and prepared my exit.

"I swear, if it's not one thing, it's another." Sue returned with an armful of rags.

"You know what?" I looked at my watch. "I really need to go."

"Don't leave. They're coming back after lunch. They always do."

"Oh, I wish I could stay," I said, unwilling to be mean. "But—"

"Thanks for calling me. I really appreciate it." I lingered a moment at the door. "Sue, how did you know I was interested in aliens?"

"They told me," she said.
"Who?"
"The aliens."

FOURTEEN

HE STOOD BY MY CAR, his skin buffalo-hide tough. Faded denim overalls, flannel shirt, dirty boots. A John Deere baseball cap obscured his face except for the unshaven chin.

"Hello," I said.

He nodded.

"How are you doing?" I said.

"Sue get you all the way out here for nothing?"

"Sort of."

"She show you the cows?"

"And your name is?"

"Abel King." He held out his hand, wrinkled and smudged from sun and work.

"I'm Sasha Solomon."

"I know," he said. "Why don't you walk with me for a minute, Sasha Solomon?"

He turned from me after he said it and headed down the road. Fields and more fields for miles. Curious, I caught up with him.

"King," I said. "Are you any relation to Mae?"

"Yep."

"And what relation would that be?"

"She's my sister-in-law. But that's not why I'm here."

He was a big man. His strides forced me to huff.

"Do you mind slowing down?"

The fraction's pause gave me no break.

"What did you want to talk about?" I said.

King stopped and said, "First of all, Sue Carter's crazy. If you haven't figured that out for yourself yet. I watch out for her. So, don't go bothering her anymore." He held up two fingers. "Second, I can show you some space alien artifacts, but I don't want my name used. Not in the paper, not on TV, not in any exhibit anywhere. Not for anything." He stooped to pick up a rock. Threw it. "And third, Mae and I don't talk much anymore. So, don't go asking me a bunch of questions about her."

"You're serious about the alien stuff?" I tried to make eye contact.

"Of course I'm serious."

"Well, let's go."

I turned around.

"Not that way," he said. "We're almost there."

We walked another few minutes. Then he stepped off the road and descended a hill I hadn't seen. I followed. We came to a large, shallow crater. It was about thirty feet in diameter, perhaps more; I've never been good at measurements. The hole was a perfect circle.

"This here is where they landed." King squatted in front of it. "The indentation's from the space ship."

"Did you actually see them land?" I said.

The wind grew stronger. I smelled the honeyed perfume of newly cut alfalfa or blossoming clover, although it was too early for either.

"Sure did. Forty-five years ago," he said, rising. "Come on, I'll show you some more."

King walked halfway around the circle and picked up something shiny. It was a smooth piece of metal.

"This came off their ship," he said, handing it to me.

Though it had been in the sun for hours, it was cool to the touch.

"Go ahead, bend it," he said.

I did. It held the shape for a few seconds then snapped back to its original flatness.

"Crumple it," he said.

It smooshed like a brown paper bag, stayed that way, then poof! It was flat again.

"That's weird," I said.

"You can keep it."

He started to climb the hill.

"Wait up!" I ran after him. "Tell me about the aliens."

"Some other time. I've got to get back to work."

"You can't do that to me. Show me this and then clam up."

He stopped, cocked his head a millimeter to the left. Smiled.

"I can do whatever I want, Missy."

"I didn't mean it that way," I said.

"Sure you did."

"Well, I'm sorry."

"Don't be." King started walking again. "You can pester me with questions tomorrow."

"Why don't you and Mae talk much?"

"I said 'tomorrow.'"

"Come on. How come?"

"We just don't."

"Do you think she's in trouble?" I said.

"You mean the murder," he said.

"Yeah."

"Nope."

"I do."

That stopped him. "You're supposed to be her friend."

"I am," I said. "I'm worried about her. About how it looks."

"It doesn't look like anything."

"Yes, it does. The police think someone might be setting her up."

"Might be," he said, hoofing it once more.

"But why?"

"Mae's got a skeleton or two in her closet."

"Like what?"

"What business is that of yours?" he said. His strides mimicked a long-jumper's.

"She's my friend. I want to help her."

"Listen, Missy, the best help you can give her is to leave all of this alone. Your job is to sell Clovis, not solve a murder."

"Why does everyone know what I'm doing here?"

We'd arrived at my car.

"I mean it," I said. "How come you and Sue know about the Chamber project?"

His eyes twinkled with amusement. "What'd Sue tell you?"

"That aliens told her."

King laughed. "She did, huh? Well, good for her."

"I don't see what's so funny."

"Then you're not looking hard enough," he said, chuckling. With a pat to my shoulder, he headed down the driveway in the direction we'd come from.

"How do I get in touch with you?" I yelled after him.

The wind carried his response. "You ever hear of a phone book?"

I finally found humor in my little adventure on the way back to the hotel. I had to share Sue Carter with someone. I thought about calling Bob, but he'd be busy at work. Mae. She'd get a kick out of the story. I picked up the phone.

Someone said, "Hello?"

"Mae?"

"Sasha?"

"That's weird. I was just going to call you," I said.

"Sasha," she said.

Then silence.

"What is it? What's happened?" I said.

"They've done it again." Urgency in her voice.

"Who?"

"The aliens."

"What?"

"They took me, Sasha. Stuck me with needles. Oh, no," Mae said.

I heard a doorbell.

"Mae? Are you okay?"

Too late. The receiver clunked onto a hard surface. Mumbled conversation. Men's indistinct voices.

"Mae? What's happening? Hello?" I yelled.

FIFTEEN

AFTER THE DIAL TONE returned, I tried Mae's number four more times. On the fifth, Charlene answered,

"King Enterprises."

"Charlene? This is Sasha. What's happened?"

"Nothing."

"That's a relief. Can I talk with your mom?"

"She's not here."

"Where is she?"

"Don't you think you've done enough damage?"

"What are you talking about? I haven't done anything," I said.

"Look. Don't call us anymore. Okay?"

"If I've done something wrong, I'm sorry. I want to help."

"The way you can help is to leave us alone. Mom doesn't want to talk to you anyway."

"She just called me," I said.

"No, she didn't."

"Charlene, let me help. Please."

"I'll give Mom your message," she said, then hung up.

Stunned, I looked at the mouthpiece as if it could tell me what was going on. The dial tone hummed. I dug out Detective LaSalle's number and called the station. He wasn't available, of course. Frustrated, I opened the laptop but couldn't concentrate.

It was after one and I needed food. I also needed to do something, anything, to calm down. After a burger at the Holiday Inn, I decided to drive to Roswell for the afternoon. Before I left, I called Mae's again.

"King residence." A man's voice this time.

"Hello. May I speak with Mae?" I said.

"I'm sorry, she's not available."

"Who is this?"

"Who is *this?*"

I sighed and said, "Sasha Solomon."

"Oh. Why didn't you say so?" His voice warmed twenty degrees.

"I wasn't sure I should."

"Why?" His confusion reassured me.

"Can I please talk to Mae?"

"I'm sorry. She's not here." Pause. "I'm Josh, by the way."

Her youngest son. I'd never met him but had heard the stories. He was a vegetarian, an animal rights activist. According to Mae, that combo didn't go well with dairy farming. She said he blamed most of the world's problems on her—starvation, drought, American over-consumption of natural resources, the energy crisis.

"I thought you lived in California," I said.

"I got in this morning. Figured Mom could use the moral support."

No kidding.

"That's nice," I said. "How's she doing?"

"I'm not supposed to tell you."

"Says who?"

"Charlene."

"Josh, give me a clue here. What did I do to Charlene?"

"I don't know," he said.

"Why can't I talk with your mom?"

"I've gotta go. I'll call you later."

"Who're you talking to?" It sounded like Charlene's voice in the background.

"Good to hear from you, too, Dick," Josh said to me. "Yeah, I'll do it. Bye."

I couldn't do anything more for Mae right now. Charlene wouldn't permit it. I got the feeling Josh would call me back, but I didn't want to hang around all day. Instead, I grabbed a couple of legal pads plus three bottles of Guinness—just in case—and split.

It was time for a change of scene.

Prince Street turned into Highway 70 as I passed rundown homes and more dairy farms. Near Portales, peanut farms came into view. On the other side of the college town, the land folded onto itself, seeming more flat and desolate than a moonscape. Strong winds buffeted my car during the journey southwest, forcing me to clutch the steering wheel. The joints in my fingers tensed white, while the tabletop of dirt and rock was interrupted only by mini-tornadoes slapping the skyline. A great horned owl sat atop a telephone pole in the middle of the commotion, unperturbed, majestic.

After more than an hour of driving, I knew Mae was in deeper trouble than anyone was letting on. Charlene's oddness had to be stress related; she was protecting her mother. I'd do the same thing if I thought my mom was in trouble.

The realization enabled me to feel compassion toward Mae's daughter. I'd try harder to convince her of my trustworthiness and motives for helping. There. That felt better.

Relieved, I grinned. Then, in an instant, hit the outskirts of my destination—Alien Central.

Let's face it: Roswell is quirky. New Mexico's fifth largest city supports a symphony, western and modern art museums, and a planetarium; it's also home to a military institute. Though the 1947 UFO "crash" site isn't in Roswell proper, the town's smart leaders have been able to exploit the public's urge not to be alone in the great dark universe. Without saying yea or nay to the reality of spaceships, bug-eyed martians, and government conspiracies, there's a thriving industry that caters to people interested in all three. And today, the town is best known for the International UFO Museum and Research Center. Green space aliens abound. From an eight-foot balloon tethered to the roof of a used-car dealership to a giant decal on the Wal-Mart, Roswell is cashing in on the world's fascination with things extraterrestrial. Best of all, the city center's street lamps are oval shaped with pointed tops and big black eyes painted on. Understated kookiness. My kind of place.

I scanned the front of the UFO museum, then crossed through its doors. Impatient to see the overall effect of the place, I declined the guided tour—only $1—in favor of my own reconnaissance, tarrying at this photo, that display.

Housed in a renovated movie theater, the museum shrieked airplane hangar, not a serious repository of knowledge. I found its pell-mell ambiance off-putting. But then, I wasn't a firm believer or nonbeliever. The existence of space aliens didn't matter to me. The informality of the place could be strategic, targeted to an audience I didn't yet understand but needed to know well enough to market the concept for Clovis's benefit.

"You know, I was chased by one of those things," said a man to a docent. The speaker sat in a wheelchair and pointed to a picture. "You oughtta write about what happened to me."

The docent, a petite woman in her thirties, asked if he'd like to fill out an incident form. He persisted, telling her about the event, getting help from a friend when he couldn't remember a particular detail, as if the telling was the most important thing.

In another alcove, two dowdy women in blah polyester pantsuits spoke in quiet tones about governmental conspiracies, their New England accents out of place in this cow town.

"It's like I said to Jim; they're keeping it secret."

"It's true. It's like that TV show about the truth being out there. Well, it is, you know. And this place proves it."

I sat on a bench to listen, to let snippets of conversation waft my way.

"He called the police that night, but no one believed him."

"Do you remember that thing we saw out the window? Everyone on the plane saw it. But when I showed the stewardess, she said it was only refracting light. Do they really think we're that stupid?"

At one point, I checked the guest book to confirm my observations. Old and young, fat and thin, male and female. American and German, Swedish and Brazilian, people by the thousands visited the museum each year. These were the same people I meant to attract to Clovis. And after an hour, I knew the keys to bring them 150 miles to the north: government conspiracy, a scientific or pseudo-scientific approach to the subject, and permission to believe in a living universe rather than an inanimate, barren one.

For cheap impulse buyers, dollar-down items bounced and bobbed in plastic containers in the gift shop. Lava lamps, puzzles, coloring books, and license plates enticed the less chintzy consumer. I bet there were silver service place settings in back.

The pens with floating space alien heads couldn't be resisted. I whipped out my wallet; these were research, tax deductible. Then came the bumper stickers, shot glasses, and the *pièce de résistance,* a glow-in-the-dark space alien mask.

By five o'clock that Tuesday, I felt I'd accomplished my goal. Seeped in the atmosphere of the museum, the kernel of a plan germinated. I'd let it grow for a day, then nurture it with writing. Anxious to get back to work, I hopped into the car. But food tempted more strongly than Clovis. After a brief skirmish, gluttony vanquished responsibility.

Driving up the hill from the downtown area in search of a restaurant, I realized Roswell held gobs more outward allure than its little cousin Clovis. Perhaps it was the size of the

place, giving it the sense of a solid *there* there. Or maybe it
was the mall-like park on the main drag and the varied architecture of its many public buildings. I couldn't quite put my
finger on it. In promoting Clovis, we'd have to make sure the
tourists we'd lured to the smaller town would feel like they
got their money's worth.

Unlike Clovis, Roswell is ranching country. You don't badmouth beef; you eat it. And the Cattle Baron is one of the best
places to dine. I could cut the filet mignon with my fork. The
salad bar took up more space than my living room. Sated after
a second bowl of banana pudding, I emerged into a dusky evening. Who wanted to drive anywhere in the dark?

What was money compared to my mental and physical
health? With a devil-may-care attitude and a credit card in
hand, I checked into the Comfort Inn.

Next morning, rested and ready, I left the hotel and went
in search of my repast. Nuthin' Fancy is *the* breakfast place
in UFO-central. The sign outside reads "Great Service—
Where you don't beg and don't pay an arm and a leg."

I ordered eggs Benedict. The sauce wasn't hollandaise. It
wasn't bad, either. Chunks of fresh pineapple, honeydew,
cantaloupe, and strawberry garnished my plate in a happy
mishmash.

Surveying my cohorts in cholesterol, I saw a puffy man
who jolted my senses. My glasses were in the car; I couldn't
get a really good look. Even a bit blurred, he resembled the
chubby guy from my interview with the Clovis Chamber.
Sensing my stare, he glanced my way, nodded, and went back
to reading a newspaper.

For some reason, he made me uneasy. I abandoned the rest
of my food in favor of putting major distance between the
two of us.

The drive out of town became more interesting simply because I paid more attention to it. Little hills sprouted in a land-

scape that the day before had seemed merely flat. A palate of browns from beach-sand light to bitter-chocolate dark stretched on both sides of the highway. Emerging greens cut through the gray of over-wintered plants whose names I didn't yet know.

Sooner than I expected, untamed land gave way to planted fields, billboards for peanuts, and dairy farms. Portales, with its ivied university in the center of town, evoked gentility. Its buildings' eastern architecture and landscaping charmed with porticos fronted by white columns and pitched roofs rather than ones designed to catch the rain. No adobe in sight.

I stopped at the Black Water Draw Museum, unenthusiastic and bored before hitting the entrance. The caretaker frowned at my sprint though. My tennis shoes squeaked on the polished brick floor until I saw the fake woolly mammoth head, its tusks as long as playground slides.

Where was Clovis Man?

Ah, here was a painting of him, there a sculpture. He wasn't much to look at, was he?

Though his thick forehead didn't make me yearn for more, an idea scratched the surface of my plan. Clovis Man and the space aliens. Hadn't they hinted at that during my interview? Had anyone drawn a connection between the big-eyed buggers and the ancient men? What a coup if I could find someone who'd put forth the theory.

Smiling, I retraced my steps to the entrance to drop a dollar in the donation jar.

Then it was back to the car and the Holiday Inn. Less than two hours from Roswell to Clovis. An effortless drive for tourists who'd come hundreds or thousands of miles already.

This might work.

SIXTEEN

THREE MESSAGES: Josh, Detective LaSalle, and Abel King. I didn't want to talk to LaSalle yet. Old man King would probably only muddle my thinking. I opted for easy street with Josh.

"King Enterprises," he said.

"Josh, this is Sasha."

"Took you long enough. I called, like, seven times. Where were you?"

The King kids excelled at grudges.

"I'm sorry. I went to Roswell and decided to spend the night."

"Oh, I forgot. You're doing that alien thing," he said.

"How on earth does everyone know my business?" I said.

"This is a small town, Ms. Solomon. Not much is secret for long."

We were buddies again. I decided to test my luck. "So, how's your mom? Can I talk to her?"

"She went shopping with Charlene."

"Is she going to be back any time soon?"

"Not likely. They're in Lubbock."

"Great. Sounds like things are getting back to normal," I said.

He snorted at my optimism. "Fat chance."

I wanted to meet him, to see the hostile tree-hugger in the flesh. "I've got a lot of work to do. Care to grab an early lunch with me before I dig in?"

"Why not? Sure. How about Poor Boys? I can be there in ten minutes."

Rather than display my ignorance, I agreed, knowing the hotel clerk could give me directions. What I didn't understand was how Josh could get to a restaurant in the middle of town in a matter of minutes. I'd assumed Mae's farm was way out, miles into the heart of the plains surrounding Clovis. Josh made it sound like it was next to the Pump-n-Snak.

Poor Boys was another steak house with a big salad bar. When Josh King walked through the door, all the women in the restaurant ceased their chitter-chatter mid-sentence. All the men searched for the cause of the silence.

From wavy brown hair flickering with red highlights, to a long, lean body that would be at ease in any setting, Josh was the most handsome vegetarian I'd ever seen. He could have been the poster boy for all things healthy and good: organic foods, free-range chickens, luxury spas.

"Ms. Solomon?" His dimpled smile was as warm and honest as the first real day of summer.

"Sasha," I said. "Yes. I'm me." *Move over Nobel laureates; I'm the next Maya Angelou.*

"Thank you for the lunch invite," he said, waiting for me to sit first.

"Glad to meet another of Mae's progeny."

"After the way Charlene's treated you, you probably think we're a bunch of ill-mannered monsters."

A plump waitress stopped at our booth, proud to be serving Josh. Nice enough to me. We both chose the salad bar.

"You've gotta understand. It's nothing personal," he said. "We're not trying to keep you away. It's…well, Mom's having such a hard time. We don't know what to do."

"How about letting her friends help?"

His grin displayed a single dimple so deep I wanted to go spelunking.

"Can I ask you something?" he said.

"Sure. Shoot."

"What did you do to Charly? She thinks you're about on par with the antichrist."

"Well, I *am* Jewish," I said.

He didn't laugh.

"Josh, I've got no idea."

We picked up our plates and headed for the food.

"It's like she blames me for what your mom's going through," I said. No one else was in line but I whispered, "The dead man would have been discovered eventually. And frankly, your mom isn't a good actress. She'd never have been able to pull it off."

"What?"

"Acting like she didn't know about him."

He took three carrots, a chunk of broccoli. My plate erupted with buffalo wings, crinkled beets, a mound of coconut-mandarin orange salad.

"I can't imagine what she was thinking, not calling the police. It looks really bad," he said. "Charly says you talked Mom out of it."

"Your sister is misinformed," I said. "I tried to get Mae to call. When she didn't, I did."

We scooted into our booth. Pieces of dilled okra fell off my plate. Josh's salad made me think of Gauguin in his Tahiti phase, lots of color but well ordered.

"Yeah. That sounds more like it," he said. "Mom's too much the reporter for her own good. I bet she thought the police would grill her." He ate a bit of grated carrot. "Charly's story sounded a little flaky to me. Mom would never let someone talk her in or out of anything." He picked up a piece of broccoli, dipped it once in the dill salad dressing. "You know, Charly's been a bit weird since Dad died."

I wanted the lowdown, the dirt on Charlene, but my mission today centered on befriending Josh.

"Tell me about your dad," I said. "I never met him."

"What's there to say? He was a businessman first. A politician second. And a father when he had the time."

"Wow. From the way your mom talks, he was the one who was there for you kids." I ate a marshmallow. "I always got the impression she felt like he was the good parent. That she thought she spent too much time on her career."

Josh's handsome smile took a dive; sadness moved up his cheeks. "I know Mom's always felt guilty about leaving us. But she was there, I mean really there, when we needed her," he said. "Dad may have been present more hours in the day but he was rarely present emotionally. You could be in his lap, telling him something important and he'd be miles away." Josh pushed a piece of red bell pepper across his plate. "I guess if you asked Charly or Theo, they'd say different. They liked working on the farm. I never did. I thought it was cruel, mean to the cows. How would you feel if you had to produce milk all the time?"

"I've got no idea," I said.

"Do you have kids?"

"No." Abstaining from pregnancy was my personal favor to the planet.

"Oh."

Josh cleared his throat, drank some water.

I wanted to ask him a gazillion questions and didn't know where to start. I said, "So, Charly and Theo liked working on the farm?"

"They loved it. Both of them," he said. "Well, you can tell Charly did. She's got her whole family there now, working like she did when she was a kid. Travis loves it, her children love it. A regular bliss festival."

That caught my attention. It played too bitter for this young, gentle man. I sought acrimony in his expression but found only earnestness, as if he strove to understand how anyone could love dairy farming.

"What about Theo?" I said. "Why did he become a lawyer?"

"That's a good question. I'd always pegged him to be a veterinarian or something to do with technology. When he was a kid, he loved that stuff," Josh said, then grinned. "He was a fanatic about science fiction, too. You couldn't get him to do a thing when the 'Twilight Zone' or 'Lost in Space' was on."

"But why did he become a lawyer?"

"Oh. Sorry." Josh fingered his fork for a second. "I think he and Uncle Abel thought they'd inherit the whole business when Dad died. Theo probably wanted to be prepared. You should have seen their faces when the will was read."

"Your Uncle Abel was at the reading?"

Josh nodded.

"Not pretty, huh?"

"Dad left him a $20 bill."

"You're kidding. Why?" I put my fork down.

"You'd have to ask Uncle Abel."

I planned to. "What about Theo?"

"We'll all inherit when Mom dies."

"Theo didn't know that?"

"Didn't have a clue," Josh said.

"Did you?"

"No. But I don't care. I don't need much."

"How did Theo and Charly take it?"

Josh ate a grape. "What can I say? They were disappointed." He nibbled at a strawberry. "Things haven't been the same since. And now, Mom's talking about totally integrated farming—"

"What's that?"

"Totally integrated dairy farming means you take the raw output, cut out the middlemen, and manage your own final product." Even though he didn't like the dairy farm, I could tell we'd moved into more comfortable territory as he answered.

"Uh huh," I said.

"What Mom's proposing to do is to take all the milk those cows produce and build a gourmet cheese factory. Then she'll sell the cheese directly to stores. It's total control, start to finish," he said.

"Sounds like a lot of work," I said.

"Mom's convinced it would assure the viability of the dairy and provide more jobs for people in Clovis. She's even talking about going more organic with the feed. That way she could sell the cheese in upscale markets."

"Bet you'd like that."

"It'd be okay," he said.

"So how much does a venture like that cost?"

"Millions, lots of millions. Don't get me wrong; if Mom sells some of her property around the state, she can finance a lot of it herself. But it'll be, like, ten to fifteen million."

"And Charly and Theo don't like gourmet cheese?"

"Nope," he said, smiling. "They're more your American, string cheese types. You know, they're the kind of people who think vintners age wine in wooden barrels because they can't afford the plastic."

"What about you? Are you a brie kind of guy?" I said.

"Dairy farming is an exploitative business that pollutes the land and causes all kinds of health problems for all of those milk consumers out there—not to mention the cows."

"Josh, that sounds like you've said it a hundred times," I said. "What do you think about your Mom's plan?"

He shrugged his shoulders. "If Mom wants to spend her fortune on the business, I can't condone it. But it's her money, her land. She can do what she wants with what's hers."

"What will happen to all of her fine plans if she's arrested for murder?"

"We're not going to let that happen, Sasha." He watched for my reaction.

"You kids?" I said.

"Us and you."

"How are we going to do it, Josh?"

"Beats me," he said.

The rest of lunch waxed uninspired. Josh must have felt like he'd said too much; our conversation deteriorated into meringue, all fluff, no substance. He did agree to tell Mae I wanted to see her. *I guess I should be glad for small victories.*

When we said our good-byes, I felt empty, like I knew less than when I'd started. Sure, Mae's kids weren't happy about her plans for the dairy farm. But what on earth did milk and middlemen have to do with murder?

SEVENTEEN

THE MEN DIDN'T MOVE like they should. Their bodies jerked to a silent music. But their feet—their feet glided, the locomotion fluid, magical, as if their toes were attached to hidden tracks. I stood transfixed. My feet ached with heaviness. I watched their arms, then legs fall off—spurting bluish blood onto the snowy ground. I couldn't stop it, no matter how I screamed. The terror continued with the malevolence of a television show that would never end.

I came to, woozy and unsure if I'd been dreaming or hallucinating. I thought about calling my therapist, Zoe, but knew what she'd say about the increased frequency of hallucinations. She'd tell me to breathe deeply, rid myself of as much stress as possible, stop worrying about Mae, and focus on my work.

Good advice. Impossible, too.

Sitting up on the bed, I realized I'd fallen asleep. The blurry, leaden feeling behind my eyes made me curse the unplanned afternoon nap. Coffee, lots of it, would dispel my mental haziness. I opened my purse to check for moolah, found my wallet. The tip of a $20 bill reminded me of Abel King.

I had to know the story. King Senior wouldn't go for subtle questions. He might not answer direct ones either. He'd already refused to be a quoted source for my space alien project.

I didn't have anything to lose.

Sure enough, his name appeared right above Mae's in the phone book. There was also a T. C. King. Probably related, too.

"King," he said. His gruff voice scraped through the phone line, growlier without the benefit of visual cues.

"Hi. This is Sasha Solomon. We met—"

"I remember you." The finality of his tone could have scared a less-seasoned interviewer.

Not me. I'm a top-of-the-line PR pro; nothing intimidates me. His rough, oyster-tight demeanor spurred me forward for the juicy prize within.

"I had lunch with Josh today. He told me something interesting," I said.

Silence.

"He mentioned your brother left you a symbolic gift in his will." I was on thin ice and half-expected him to hang up.

"Symbolic? Is that what Josh said?" King laughed.

"Actually, that was my word for it."

"He tell you how much?"

"Yes."

"What else do you need to know?" King said.

"Why he did it."

"Now, why is that any business of yours, Missy?"

He had me there.

"I was curious," I said.

"I suppose you know about the cat," he said.

"What cat?"

"The one that got killed from being too curious."

"Is that a threat?"

"Nope."

"Are you trying to tell me I'm not getting an answer?"

"I'm not trying. It's none of your beeswax." A sniffle, a cough, a change in tone. "Now, was there anything else you don't need to know?"

"As a matter of fact there is," I said.

"I was afraid of that."

"I know you told me not to ask you about Mae, but I have a couple of questions."

"You always do this?"

"What?"

"Ignore what people ask you to do?"

"Pretty much," I said.

That earned a chuckle. "What do you want to know?"

"Can you tell me about those skeletons you referred to?"

"Ask Mae."

"I can't, Mr. King. Charlene won't let me near her."

"I tell you what, Missy. I've got work to do. I'll call you when I'm done. You're there—we'll talk. You're not—too bad."

With that, the line disconnected. Only then did I remember I'd been returning his call from earlier that day; he had wanted something and I hadn't let him ask. I sighed.

Two o'clock and I needed to work. I knew I should telephone LaSalle. Instead I decided to hit the Pump-n-Snak for another can of whipped cream.

In the lobby of the hotel, I noticed the same man I'd seen in Roswell. At least it looked like him. He straightened a newspaper, his stumpy legs crossed at the ankle like a girl at a cotillion. He glanced up at me, then turned a page. Too nonchalant. I stopped by the desk to ask the clerk for the name of a non-steak house for dinner. The man came up, stood next to me.

"Ms. Solomon, isn't it? What a pleasant surprise," he said.

"Hello, Mr.—"

"Johnson. Bud Johnson. We met at your interview."

"Yes."

His chumminess didn't fool me. He wanted something.

I moved a step away from him.

"Are you enjoying Clovis? Have you had time to see much?" He emitted false bonhomie. "How'd you like a little tour? Why, you probably don't even know about Sandzen, or the community college, or our great zoo. We've got a real Bengal tiger. Retired from Las Vegas."

"Actually, I've visited all those places already."

"You get around, don't you?"

A prickly edge of paranoia made me inch farther away from him. I forced myself to be rational. He was being courteous. He was with the chamber of commerce; Jan Cisneros must have told him to find me, to make sure I felt welcome.

And then, out of the blue, he said, "You're friends with Mae King. Right?"

"Yes." I waited, not blinking.

"You know about the murder on her land. Right?"

"Yes."

"You know who she killed?"

I opened my mouth.

Johnson raised his voice to drown out my objection. "The new Singaporean commanding officer of the four-twenty-eighth fighter squadron at Cannon Air Force Base. That's who," he said. "The guy hadn't been here two weeks."

"Mae didn't kill him." I whispered, trying to quiet him.

I headed to the plush lobby chairs hoping we could finish our conversation away from the gossip-greedy ears of the desk clerk and passersby.

"You don't seem to understand what's at stake here, Ms. Solomon." He followed me to the sitting area. "Cannon brings money, real money, into our economy."

"Mae didn't kill anybody," I said.

"Madam, you believe in your friend. That's admirable." He strained forward, his elbows resting on his thighs. "But friendship doesn't matter here. Don't make a mistake by throwing in your allegiance with a murderer."

"That sounds ominous, Mr. Johnson."

"Take it as you like. Just remember what I said."

Finished, he pushed himself up out of the chair, the bottom

button of his shirt popping with the effort. It flew onto the tiled floor, landing with a plink. Embarrassment followed its trajectory like a heat-seeking missile. We stared at it, neither one daring to speak. He nodded at me once, turned and left.

A drink. I needed a drink, something strong enough to erase the encounter from my mind. I had to work; booze was out. When in doubt, opt for caffeine, good caffeine. I headed to the Coffee Connection for my millionth double espresso. I'd be jittery but focused.

The oversized white wicker chair made a satisfying crunch when I sat down. I opened my notebook and tackled the PR plan. Based on my previous work, I free-associated and diagrammed concepts, a mess of arrows and lines, to capture flashes of insane possibility. I was rephrasing a particularly clever idea about networking with the Roswell museum when I heard the harsh cadence of Cantonese.

Factoid: My undergraduate degree is in Chinese. I earned it at the University of Michigan and even spent a year in Hong Kong learning the language. My graduate degree in social work is from the same lofty establishment—hey, Ann Arbor is a great town. And it starts with "A" like Albuquerque. I live my life in an alphabet theme.

Anyway, to hear Cantonese in Clovis could be neural fabrication as easily as reality. But this was no hallucination. The speakers ensconced at the table to the right of mine argued in nasal tones that climbed and descended a vast musical scale. He, referring to *gwei los* (nicely translated as *foreign devils*). She, panning all Americans as stupid.

Buddha plump, the man's moist skin betrayed his recent arrival in the Southwest; people who've been here for a while wrinkle like raisins. Her moon face, emphasized by a tight, perfect bun, crinkled in disapproval. She wore a casual chic sweat suit of auspicious red and more gold on her arms, hands, and neck than you'd find in most jewelry stores.

"Don't treat me like a baby!" she said, bracelets clinking. *"Ai yah!"*

"You're acting like one, little sister."

This was too good to pass up. Chinese speakers right here in the Coffee Connection.

The woman saw me staring.

"What's she looking at?" she said to her brother.

He returned my stare with open rudeness; I recognized it and wasn't offended. In Hong Kong, my skin had thickened from the experience of being a visible minority. I knew the man assumed I couldn't read his expression or understand their conversation.

"*Leih ho m ho ah?* (How are you?)," I said.

Oh, it was worth it to see their reactions.

"What did you say?" the woman answered me in English.

I repeated the Cantonese greeting.

"You're speaking Cantonese," she said.

"Yep."

"How can she be speaking Cantonese?" Not waiting for an answer, she put the same question to her brother in Chinese.

"Watch out, this gwei lo understands Cantonese," I said. "I learned it in Hong Kong."

This side of hysterical, she laughed and then stood to pull out a chair for me.

"Come," she said. "Come sit with us. The first civilized person we've met here."

A ripple of offense fluttered from one customer to the next in the open room. The insult wasn't intentional; she called it like she saw it—no more, no less. And as a civilized person, I accepted the invite. It sure beat sitting alone and working.

The woman introduced herself as Becky Tan, most recently from Singapore. The man, Mike Cho, was a prominent import-export magnate who'd flown in the day before.

"Are you here for a visit?" I said to him. Standard chit chat.

"For a short visit, yes. I'm here to help Becky move back home."

"Decided to leave already?" I said.

"There's no reason for me to stay any longer," she said. Mid-afternoon sunlight caught her fish-wet eyes, making them glisten.

The room felt cold of an instant. I wanted to ask but didn't dare.

"My sister has suffered a terrible loss," said Mike Cho. His gaze went beyond me to the window and then to his immaculate hands. He twisted a large gold ring on his middle finger.

"Oh, I'm so sorry," I said.

Too much of a coincidence, this can't be happening.

"Perhaps I should leave you alone," I said.

Becky Tan's focus went inward. She paled. Once restrained tears flowed.

"Mrs. Tan?" I said.

She murmured to the air by her shoulder, "Not here. Not now. Please." And then, oddly, "It's her, isn't it?"

"*Chutt!* None of that," Cho said in Cantonese.

"He's here," she said.

Taking his sister's hand, the Chinese businessman tried to yank her out of the chair, but she resisted, as if woven to the wicker.

"My husband's murder will be avenged." Her eyes focused on mine. "And you will help."

"Excuse me?" I said.

Without a word, Cho snatched his sister from her seat, then let her hand drop. She followed, head bent, submissive. Their drinks still steamed on the table when they walked out the door.

EIGHTEEN

BACK AT THE HOTEL, I walked past the front desk. My mind circled the two weird encounters I'd had in less than an hour. Bud Johnson's verbal assault smacked of planning; the man had waited for me, waited to pounce. The parley with Becky Tan and Mike Cho hinted at kismet, a cosmic blip. While I wanted more of the one, I wanted none of the other. Tomorrow morning, I'd ask Jan Cisneros at the Chamber to tether him.

Detective LaSalle tapped my shoulder.

"Hello," he said. "Got a minute?"

"God," I said. "What now?"

He winced.

"What?"

"Why do you have to take the Lord's name in vain?"

I stared at him for a full minute. "The Lord's name? You're not a Baptist, too?"

"What does that have to do with anything?"

He tailed me through the atrium to my room. I unlocked the door. What a mess. I'd forgotten to remove the *Do Not Disturb* sign. Clothes lay everywhere, deflated fish in a sea of carpet and upholstery. The bed I'd napped in gaped unmade, obscene in its disarray.

"This is a real Jesus kind of town, isn't it?" I said.

"We believe in God, if that's what you mean."

"Never mind."

Fidgety hands, quick irritation, racing heart. Too much coffee. I took a deep breath.

"Sasha, you don't have to believe in Jesus to honor the Ten Commandments." He surveyed my room. "Not much of a housekeeper, are you?"

"I don't suppose you drink, do you?" I walked to the cooler, got a Guinness.

"Rarely. But you go ahead. You look like you could use it."

"Gee, thanks," I said, wondering if I looked as caffeine-cranky as I felt.

"Anytime." The detective waited until I sat on the bed, then moved my high heels from a chair and sat across from me. "We've confirmed the identity of the dead man. Like I thought, he was from Singapore."

"I know. I met his widow."

"Mrs. Tan? Where?"

I gave him a rundown on the scene at the Coffee Connection.

"I didn't know you spoke Chinese. That's something." He got a funny look. "When did you say you got to town?"

"Sunday evening around eight. Why?" The realization slapped me upside the head. "You've got to be kidding. Just because I speak Chinese?"

"Don't jump to conclusions," he said.

I took a swig of Guinness, hoping the alcohol would ratchet down my jitters a notch. The beer fizzed out of the bottle.

"Marvy," I said.

LaSalle went to the bathroom, wet a washcloth, came back and handed it to me.

"Refresh my memory. How did you know his name was Tan?" he said.

"I told you, I met his wife."

I swiped at the brown liquid on my hand and leg. The Guinness didn't taste as good as I'd hoped; bitterness coated my tongue. Must have had something to do with the conversation.

"Okay. Don't get upset." LaSalle held up his hands. "Professional habit. I was fishing." He pinched his nose to suppress a sneeze. "We've spoken with Mrs. Tan. And I had the pleasure of being lectured by her brother today. Apparently I'm not doing enough to solve this case."

"Yeah, well. I've met his type before in Hong Kong," I said.

"When were you in Hong Kong?"

"When I was in diapers."

"Really?"

"Nah. I studied Chinese in college." I took another sip, feeling a tad calmer. "Anyway, I bet he's worried about his sister and thinks Americans, especially ones in small towns like this, are too provincial to know what they're doing." Another swig. "Is Mrs. Tan a suspect?"

"You know I can't tell you that."

"Right. Professional habit, I guess." I winked. "So, was that why you stopped by? To tell me about Tan?"

"Not entirely." He had that look—the one that implied he had a lot more to say but I'd have to twiddle my thumbs until he was ready to say it.

I scratched my head, hid a pair of panties under the covers, shoved a bra under there, too.

"We've got to solve this one soon," LaSalle said. "The FBI, OSI, the sheriff, everybody's involved. Just like I predicted. And we have to consider everything."

"Like me?" I tilted the bottle this way and that. "Because I'm Mae's friend?"

"We'd have to be pretty desperate to consider you."

"Gee, thanks."

"That's not saying it won't happen at some point," he said, scooching back his chair, and stretching his legs. He straightened. "Sasha, I need a favor and I don't like asking for favors."

The Guinness bottle had become lighter somehow. I waited.

"I want you to be another set of eyes and ears for me," he said. "I was going to ask in relation to Mae and her family, but now, I'm going to include Mrs. Tan and her brother."

"If blind and deaf will do you any good," I said. "Mae's kids have circled the wagons. I can't get near her. And Mrs. Tan? We've met once. I don't see how I'd be any help at all."

"You never know. If you could just keep your eyes and ears open. Tell me what you pick up. I don't know if it'll help, but you're a unique source of information," he said. "Mae's your friend. You speak Chinese and have an in with Mrs. Tan."

"It sounds an awful lot like being a spy or a tattletale." I went for another beer.

"Not very honorable, is it?" LaSalle said. "But I'm asking for everything, for more than the information that would get someone in trouble." He pinched the tip of his nose. "Don't edit. Don't censor. Just tell me what these people say to you as close to verbatim as possible. There might be something in there that will help the investigation."

"And I should do this because…?" I said.

"It's your civic duty."

I rolled my eyes.

"There's also the issue of contaminating a crime scene," he said.

I bristled, got up, sat down again.

"Look, I dislike threats," he said. "How about I throw this in? I'll try—within reason—to let you know what's going on with the case. And, if we decide to pick up Mae for the murder, I'll give you a heads up before it's common knowledge."

Sasha Solomon, police stooge. I didn't like it, being an informant. But what did I owe anyone but Mae? Charlene, at best, was a ditz. I felt no obligation toward Josh. And the Singaporeans? Who knew? They might be the murderers. Then I remembered someone who might be quite angry at Mae.

"Hey, what do you know about Abel King?" I said.

"Abel?"

"Yeah."

"He's a businessman," he said. "Why?"

"Do you know Damon only left him a $20 bill in his will?" LaSalle watched me.

"Pretty rude, huh?" I said.

"You're thinking he'd be angry at his brother? That he'd take it out on Mae?" LaSalle frowned. "That's grasping at straws. He's a good, strong citizen in this community."

"Like Bud Johnson?"

"Bud?"

"Guess who knew details about the murder this afternoon?" I said.

"That's ridiculous. He wouldn't know anything."

"Oh, but he does." I put down the bottle and leaned forward. "He staked out the lobby, like you did, and waited for me. Then he started yelling about Mae killing a guy from Singapore. And then he threatened me not to—oh, what did he say?—not to cast my lot with Mae or something like that."

Pulling out a small notebook and pen, LaSalle held my gaze, serious. With a clinical voice devoid of emotion and chilling with its singular focus, he said, "Stop, Sasha. Take a breath."

I did.

"Start at the beginning. Tell me exactly what happened," he said.

NINETEEN

REVENGE IS BETTER in the abstract. I enjoyed the idea of getting Bud Johnson in trouble but the interview made me feel sleazy. I could imagine the thin film of dirt around my soul. With LaSalle gone, I downed the rest of the now-warm beer. The Guinness had worked its magic; I'd be able to concentrate on the PR plan.

I decided to unpack my paraphernalia from Roswell. First out of the bag was the mask. I tried it on in front of the large mirror in the dressing area, laughed, and then put it face down on the guest bed. Next came the pens—purple, pink, and blue—with their itty-bitty space alien heads floating up and down in water. I put them by the laptop for inspiration when my creative impulses waned. Last, but favorite among the purchases, was a photo of a road sign. The graphic, black against ochre, showed a cow being transported into a flying saucer. The picture deserved a place of honor. I propped it against my dictionary and thesaurus, mere inches beyond the computer screen. I wanted to be able to see it while I typed.

For the next three hours, I worked, putting myself in the mindset of people who'd shell out good money to go to Roswell or that place in Nevada. The modem tweeted. I keyed in *UFOs, alien abductions,* and *space aliens.* Each search referenced hundreds of thousands of sites. Our audience was out there. What made it tick?

I checked out a couple of sites, but the Internet connection was slow and my heart wasn't into exploring more than a few.

Instead, I let my imagination float. I thought about the people I'd seen in Roswell. And about what I'd watched on television over the years. One thing had always bugged me. If aliens were so advanced, with technology that far exceeded our own, why did they make a habit of snatching dowdy girls and pasty boys for their experiments? Why didn't they go for nuclear physicists or Nobel Prize winners? And why was it always small-town hicks? Less attention?

From there, I thought about science and science fiction. Which led me to Creationism and Bible Belt communities. How would the deeply religious community in Clovis feel about space aliens? Would they be more acceptable than evolution? Another confirmation of God's glorious plan?

One thing the Roswell Museum did well was to present the information as if it were scientific. The approach validated the whole idea of aliens and abductions. I sensed from my eavesdropping that our target audience needed the appearance of objectivity. How were we going to achieve the same thing in our Clovis project?

I picked up the small piece of metal Abel King had given me. Maybe we could use the site he'd taken me to as our base. Or if, as Jan Cisneros had said, there were more sites, maybe we could do a bus tour ending in a freestanding museum. If we could find more artifacts, people could actually touch them. I looked at the shiny object, scrunched it, watched it pop back to its original shape. A couple of bigger pieces would be pretty convincing.

My main problem was that I wanted to gather more information before nailing down the plan. I had enough text—with some editing—to present an idea. In order to get the job, it would have to be stronger—more Clovis-focused, less generic.

I disconnected the modem and stood up, thinking hard.

The phone could've rung a hundred times before I noticed it. Answering, I heard three musical tones, then a robotic voice directed me to hold the line for a prerecorded message.

"Sasha, how could you?" It was Mae. She sounded awful.

"Mae?" I said, concern causing my heart to thump.

"If you'd like to repeat the message, press one," said the she-robot.

I pressed *one*.

"Sasha, how could you?"

I pressed *one* a second time.

"Sasha, how could you?"

I dialed Mae's number. The phone rang and rang, a sound made lonelier by its own insistence.

At the computer again, I tried to focus on the plan. I looked at the cow picture, then at a small desk calendar. Wednesday. Two days left to complete my proposal. I'd have to work straight through to get the thing done. The more I scolded myself, striving to reign in my worries about Mae, the more my thoughts shifted toward paralysis.

Why had there been accusation in her voice, the strained pitch of betrayal?

Obsessing is like an endless loop; you've got to snap it somewhere. I decided to go for a quick dinner in the hotel restaurant. Outside the entrance, the afternoon paper had a large photo of Mae. I bought one.

Along with the waitress's smile and my water came the explanation. The headline splashed across the newsprint like spilled coffee.

KING TAKEN INTO CUSTODY

Clovis, NM—Local dairy farmer Mae King was taken into protective custody this afternoon after an apparent nervous breakdown. According to her daughter, Charlene Simpson, Mrs. King had been confused and despondent since the body of Colonel Tan Li Piao was found on her land earlier this week.

"When Mom started talking about space aliens, I

knew something was wrong," said Simpson. "And then, I saw those cuts on her, and, well, I had to do something."

I read the paragraphs again. What cuts? And why did Charlene believe there was a causal relationship between Mae's finding Colonel Tan and her claims about being abducted? That event A led to event B?

A three-column-wide photo of a smiling Mae and Damon graced the next page.

"Mom's claiming she's been in a space ship, not once, but three times in the last couple of days," said Simpson. "She says the aliens cut her on her stomach and chest. When she told us that, we knew she was a danger to herself. We had to do something. Thank goodness the police were here to help."

Hold on a minute. The aliens cut her? Mae had never said anything about torture.

And what was this about being abducted multiple times in the last few days? That didn't make sense. The only recent abduction I knew about was yesterday's. Were there others?

Charlene's chronology bothered me. If Mae had been taken into custody earlier today, then what about the supposed shopping trip to Lubbock? Was Josh lying? Did he know Charlene was going to call the police? Or the ambulance, or whomever she called? And LaSalle! Was his eyes-and-ears routine a ruse?

I thanked the waitress when she served my grilled cheese with green chile, speared a French fry, and read on.

Acquaintances and business associates expressed shock. "You'll never meet a more stable person than Mae King," said Roc Johnson, former mayor of Clovis. Simpson revealed her mother has been fighting depression and mental fatigue since her husband, Damon King, died four years ago. "Mom hasn't been the same since Dad died. Sure, she's acted normal to the rest of the world, but in private she's a shattered woman. Most people don't know she can hardly do anything for herself. I think this murder put her over the edge."

Mrs. King is being held at the Northwest Regional Medical Center awaiting evaluation.

My grunt of disgust suspended conversations at the two tables nearest me. I gazed mid-distance in disbelief. All through that horrible night with Mae—the body, the discussion afterward—she'd never seemed *shattered*. Upset? Well, duh. But crazy? Clinically depressed? Not on your life. She'd been as lucid as anyone could be given the circumstances.

Charlene was lying.

The food could have been soap flakes for all the attention I paid it. I rushed back to my room, phoned LaSalle's office, his home. Wasted efforts. I kicked the chair he'd sat in a few hours before. He'd asked for help and lied through his teeth. The man was as mercenary as a five-year-old who wanted a candy bar.

Charlene's betrayal loomed monumental. A daughter lying to get her mother committed. Why had she done it? Did Mae even have cuts? Had Charlene made that up, too? I massaged my forehead. My mom could make me furious. She often did. But I'd never, ever, do something this odious to her. Charlene would, and had. Thanks to her, Mae was stuck in a loony bin.

I punched LaSalle's numbers again and paced the room, feeling like the cougar at the zoo—trapped, mean, and no place to go. I thought about Mae's last message, her tone. The epiphany hit like an open-handed slap on a sunburned face: she blamed *me!*

Why? Her two-faced daughter, that's why.

I flopped onto the bed, sat up, and dialed Mae's place again. The answering machine, with its garbled recording, picked up. I continued my pacing.

"Charlene, this is Sasha. Call me back, please. I'm in Room 111 at the Holiday Inn. Thanks," I said.

The laptop lured me, a life-rope for my swirling emotions. If I could find information on the Internet about protective custody, I could help Mae. Uneasy in my skin, I leaned against the dresser for support and drank the remnants of cold, metallic coffee from this morning's brew.

Twenty minutes passed. I called again.

"Charlene, it's Sasha. I really need to talk with you."

An hour later, I'd abandoned the nice messages.

"Charlene, if you don't call back within the next ten minutes, I'm calling the police."

That did it. My phone rang.

"One more call from you and *I'm* calling the police!" she said.

TWENTY

"Fine by me," I said.

"You're insane," Charlene said. "What do you want from me?"

I wanted *her* in the loony bin. And Mae free.

"That was a fascinating article in the paper today. You're quite quotable," I said.

She slammed down the phone.

What tiresome behavior.

I dialed once more, got the recording.

"Charlene. I know you lied. You know you lied." I sat on the bed to remove my shoes. "Two questions remain. Why did you do it? And, do the police know what a crock you're handing them?" I cleared my throat. "Courtesy of your mom, I've recently learned about felonious withholding of information."

The machine beeped to disconnect. I redialed.

"Me again, Charlene. One more question. What happens when the police find out you've made them look like fools?" I hung up, not feeling very proud of myself.

The phone twittered. I waited an extra ring to make her squirm.

"Sasha, please stop it. Charly can't handle any more. She's falling apart," said Josh.

"You can't be defending her."

"Someone has to." He took a breath. "What has Charly ever done to you?"

"I thought you wanted to help your mom."

"I do. But can't you understand that when they take your mother away kicking and screaming she's not crazy, can't you understand that that's upsetting? Charly's a mess."

"*Charly* is the reason your mom's in trouble in the first place."

"Mom said it was you."

"Josh, how could I get your mom committed?"

He thought about that for a minute.

"You're not going to tell me you didn't know Charlene lied to the police," I said. "Your mom told me Sunday night she'd been abducted several times before. *Ergo* she's not suddenly having a nervous breakdown. Your sister is a blatant liar. And you too, Josh. You must have known she was going to do this when we had lunch."

"I didn't! I thought they were in Lubbock."

"So, what happened?"

"They had to come back early. Charly said Mom started flipping out in the car."

"Since when does your mother flip out?" I said. "Have you ever seen her flip out, Josh?"

There was a long silence.

"Josh?"

"Yeah."

"Do you believe me?"

"*When* did Mom tell you about the abductions?"

"That night at the hotel. Have you even read the paper? Have you seen what Charlene said? She makes it sound like Mae's been depressed for years. Ever since your dad died."

"Well, that's simply not true."

"You're preaching to the choir," I said. "Weren't you there when this went down?"

"No. It happened while we were at lunch."

"So, you haven't seen the paper or heard what Charlene's saying?"

"Not yet. Can I call you back?"

"Only if you promise to tell your big sister we need to talk."

"I'll see what I can do."

I tried to work, honest I did. *Roswell. Clovis Man as a space alien. Cannon Air Force Base attracting extraterrestrial attention. Interviews with old-timers.* How was I ever going to get this done? I needed more time, the weekend at least. And I'd spent money like an idiot. Was Mae still paying for the hotel? I'd have to find cheaper digs if she wasn't.

I took a deep breath to regain my perspective. This was a PR *plan,* not the implementation of it. All I needed to provide was a framework, a general scheme, not all the nitty gritty details. The Chamber could have those when I was hired.

Why hadn't anyone called back yet?

Come on. Focus!

Truth: I didn't want to talk with Charlene; I wanted to spear her.

I tried LaSalle's numbers again. He should be the one to question her. Because of Charlene, Mae thought I'd violated a confidence. I was upset and hurt. How could she believe such a terrible thing of me?

This isn't about you, Sasha. I picked at the pain until it was numb.

A knock on the large window outside the room distracted me. It sounded like a bird had hit the glass. I peeked out the curtain, then opened the door. In the faint light, I saw a small parcel at my door. Quickly, I looked both directions down the darkened walkways, then picked up the package. Someone had written my last name in black marker across the top. I ripped open the wrapping. It revealed a white jewelry box within. Unfastening the clasp, I found a piece of paper, folded and then folded again. Inside, typed in Times Roman, was a message.

"LEAVE WELL ENOUGH ALONE."

TWENTY-ONE

My POINTER FINGER HAD a permanent kink from dialing. I tried LaSalle's house one last time though it was past midnight. No go. I punched in his office number again. A woman answered, emanating impatience. Bottom line: LaSalle was unavailable.

"I need to talk to him about the Singaporean case. You think he'll be available for that?" I didn't bother concealing my testiness. Exhaustion knuckled my brain. My tense neck ached.

"I'll give him the message as soon as I can, ma'am," she said. "He's been in meetings since before I got here and hasn't come out once. It may be a while before he gets it." Frustration permeated her words.

We mumbled our good-byes, allies in aggravation.

I turned the unfolded note in my hands. Reread it. The message didn't upset me. Its sophomoric delivery contained no real threat or danger. I knew who'd left it. Bud Johnson. Come to think of it, he'd done me a favor. The chit would help with my work. Paranoia was a key factor in the UFO/abduction industry. I decided Bud's handiwork could serve as additional inspiration and placed it on top of its box next to the flying saucer and cow photo.

I felt as dingy and colorless as overcooked meat. I rolled my shoulders to release tension, got a cup of the hotel coffee, and set to work. The plan was coming into focus. I knew what I'd do once they'd hired me: I'd interview all the people I could find in and around Clovis who'd seen UFOs or who claimed to have been abducted. I'd concentrate on the really credible sources, the policemen, retired air force pilots, professors, prominent businesspeople. I frowned. Mae would have been such a great source. Abel King, too.

Waitaminute. King was supposed to call me back. I looked at my watch. He might not appreciate a call at one in the morning. I plunged forward, tap-tapping on the keyboard, making solid progress.

After I had a plethora of good stories and facts, I'd get on the Web—or hire some college kid to help me—create a site and link to every other UFO-extraterrestrial-abduction-conspiracy outlet in the ether. I'd also propose a *there* there; the city would have to invest in a destination for visitors to come to—be it a museum, a tract of land, a theme park. And, I still liked the idea of a guided bus tour to crash sites—if there were more like the one King had shown me.

When the location was established, I could use national media—credible or not—to publicize a grand opening. Along with tourism outlets, newspapers, *New Mexico Magazine,* I'd target more sensational outlets: *Weekly World News, National Enquirer.* This was going to be a blast!

Of course, there would have to be some preliminary work with the public information office at Cannon Air Force Base to make sure no one got blindsided. Jan Cisneros had told me about a group of prominent citizens who'd formed a committee that spent its time making sure Cannon was well funded and well-respected. I'd include them as a critical part of the plan, using one of their members to make sure we didn't endanger funding to the base. That'd impress the locals.

I still didn't have an angle for Clovis Man, wasn't sure how to work him in. I suspected he wasn't too popular with the fundamentalists in town since scientists used him to prove the theory of evolution. But I wanted to use the guy, too. Perhaps if we posited that his origins were extraterrestrial. Who could really say how he'd come to the high plains of New Mexico?

I dozed off at some point. I know because the phone rang at six a.m. and I jumped. The chair I'd been in tumbled backward. Rubbing my eyes and banged-up back, I answered.

"Ms. Solomon?" The male voice dripped with ego and arrogance.

"Speaking."

"This is Theodore King." *Basso profundo;* I was supposed to cower at the name.

"Yes."

Though we'd never met, I could picture him. Oily, self-satisfied, and full of enough hot air to power a balloon to China.

"Charlene Simpson's brother," he said.

"Ah. You mean Mae King's son?" I said.

"That, too."

"Okay. Well, how can I help you, Theodore?"

"Mr. King."

"Excuse me, Mr. King. So sorry."

"Are you being sarcastic?"

"Mr. King, the sun hasn't come up yet. I'm working under deadline and I don't have time to play games. What do you want?"

"You'd better leave my sister alone." He paused for effect. "I will not have you impugning her good name for your nefarious personal gain." He'd have made a great bit player in a melodrama. "You're perilously close to a slander suit."

"Mr. King, 'nefarious personal gain'? You've gotta be kidding," I said, snickering. "I'm more at risk for a felony if I withhold any more information. You know that. And, I'd like to remind you I'm not at fault here. Your sister is the one who should be worried. Not me."

He didn't say anything. I heard muffled sounds, as if he held his hand over the receiver. I imagined the King kids conferencing in the kitchen or family room, trying to save Charlene from inevitable consequences.

"Why can't you leave me alone?" Charlene whined a minute later.

"Why should I?"

"You just should. And you better stop butting into our business."

"Charlene, you're not exactly on high moral ground here," I said. "Don't you have any sense of shame?"

"Me? What about Mom? She's crazy!"

"Because she thinks she's been abducted?"

"And, that the aliens cut her," she said, waiting for me to bite.

"You made that up," I said. "Just like you made it look like this alien abduction thing was caused by Colonel Tan's death. You know you lied to get her taken into custody."

"So what? Getting her committed is a lot better than having her stand trial for murder. I was doing it for her. To protect her."

"I don't know what game you're playing, but I'm going to find out," I said.

"This isn't a game, Sasha. It's my mother's life." Charlene coughed. "Don't you get it? When they see she's crazy, they won't blame her for killing that man."

I didn't answer. Mae's own daughter thought her mom had committed murder.

"Sasha?" The voice had changed.

"Josh, did you hear that?"

"Yeah."

"What do you think?"

"I don't know. It's pretty sick, if you ask me."

Theodore and Charlene both exclaimed in the background.

"I wouldn't blame you for telling the police, Sasha. Not one bit," Josh said.

"I don't know what else to do, unless you do it instead."

"I can't. I don't know for a fact that Charly's lied."

"I didn't," she yelled.

"Mom's never talked to me about the abductions," Josh continued. "Our phone conversations are usually about me. The first time I heard any of this was yesterday, after our lunch." He stopped, cleared his throat. "I'm disgusted."

"Me, too."

There was another conference before he spoke again.

"I'll call you later. Maybe we can meet somewhere and figure this out," Josh said.

"What are you going to do?"

"I don't know. To be honest, I'd like to hop on a plane and go back to Napa. Let everyone fend for themselves," he said. "But with Mom locked up, I can't leave. Not until she's out. Not until the police decide she's not a suspect."

"Okay. Well. Will you call me back if you have a brilliant idea?" I said.

"I'll call you either way. Tonight, if I can. Tomorrow at the latest."

I returned to the computer and picked up the little white note, wondering if Charlene and Bud Johnson might be in cahoots. Nothing would surprise me now. Charly made it sound like she had been acting nobly, trying to save her mom. I knew she was a liar. Could she be involved with Tan's murder? I still didn't see how.

But why not?

If Mae didn't make sense as a suspect—and the police were looking at her—why not Charlene? I had to talk with LaSalle. He was the one to figure out this muddle. Not me.

The sun tickled the night sky. I showered, dressed semi-professionally—not jeans, but not heels either—and went for breakfast. After biscuits and gravy, I tried to work for another hour, but it was a bust. I knew I couldn't get anything done until I'd gotten this Charlene mess off my plate and onto LaSalle's.

I unplugged the computer, packed it up, and headed downtown.

TWENTY-TWO

THE DETECTIVE DIVISION receptionist was young, sweet, and wholesome as a sun-kissed apple. She told me LaSalle had slipped out for breakfast but was expected back in a "jiffy." I opened the laptop, hoping a dose of the criminal element would get my creative juices flowing. I was rereading a sample press release when I heard the gutturals of Cantonese. Mike Cho had entered with his sister in tow. Becky Tan recognized me right away. Came over. I closed the computer.

"Ms. Solomon. How are you?"

We spoke our greetings in Chinese. Cho nodded, went to the front desk, then returned.

"Why are you looking for Detective LaSalle? What has he to do with you?" he said.

"I know the woman who owns the land where your husband was found." I addressed Mrs. Tan, ignoring her rude bother. She deserved to know what I was up to more than he did, her loss being greater.

"The one who murdered my brother-in-law?" said Cho.

"Mae didn't kill anyone." I felt like a recording.

"Of course she did," he said.

"How do you know that? Why does everyone assume Mae killed a man she'd never met, knew nothing about, had no business with?" I said. "I'm stumped. Perhaps you can enlighten me since you know so much."

The widow put a hand on my arm. "My husband says she did not do it." She turned to Cho. "Big brother, you know that."

"Your husband told you this?" I said.

"Certainly. His ghost is still wandering." Her hand remained on my arm. "We need to take his body home. The monks need to guide his spirit."

"Hush!" Cho's cheeks had lost the flush from his earlier outburst.

"He mocks you, big brother. He says you are a fool. Can you not hear him?"

"Ms. Solomon, please forgive my sister. She is mad with grief."

"Do not make excuses for me," she countered.

Their conversation lapsed into rapid and passionate Cantonese, making it difficult to follow.

In English, Becky Tan said, "My husband says you can see him, too. He visits you in your dreams."

Cho regarded me, his eyes small with suspicion. What should I say? She sounded like another member of the crazy club. But I had dreamed about her husband and seen him that first time in the *Bosque del Apache*.

"There is no need to answer silly questions," Cho said. "We are leaving. This minute."

He tried to pry his sister from the chair, the action déjà vu familiar. She gripped both of the armrests, her fingertips white with effort. This was an old, old dance between them. Letting go with an audible grunt, he went back to the receptionist.

"My husband, my beautiful husband needs your help," she whispered, watching her brother's back. "You must call me. Here is my number." She handed me a piece of paper. "Call between three and four today. Big brother always takes his walk then. We must talk."

I nodded, half-listening to her and to Mike Cho bullying at the counter.

"None of you know a thing. Not a thing," he bellowed. "This is no way to conduct an investigation."

"Sir," the receptionist said.

"No arrest? Pah! You know who did it and still nothing has been done. My government will hear about this!"

A crisply suited man—I assumed he was a detective—appeared from the back, opened the locked door, and addressed Cho. The businessman's shoulders slumped forward. A minute later, he pivoted around and faced his sister.

"Come! These people will learn they cannot treat us with such disrespect," Cho said.

"Why must you make enemies? You are doing no good," said Becky Tan. With a sigh, she gestured a quick good-bye to me, her smooth hand moving less than an inch in the wave.

When they left, I got a clear view of the young girl who'd been the brunt of Cho's ire. Her body shook from crying though I heard no sobs. The detective consoled her. She nodded, tried to be brave.

"Don't take it personally. Cantonese is a loud language. Some people forget that when they switch to English," I said from my chair.

It sounded flimsy but she was gracious enough to attempt a smile.

"Hey, you got in the line of his fire. That's all. It was really meant for the person who killed his brother-in-law." I tried to will her mood back to perkiness.

The phone rang and she answered it.

The "jiffy" turned into more than an hour. My fieldtrip at the station hadn't unleashed massive creativity. I handed the receptionist my business card.

"Please tell Detective LaSalle I give up," I said. "If he wants to talk, he knows where to find me."

TWENTY-THREE

WITH A BIT OF MONEY in the right places, downtown Clovis could be a draw. The Lyceum Theatre, completed in 1920, sported a grand old façade and had been renovated for contemporary use. Down on Seventh Street, you could almost hear Buddy Holly's "Puh, puh, puh, Peggy, Peggy Sue-ue-ue" bursting from the restored Norman Petty Studio. But music wasn't on my mind; ghosts, lies, and Bud Johnson were.

I decided to visit the local library.

Small-town newspapers are big-time resources. The *Clovis News Journal* gushed with information on my particular subject. Bud liked media attention and managed to get his picture taken at every Chamber event the publication covered. Though his political stances might have been popular with some in this town—he supported instruction of Creationism and opposed sex education in public schools—Bud couldn't garner enough popularity to push his ideas into action. Both of his runs for mayor had ended in defeat.

When Bud couldn't get his mug on the front page, he advertised his dental practice. The lousy graphic of a smiling mouth with a cross at its center was bad enough. The tag line put him over the top: *Beautiful smiles for Jesus.*

Mind you, I've got nothing against religiosity. It's intolerance that activates my gag reflex. And Bud reeked of it.

Born and bred in Clovis, educated in Portales and then at the University of Kansas, Bud was a Bible-thumping, never-been-married Baptist who probably felt out of place without a wife and kids of his own. From what I read, it looked like my fellow baby boomer still lived with his mommy and daddy. If I didn't like him before, I liked him even less after my research.

Since I had the microfiches out anyway, I decided to search the newspaper's coverage of UFOs. What I found focused on Cannon Air Force Base. In one of the articles, The Clovis 25 was mentioned. Jan Cisneros had told me about this group working to save the base. Redirecting my search to the new topic, I found more than a hundred articles in the last two years.

And then it clicked: Bud Johnson was upset about bad PR propelling Cannon onto the governmental butcher block. He must be a member of The Clovis 25.

I remembered the fights to save Kirtland Air Force Base in Albuquerque. The base had come up a few times as a tempting target for military cuts. If that ever happened, tens of thousands of people would lose their jobs. It would be horrible. But Albuquerque is a big city, at least by southwestern standards. We'd persevere. Clovis was a different story. If Cannon went under, it would drag the town right down with it.

I scanned for Bud's name in the new articles. He wasn't mentioned in connection with the group. How could I find out if he was a member? LaSalle would know, but I didn't want to involve him in this. Bud wasn't dangerous; he was irritating and a crummy writer. Witness the cliché note he'd left. All I wanted was to find enough dirt to irritate him right back.

I copied down several names of Clovis 25 members and found them in the white pages of the local directory. With quarters in hand, I headed for a phone. What was I going to say to these people? I cast the money back into my purse.

Plan B: food. I found a Blake's Lotaburger—the New Mexico version of Mickey D's or Wendy's—and ordered a green chile cheeseburger, fries, and a chocolate milkshake. Traffic flowed by while I ate the burger, enjoying the hot spiciness of the roasted peppers.

After lunch I decided to stop by the Chamber to talk with Jan Cisneros. I wanted to sniff out details about my competition and get the skinny on Bud. A handwritten sign on the front desk in the lobby announced Sandra had gone to lunch. I strolled through the low-lit hallway and found Clovis's chief marketer at her desk, eating.

"Oh! Excuse me," she said, wiping mustard off her lips.

"I'm sorry. I can come back later," I said.

"No, no, no. My hamburger and I would love some company." She brightened. "No, really. It's fine. Sit down. I left you a message this morning. How's the plan coming?"

"Great. All that's left is getting it in presentable order."

"That's what I wanted to talk with you about. How quickly do you think you could get it to us?" My prospective boss selected a long French fry, dipped it in catsup, and dripped some on an official-looking piece of paper. "Oh, drat."

"The plan," I said to get her attention. "Do you need it now?" If she did, I'd go back to the hotel, lock the door, and unplug the phone. Mae, and everything else, would have to wait.

Her face crumpled into a jumble of emotion. She wiped at the catsup with frantic motions, spreading it into bigger streaks.

"It's just that—that—we've had some changes happen," she said, covering both of her eyes with her hands and hiding her face.

"Ms. Cisneros? Are you all right?"

"Oh, I'm fine." Her red eyes blinked back barely contained sorrow. "Don't mind me. This job can have a lot of pressures."

"Is there anything I can do?"

She shook her head, rubbed her hands together.

"The other finalist has asked for an extension," she said. "I gave him until Monday. I suppose you'd like one, too?"

"That'd be fine." Yippee! Hallelujah. "Is there anything I can do to help you?"

"What? Oh, no, no. I'm fine." A fat tear rolled down her cheek. She sniffled, blew her nose. "I'm sorry. A couple of hours ago, I found out our City Manager is leaving. And Cannon's threatened again. And this murder case. Everything is hitting at once."

"The murder and closing the Air Force Base are separate issues," I said.

"Of course they are." She took a sip of her drink. "But tell that to a bunch of congressmen who're looking for any excuse to save their hides and get votes." She tossed the tissue she'd used into the garbage can. "Kirtland gets all the positive PR. Clovis is too small. We're really at risk this time."

"What about The Clovis 25?"

Pride replaced anguish. "If anyone can save Cannon again, they'll do it."

"I bet Bud Johnson's a real help there," I said.

"Bud?"

"He strikes me as very assertive. He must be a big player in The Clovis 25."

"Noooo," she said, her voice stretching the word like taffy. "He's not part of the 25."

"He's not?"

Jan Cisneros shook her head.

"That's strange," I said. It'd been tidy, the way I'd figured him out.

"Has Bud been up to something?"

"I think so." My face felt tense. "I'm pretty sure he's been following me. And I got an anonymous note that has his style all over it. Anyway, I kind of thought Bud was worried about the wrong kind of PR for Cannon. And that led me to The Clovis 25."

Her eyes took on an expression I couldn't decipher. Something had changed. She'd retreated to a place I couldn't fathom.

"How awful for you," she said with brittle sympathy. Cisneros ate another fry, not moving the paper she'd ruined. "You're sure it's Bud?"

"Reasonably sure."

I told her about Roswell, the encounter in the hotel lobby, the little white box.

"It's not particularly upsetting. Just annoying," I said. "Can you call him off?"

"I know someone who can."

"Well, I'd appreciate it." I cocked my head a tad to the right. "Why were you surprised when I asked if Bud was part of The Clovis 25?"

"That gets into city politics. It would only bore you," Cisneros said.

"I bet it wouldn't."

Her response was a light stare, held a moment too long.

"I know he ran for mayor twice and lost," I said, hoping to convince her to talk.

Instead, she got up, excused herself, and disappeared down the hallway. She returned a moment later and closed the door.

"I needed to make sure someone was out front," she said in a semi-whisper. "Bud's what I'd call a loose cannon. He thinks he knows everything about everything. You've met the type."

I nodded.

"The Clovis 25 is prestigious, about fifty men—mainly men—and in addition to contributing substantial money to the project, there's another requirement. You have to be voted in. Think about it. Bud can't even get himself elected mayor of a city run by a city manager. How would he pass muster with the most respected people in town?" she said.

"He's on your board. That's got to count for something."

Her expression was more cynical than I would have thought possible.

"Yes, he's on the board. That's as a favor to someone a lot more important." She scratched at the back of her neck. "Let's leave it at that."

"So there's no way he'd bother me on behalf of the 25?"

"No way." She dumped the rest of her fries in the garbage. "These guys have breakfast with five-star generals. They have lunch with the Singaporean Ambassador. They wouldn't play games with you. They're too classy. I don't know what Bud's up to. If it is Bud."

She looked at her watch.

"Who else would it be?" I said.

"Ms. Solomon, I really don't know. Have you spoken to Henry about it?" She mistook my momentary silence. "Detective LaSalle."

"Not yet. He's hard to track down."

"Well, he's been awfully busy lately." She sounded like they were bosom buddies.

"Really?"

"Everyone's breathing down his neck. He told me they're even thinking about bringing in the CIA." She bit a fingernail, then wadded up the paper from her burger. "It's like he's got twenty bosses. No wonder you can't find him." She stood to open the door. "But I can tell you this. He really respects you."

Big whoopee. "That's nice."

She lingered half-in, half-out of the doorframe, the hint obvious. I could have pushed the conversation further but didn't bother. Jan Cisneros had given me more information than I'd expected.

"Thanks for talking with me." I got up, held out my hand for a shake.

She didn't extend hers.

I stalled, said, "Soooo, Monday then for the PR plan?"

"What? Oh, yes, that'll be fine."

She glanced at her watch. Looked at me. Glanced at her watch again.

I got the message and bid her *adios*. In the lobby waited a well-dressed man. His veneer shone more polished and pressed, clipped and tucked, than I'd seen anywhere in Clovis so far. Formal, like he'd just arrived from New York or D.C. At his feet sparkled an auburn leather briefcase. His shoes showed not a single scuff.

We assessed each other, disliking what we saw.

Unwilling to cower before his disdain, I looked straight at him again before leaving. He narrowed his eyes, set his jaw, then turned his head away.

TWENTY-FOUR

WIND JETTISONED pieces of litter across the street. I tramped back to the police station. It was a little after one o'clock. If LaSalle wasn't in, I planned to cozy up to my laptop and camp in the waiting room until he returned. I didn't have anything better to do.

When I entered, the receptionist smiled at me, nodded, and spoke into a headset. LaSalle opened the locked door to the inner sanctum before I had time to get comfy.

"You've been busy," he said.

"Sounds like you've been busier." I followed him to his office. We passed a conference room where several men sat at an oversized white table. Giant pieces of paper jammed with scrawls in red, blue, and green hung from strips of masking tape on the walls. Dry-erase boards covered with text and grids filled out the rest of the space. It looked like a hyper-literate decorator had gone mad.

"Is that Homicide Central?" I said, pointing.

"Part of it." We sat down. He raised his chin, inviting me to speak. "What do you have?"

Innocuous enough, but the tone rang false, a studied cross between patronizing and bored. For a second I couldn't remember why I'd been so intent on speaking with him. To buy time, I scrunched my eyes shut. Most people would have asked if I were okay. LaSalle didn't.

"Boy, that was some article in the paper about Mae," I said, using the aw-shucks approach he'd thrown my way when we'd first met.

"Yes, it was."

"Gee. I thought you were going to call me if Mae was arrested."

"She wasn't arrested."

"Arrested, in custody, call it what you want. She's still someone's prisoner."

"I don't have control over everything," LaSalle muttered.

The off-kilter response made me watch him more closely while he reigned his anxiety, forcing it through a sieve into gentleness.

"It would have helped if you'd told me about those abductions," he said.

"I didn't think they were important."

"But you knew about them, right?"

I looked at my hands. "Yeah."

"You decided they weren't important?"

"Sort of."

"Sort of."

I scootched in the seat, feeling sheepish. "Mae told me in confidence. I didn't want to betray her trust."

"That's not what we agreed on. You said you'd tell me everything you know."

"That was before."

"Before what?"

"Oh, never mind."

"So, what do you know?" LaSalle said.

"I don't know what I know," I said. "Yes, I do. Mae's not crazy."

"Let's see what the psychiatrist says."

"Did she really have cuts like Charlene said?"

LaSalle nodded.

"Really?"

He tapped a pencil against the edge of his desk, rattattatt, rattattatt. The room was hot, overheated for windy, spring-like weather.

"How long will they hold her?" I said.

"Up to a week. I hope for everyone's sake it's not that long."

We gauged each other, miserable and wary. Both of us with unexpressed agendas.

"You know, this seems like a bad time for you," I said, getting to my feet.

"No, no. It's okay. I'm tired. Go on. What else have you got?"

I perched on the chair's metal arm. "I think Bud Johnson is up to more tricks."

LaSalle grimaced, crossed his hands in front of his face and rested his chin.

"I spoke with Bud myself. He claims you made everything up. It's one of those he-says, she-says deals," LaSalle said.

"If he wants to go incognito, he should get rid of that sapphire pinky ring."

The detective gave a single nod.

"And what did he say about the note? Did I write it myself?" I said.

"The note."

The phone rang. He picked it up, listened, said, "I know. Frankie, could you hold my calls for fifteen more minutes? I know. This is the last time, I promise." A tiny smile, then a frown as he hung up. "What note?"

I told him.

"I don't have time for this."

"You think I do?" I said.

"Sorry." Rattattatt, rattattatt. "I'll check into it."

"Thanks." Conciliation dangled in the air. "Can you tell me what happened with Mae?"

He shook his head.

"Can I see her?"

"Not right now." He got a sly look on his face. "And you'd have to drive to Albuquerque not to do it."

"Albuquerque? Why?"

He stared at me as if I should understand.

"But the newspaper said—"

"Since when do you believe the paper?" he said. "Our local psychiatrist is on vacation. We thought it would be good to get her out of town anyway. Keep her safer."

"The whole protective custody thing is just a cover?"

"No. She hurt herself. She's under observation."

"And there's no way I can help her?"

"You forget. You're my eyes and ears."

"I've got more than fifteen minutes' worth of information," I said.

"But I don't have fifteen minutes to listen." He looked at his watch. "In ten, I've got to be in a meeting." He picked up a picture from his desk, wiped imaginary specks off the frame, put it down. "You see, Sasha. This whole situation is problematic. I'm titular head of the homicide team but no one bothered to tell me about taking Mae into custody until after it'd been done." He snorted. "The guy at the paper knew before I did."

"I bet Charlene is feeling pretty proud of herself right now," I said.

"Charly? Why?"

"You know I know how the media works."

He nodded.

"She had to have called the paper," I said.

"Why would she do something like that?"

"To turn people against her mom."

Though fatigue smeared his face, he radiated more energy than I'd seen during our entire conversation.

"Keep talking," he said.

"I…. She's lying."

"About what, Sasha?"

"If you read the article closely, you'll see Charlene's version of what happened is all wrong. She claims Mae started talking about abductions after Colonel Tan was discovered." My nose itched; I rubbed it with my wrist. "But that's not true. Mae told me about them on Sunday night. She said she'd been abducted a couple of times already."

"Stay right here," LaSalle said, voice frosty and face pale.

He pushed back his chair, stood with the rigidity of a soldier at attention, then left the room. His quick footsteps clipped down the hallway. I heard chairs screech, scraping on uncarpeted floor.

LaSalle returned with several men in his wake. They stared at me, faces bland. In the undercurrent, I felt them measure me against other informants.

"Tell them what you told me," the detective said.

I did.

No one responded. Not a wink, not a smile. It was like talking to breathing photographs. Their thoughts impermeable as lead.

"See what I mean?" LaSalle addressed the group. "She's got all this information and doesn't know what's important. What's not. I don't think it's deliberate sabotage."

"Of course it isn't," I said.

"She's too interested in helping her friend," he said, ignoring me.

A couple of subtle nods I would have missed if I'd blinked. One of the men moved his head a millimeter toward the door. They all got up without a word. LaSalle stopped before walking out.

"Stay right in that chair," he said.

The table in front of his couch offered more space to work. I plopped myself down, opened the laptop, and attacked the PR plan. While composing brilliant prose, I waited, imagining the worst. Space aliens, the plan, my money problems reeked of triviality in the face of this murder.

The sheer scope of the investigation daunted me. Those emotionless men represented a plethora of governmental agencies all called in to find the person who'd killed Tan. I wondered who was who. Which one came from the FBI, which one from the state police? Had one of them been from the CIA?

Because Tan was Asian, someone was probably checking out an international smuggling angle. Or drugs. Becky Tan didn't fit my image of a drug lord's wife. However, one explanation for her pesky hallucinations could be that they stemmed from flashbacks, the residue from bad trips.

Wait a minute. With all this stress, where are my hallucinations?

I looked around LaSalle's office, at the rug, at the paintings here and there with their schlocky New Mexican landscapes, cowboys by the campfire. I tapped the keyboard without typing. If this whole murder case wasn't high stress, I didn't know the meaning of the term. With all the drama around me, the pressure, I hadn't had a hallucination since—when? Yesterday? The day before?

Maybe I was cured! Wouldn't that be a kicker, a bright note in all of this? A surge of relief flowed through me.

Back to the computer. The Internet searches I'd done were filled with governmental conspiracies. The irony of my current situation evoked a tiny giggle. It was the old seek-and-ye-shall-find principle: I wanted to understand paranoia and had landed in the middle of a conspiracy myself. A gaggle of guys from some of the most secretive agencies in the world conferred down the hall, deciding my fate.

Adobe bricks had more humanity than the G-men I'd just encountered. Imagine the impression these guys would make on a person who thought she'd been abducted by aliens. Imagine talking to those impassive faces. It'd be intimidating, upsetting, disturbing, horrifying—none of the words I came up with touched what *I'd* felt while talking to them. They hadn't even tried to put me at ease. Was this how they treated everyone? No wonder the government had such a bad name in the alien conspiracy subculture.

I sighed. While this was an interesting tangent, it didn't help with the plan.

Oh, yes, it did. The people we wanted to attract to Clovis believed in the outer edges of reality. Many concluded the government had lied for years and that there was substantial science to prove it. If I believed that, then even if the government guys started making nice-nice, I'd be suspicious. It was a question of loyalty. These agency men scorned individuals—at least that's how it looked. They worked for ideals, for democracy, the government, the FBI. Meanwhile, thousands of people had experienced inexplicable happenings—alien abductions, UFO sightings, close encounters—and no one cared.

That was another big theme. Our own government ignored individual rights and concerns. In my professional life, I'd had some bad encounters with the FBI. The most recent involved one of my former clients who'd had trouble with a money-launderer. The FBI agent I'd met shredded my client's business and life to investigate the crime.

"What are you doing?" LaSalle said, standing, framed in the doorway. "Didn't I tell you to stay in the chair?"

"I couldn't balance my computer and work there. I assumed it'd be okay." I picked up an old *Readers Digest,* waved it. "Unless you've got coded material in here."

He sucked in his left cheek, chewed on it. "You can go now."

"Do you have a few minutes?" I put down the magazine.

"No. Got to check something out."

"I really need to talk with you."

"I know we need to talk. I just don't have time right now." He picked up a pad from his desk. "Why don't you go get a cup of coffee, eat an early dinner? Go to your hotel and watch TV. I'll be in touch as soon as I can."

"I'm tired of waiting," I said.

"Give me a break. You're a piece in a major investigation." He held up his hands. "It's a whole, giant jigsaw puzzle and you're a piece of it."

"Marvy."

"Look, you're an important piece." LaSalle pointed at the laptop. "Why don't you take that fancy computer of yours and write down everything you can remember that's happened since you arrived in Clovis." He slapped the doorframe. "I've got it. Why don't you write me a book? Don't edit. Don't censor. Give me every detail—don't leave anything out. That way, when we talk tonight, it'll be worth both of our whiles."

A man stopped to talk with him.

After they finished, LaSalle said to me, "Go back to the hotel. I'll call you when I can."

"Yes, Master," I said.

He didn't notice my mock salute.

Minutes later, I was back at the hotel. The maid had done her magic and the orderliness of the cleaned room almost soothed my out-of-sorts mood. Almost. The phone's message light blinked. I sank onto the straightened bed and felt sorry for myself. My eyes scanned the dresser, the silent television, the table with the cow photo. The little white box with its amateurish missive. And, what was that? Another one?

I sprang off the bed. Opened the second box, found another computer-generated note. "MIND YOUR OWN BUSINESS."

Furious, I stormed to the front desk. A young man named Carlos met me at the counter. I asked if he knew Bud Johnson. He nodded; everyone knew Bud.

"Was he here today?"

"Oh, no, I haven't seen him, ma'am," said Carlos.

"Really?"

When I showed him the note, he stammered, "What is it?"

"A little something for my reading pleasure. I found it in my room."

"Are you sure?"

"Trust me. Something like this—I'd remember it."

"Excuse me. Of course, you would," he said. "I'll call the maid who cleaned your room." He picked up a phone receiver. "We have policies about this kind of thing. I can't believe any of our employees would do something like this." More head shaking, a trembling hand. "I'm very sorry. I'll find out what happened. I'll let you know as soon as I can."

Bud Johnson deserved a kick in the pants. Some poor woman would get fired over this.

Unenthusiastic about food, I went into the hotel restaurant, ordered a chicken stir-fry, ate like a person with no taste buds. I was getting sick and tired of Clovis even before signing on any dotted line. What if I got the job? Would I be able to stand this town for weeks or months on end? How would I work it? Would I commute from Albuquerque? I hadn't thought any of this through. And I needed to. It had to be part of my plan—or at least hinted at in the bid. Five-thirty and dinner lay heavy in my stomach.

I wanted a drink, a real one with throat-burning liquor. Lucky for me, the Holiday Inn's bar was open. I walked in. An ambient hostility hung in the air. The darkness was cut by streaks of light from the big screen TV. Smoke hovered dense and malodorous. I ordered a Glenlivet, earned curious stares from three men in army fatigues sitting a few tables down from mine. An older couple entered, looked at me, said something to each other and looked at me again.

I downed my drink, headed back to the room.

For the first time in a long time, I didn't know what to do.

TWENTY-FIVE

YEARS AGO, WHEN I lived in D.C., my bedroom was close to the street. Every few months I'd wake to flashing red lights. Scared but interested, I'd sneak a look from behind the curtain to see police cars surrounding the vacant building across the road.

Tonight, the message light on my phone reminded me of the minutes before curiosity conquered fear and I looked out, wondering if horror awaited. Would someone shoot? Someone else return fire? Would the bullet zip past its mark, shatter the window and pierce my heart?

No real bullets here, only metaphorical ones. I steeled myself, punched in my code and listened. Words—accusing, distraught, unassuming—vied for my attention. Bob, Jan Cisneros, Abel King. Charlene wondering if I'd told the police, pleading for me not to. The owner of the hotel calling to apologize for the notes left in my room, saying he'd investigate the matter himself. Becky Tan. I shut my eyes. I'd forgotten to call her.

Choices, choices. If I called Bob, I'd be tempted to tell him everything that had happened. He might run right out of my life; I wouldn't blame him. A conversation with old man King could be interesting, but I wasn't up to his crustiness. Not quite yet. I could throw the phone across the room in frustration with Charlene. Or I could call Becky Tan.

She answered on the first ring. "Hello?" Her voice shimmered with years of education behind the careful enunciation.

"Mrs. Tan, this is Sasha Solomon. *Lei ho m ho ah?*"

"*M ho,* Ms. Solomon. *M ho.*" Not good.

"Anything I can do to help?"

"I would like to talk with you. If I may."

She gave me an odd feeling, like she was teetering on a cliff, madness an easy fall away. Did I really want to get involved in her story? Wasn't Mae's enough?

"I need to stay here at the hotel. Would tomorrow be all right?" I said.

"I am afraid not. May I come to you now?"

I bent to pick up the clothes I'd just thrown down. "Uh—"

"Please, Ms. Solomon. I promise you will want to hear what I have to say."

"Okay. I'll be here."

"Thank you."

"Is your brother joining you?" I crossed my fingers, hoping for the contrary.

"Most definitely not. He is in Scottsdale, Arizona, meeting with an embassy representative tomorrow morning." She cleared her throat, the sound abrasive compared with the mild cadence of her English. "May I come now? Please?"

I gave her the room number, observed my realm and found it lacking. I'd been back only minutes and my mere presence had rumpled the bed and put a water ring on the dresser. Seeking an excuse not to clean up, I called Bob. At a little after six o'clock, I knew he'd be at the office. I was wrong. Thursday night. He never left work earlier than seven. Worried, I called his house, left a message about getting too involved in other people's business.

And that brought me back to Bud Johnson. I liked the idea of Bud being evil incarnate. I remembered the night at the Roadrunner Motel, the rattling doorknob. Someone claiming to be my husband. Had that been him? It didn't make sense. Nothing made sense since I'd arrived in Clovis.

Not wanting to lose the thought, I turned on the computer, keyed in what I remembered from my first night. Wow. Could Bud be the murderer? I tapped that question in, too. What was his motive? He and Charlene were having an affair! That might be enough to set up Mae. But a murder? And why Colonel Tan? Did Bud suffer from Clovis 25-envy? He could be trying to kill Cannon. God, save me from my imagination.

A faint knock at the door dismantled my concentration. Through the peephole, I saw Becky Tan. Her body could have been marble, she stood that still. Her pseudo-calm turned to jitters when she entered. She glanced over her shoulder as if worried about being followed.

"Shhh!" she said.

"Excuse me?"

"Not you."

Discomfort marked her features in a strained grimace that disintegrated when she drooped into the chair I offered. She jerked, marionette-ish, her motions dictated by someone else. She nodded to commands only she could hear.

I balanced on the edge of the bed across from her, marveling at her bizarre behavior.

"You are refusing to see him," said Becky Tan. "You have closed him out. As if he no longer exists. Why are you hardened against him?" Despair rendered her words sparrow-bone thin and excruciating to hear. She didn't meet my eyes.

"Your husband?" I said.

She nodded.

"What?" I said.

"He is struggling to reach you. Why will you not listen?"

Oh, boy. I'd spent the last few months battling hallucinations and this woman was pleading with me to backtrack, to give in.

"Mrs. Tan. I dreamed about your husband a few times, but—"

"You lie. You saw him. He begged for your help," she said. "Oh, Ms. Solomon. Without you, the truth will vanish. No one will ever know how he died."

Elbows on thighs, I rested my head in my hands and leaned forward. The woman was crazy. No sense sugarcoating reality. "Your husband's dead, Mrs. Tan. And I don't see how I can help him or you either."

"You are wrong, Ms. Solomon."

A small warmth floated past me, a scent of orchid.

In an instant, Becky Tan smiled. She patted her left hand on her right shoulder as if someone were standing behind her.

"He is here. By my side," she said, closing her eyes and breathing the perfumed air. She looked past her shoulder, eyes full of love. I watched her face in profile.

"You must help us."

"How can I possibly help you?" I said.

"You can tell the police what happened the night he was killed."

"I don't know what happened that night."

"The police will believe you," she said. "You have to do it. Or your friend will be punished for a crime she did not commit."

A flash of white rested on her shoulder, disappeared. Goosebumps prickled my skin. I could feel him. I fought with my curiosity. This was ridiculous; I didn't want to hallucinate. No, I didn't want to see him. I squinted for a closer look at another shimmer of white.

"Do you really know what happened the night he was killed?" I said.

Mrs. Tan nodded, opened her purse, and fumbled with a handkerchief. "My husband always dreamed of being a pilot, of helping our country." She morphed into a Chinese schoolmarm. "Do you know how young Singapore is?"

I shook my head.

"Li Piao was born the year of its birth, in 1965." Her eyes

became moist. "As a small child, he went out at night to study the stars, learn their patterns, their names."

She blinked several times.

I didn't dare speak.

"My husband was an astronomer from the time he was born. We met in high school, shared a love of the night sky. That love, our love, grew through college, graduate school."

Tears rolled down her cheeks, her handkerchief a useless prop. They dropped onto the turquoise silk of her shirt, staining it.

"The night Li Piao was killed, we had had a fight," she said. She closed her eyes, then opened them. "I hate Clovis. My friends in New York, Los Angeles, they laugh at me for being here. There is no culture, nothing to do. I told him I was going back to Singapore. He said my place was with him. All we had was each other."

A tear clung to one of her lashes.

"We had no children," she said. "Do you have children? Are you married?"

"No." I reached behind me to get her a tissue.

"Have you ever been in love?"

"A couple of times."

"Ah."

"You were telling me about your fight," I said.

"It was nothing. We disagree often. He is a dragon and I am a tiger. These signs are strong, both wanting their own way and fighting to get it."

I waited, watching her momentary turmoil when she realized she'd used the wrong tense for her husband.

"I locked myself in the bedroom," she said, taking a long, strengthening breath. "When I came out, Li Piao was gone. He had taken his telescope." She focused on me. "He always looks at the stars to calm down. It helps him remember his place in the universe."

Telescope? I hadn't seen a telescope near his body.

"You told the police about all of this, didn't you? About the fight, the telescope?" I said.

"The fight, yes. The telescope? I do not remember. They were not interested in my story. Their questions were about drugs and enemies. As if my husband were a common thief."

"Was that the last time you saw your husband?"

"No. I saw him in that drawer." She shuddered, more tears falling. "Dead. Oh, he is wandering, so sad and confused."

"And you actually see him? Right now? Like a ghost?"

She strained a smile, lips white with the effort. "A ghost," she said. "You've lived in Hong Kong, you know about Buddhism. Don't you?"

"I think so."

"In my faith, death is not a bad thing. It is an opportunity to leave this cycle of suffering. We celebrate it." She picked at the pearl-colored nail polish on her thumb. "But there are rites, ceremonies that must be performed.

"My husband's body lies in a refrigerator like meat. They cut at him, disturbing his soul. He should be home, prayed over by monks." She looked up. "I tried. I tried but I could not find a single monk here or in Lubbock. The closest ones are in Albuquerque and Dallas. He needs help. We have only little time before his soul must wander forever."

Becky Tan passed a hand over her hair.

The white essence became more defined. An arm, two legs.

"The sooner they find his murderers, the sooner I can take his body home, free him for the next cycle," she said.

His face was almost visible. Empty air where there should have been eyes.

She said, "Yes. I must tell her."

In response, I listed away from her, as if bracing myself for an explosion.

"My husband grows impatient with my words. I must tell

you about the murder," she said, inclining her head and listening. "That night he drove for a long time, finally finding a tempting dirt road off the main one."

She reminded me of an interpreter, pausing after each sentence to grasp the next.

"He parked his car and set up the telescope before he noticed the small house or shed, in the distance. It was unlit. He stayed where he was. Some time later, he heard noises. A truck passed, continued down the road to the shed."

Confusion nipped at her features, constricting them.

"This part does not make sense." She batted something away from her face and said, "*Ai yah!* Let me tell the story."

Then she resumed her narrative, her ruffled feathers settling before my eyes.

"Two people stepped out of the truck. Only they were not people. Where human faces should have been, there were green ones, glowing. Big black eyes like rotten lichee nuts. They had no hair on their heads. None anywhere." She swatted the air again, mumbled in Cantonese, but I didn't catch it. "The two of them carried something. They struggled with its strange shape. My husband trained his telescope on them and realized it was a body they carried. They dropped it twice, and dragged it for a time."

I imagined the scene: the deep darkness of the night, the strangeness of what Tan witnessed.

"You must understand, my husband has been in the military for many years," she said, picking at the nail polish on another finger. "He knows what is right and what is wrong. He could not stand by silent, when he saw what he knew was a crime."

She studied her hand, pulled the top of a nail off.

"Li Piao yelled at them, demanded they stop. In Singapore, they would have obeyed the moment he spoke. His voice carries such authority. But here, they ignored him, so, he followed them to the shed. They noticed him then. At once, they stopped and put the body down."

Her breathing was fast, unnatural. She shook her head several times.

"And?" I said.

"He saw the flash before he felt it," she said. "And then another, and another. Five holes in his chest. They shot him like a pig." She glanced beyond me, filled with despair. "He fell to the ground, trying to staunch his draining blood."

She stood halfway, but her legs lacked strength and she sank back into the chair.

"He heard their footsteps crunching on the loose gravel and dirt," she said. "They dragged him to our car, shoved him in the back seat. One drove while the other must have gone in the truck. They traveled for a long time, the bullets rattling in his body like parasitic eggs.

"Even then, he hoped they were going for help, that they realized their mistake. But no. They pulled him from the car, removed his clothes, called him names he did not understand."

Her gaze held emptiness, a loneliness so profound nothing could console it.

"They hauled him to the water container and threw his head in," she said. "Too much blood, too much confusion had flowed inside his body. He could no longer fight, no longer move." She shook her head. "As my Li Piao suffocated in the cold water, he felt the snow caress his bare skin. His last thoughts were of me, of us. And when his spirit left his body, he met our unborn child."

"You're pregnant?" I said, sickened.

Oh, God, the horror of it. To live with her husband's death memories, to be carrying a baby with this legacy.

She nodded, her face wet. "And old. Too old to have a baby. To have a baby alone."

I closed my eyes on her shaking form. My push-pull emotions high, I yearned to run away from her and what she represented, to flee from her misery. I also wanted to reach out, to hold her. Impotent before her grief, I focused on the facts, the blessed details that offered an escape into objectivity.

Her story rang true.

LaSalle had neglected to mention things like the telescope, the missing car. But then, why would he tell me? I wasn't a member of the investigation team; I was a mere stooge, an informant. Mrs. Tan had calmed down during my introspection. Her breathing had slowed and the tears left traces in the remaining powder on her face.

"Did you tell the police all of this?" I said, cracking the silence.

"No."

"Why not?"

"Do you believe me? Do you know that my husband told me this?"

"I know you believe it."

Her breath came out as a scoff. "My husband told me to trust you. I told him we could trust no one here."

"Please, give me time to think about this," I said. "I've never really believed in ghosts."

"*Pah!* My husband says you are lying. He says you *have* seen ghosts before."

I turned away from her accusation. How could she possibly know that? Was she bluffing or had her husband really said it?

Nausea inched its way up my throat.

She pursed her lips, then in anger said, "*Ai yah!* You have even seen my husband. I know you have." Her face reddened. "You know he is here. You know I am telling the truth!"

"Calm down, Mrs. Tan. I didn't say you weren't. Please. Let me concentrate."

How could I recount this to LaSalle and expect him not to laugh in my face?

"You must tell the police," she said. "But you cannot say where you heard it."

"I have to," I said. "At least let Detective LaSalle hear it in your own words. He'll be reasonable. He'll listen."

"I must leave," she said.

"Are you talking about leaving this room or leaving Clovis?"

"I must leave." She stood up.

The room had grown dark during her recitation. I couldn't read her face well enough.

"You can't leave," I said. "They'll think you had something to do with the murder."

"They will think that if they hear Li Piao's story from my lips. That is why you must speak for him. For me."

"Mrs. Tan, did you kill your husband?"

"How could you ask such a thing? How could I kill my husband? How could I kill the father of my child?"

She put her hands on her stomach as if to shield her unborn child from the thought.

I felt lowdown disgusting. "Then you have to stay. Detective LaSalle's supposed to call me tonight. Stay here and I'll get him to come over right now. This has got to be in your own words."

"All right," she said. "But let me go home. My stomach is bad with this baby. I have pickled ginger at home. It makes me feel better. Tell him to come to my house."

"You're sure you want to go home? I could get you some soda pop." My gut told me she'd given in too easily, but I couldn't force her to stay. "Please don't do anything foolish," I said. And again, "LaSalle's reasonable. He'll listen."

Becky Tan shook my hand and thanked me. She left soon after. I had a bad feeling as I watched her head toward the lobby. A feeling that I wouldn't see her again.

She walked through the courtyard, went into the building and disappeared from view.

I closed the door and stared at the overturned alien mask on my bed. I put it on and went to the mirror and turned off the light in the dressing area. It didn't take a brain surgeon to figure out the two people had used something like it to hide their identities from Colonel Tan—and Mae. Tan must have seen Mae being abducted. It had to be. That was the connection. Why else had he been left on her land? I knew it in my bones even though it made less than no sense.

The room felt close. Dizzy, I groped for a light switch. The ringing phone stabbed my senses along with the brilliance of the overhead lamp. LaSalle's weary voice nudged the tip of my awareness. I yelled at him, cursed his awful timing.

Five minutes earlier and I could have stopped her.

TWENTY-SIX

LaSALLE STARED AT ME, his face bisected by steepled fingers. *Here is the church. Here is the steeple. Open the doors to see all the people.*

"A ghost? You're talking about a ghost," he said.

"Yes. Her husband's ghost told her how he was killed."

This was the fourth time we'd gone through it.

"In her culture ghosts are real. You're not crazy if you see one," I said. "Especially if a murder is involved." Ever the closet cultural anthropologist, I wanted LaSalle to understand, to really understand.

"Okay. Let me get this straight. I'm supposed to go to the homicide team and tell them a ghost has come up with crucial evidence?" He took a long breath, ran a hand through his hair. "I understand why you wanted to tell me this in person."

I moved toward the phone. "Do you want me to call her? Tell her you're coming over?"

"No. I think I'll stop by. See what she's up to."

"I'd do it soon. I think she's planning on leaving town."

"I tell you what. I'll go over there. Have a little chat." At the door, he rolled his eyes and said, "Ghosts. I've got a ghost for an informant."

"Would you mind calling me after you talk with her?"

One nod and he was gone.

Unable to focus on the PR plan, I typed out what I could remember of my conversation with Becky Tan. I keyed in everything, all the details. This was too important to lose even a sigh. My little portable printer chugged away, its sound comforting. If LaSalle decided to take the story to the homicide team, I wanted him to have hard copy.

Twenty minutes later, the knock at my door was soft, deferential. LaSalle came in, smelling of cigarette smoke.

"There's no one at her house," he said. "The lady across the street saw Mrs. Tan put a suitcase in her car late this afternoon. We were set up. She planned to leave all along."

"Wonderful. That's just wonderful."

I plopped onto the bed for emphasis.

"I agree," he said.

"Can't you stop her? Put out an all-points bulletin or whatever you call it?"

"You watch too much TV."

He sat down in the chair where she'd been less than an hour before.

"Well, can't you? Isn't she a suspect?" I said.

"About on a par with you or me." LaSalle sucked in his cheek, made a smacking sound. "Who knows? She might be visiting a friend right here in Clovis." He shrugged. "I called our Singaporean contact. His guess is that she'll head home. She's not used to roughing it. She'll use her credit cards and there'll be a trail. We'll know where she is if we need her."

"What about this?" I held up the space-alien mask. "They cost five bucks down in Roswell. In the dark, with this black cloth in the back, all you'd see would be the face."

He pulled out a pack of cigarettes. Camels. Tapped it on the table.

"Uh unh. Not in here, you don't," I said.

"I wasn't going to." Defensive. Tap, tap.

"I didn't know you smoked."

"I don't."

"You smell like cigarette smoke."

"Can we drop it?"

"Sorry."

He rose, leaving the cigarettes on the table.

I watched him pace the short stretch in front of the beds, from front door to dressing area and back. He picked up the mask, put it on.

"It's even comfortable." Taking it off, he said, "Can I borrow this? Show them?"

"Sure." I handed him my printed notes.

"What's this?"

"Cheat sheets. Everything I could remember from my talk with her. You know, the telescope, the car, that kind of stuff."

He dropped back into the chair, befuddled. "How am I going to do this?"

I shook my head.

He sighed, gazed at my impromptu worktable and noticed the two white boxes. Bending forward, he picked up the first one, opened it and read. Eyebrows scrunched, he said, "You got another one?"

"Yep."

"When?"

"Today. Yesterday. I don't even remember."

"Sasha, how do you do it? Ghosts, anonymous notes. I ought to have someone follow you twenty-four-seven." He was almost amused.

"This isn't funny."

"You're right. None of this is funny. I've got an international incident, a crazy suspect, a crazy widow, seventeen agencies telling me I'm doing my job wrong, and a PR consultant who has no business knowing anything giving me leads from a ghost. It's either laugh or cry."

I bit back my response. No need to antagonize someone under this much pressure.

Time moved, sticky as old molasses. While LaSalle read my notes, I went back to typing. So much had happened in the last couple of days; it was difficult to keep it in order. I scoured my memory for important information. There was the phone dance with Charlene. Something else, oh, Josh was supposed to call back and hadn't. I looked up at LaSalle. His expression was too serious. An interruption would only aggravate him.

I typed in the word *Josh*. Then *Charlene*. Had I told LaSalle about the lunch with Josh? About the—what was it?—totally mixed, no, totally integrated farming? Oh yeah, and I wanted to ask about The Clovis 25. I heard a hum, looked up.

"I've gotta go." LaSalle said, glaring at his pager. He gripped the papers. "Thanks for these. They'll help." He went to the door. "Oh, and do me a favor. Stay close for a little while. I may need you to come down to the station and talk to the guys yourself."

He walked out, but I sensed him standing there, waiting.

I opened the door.

"What?" I said.

"Don't take this wrong. Okay?"

"What?"

"Why don't you take a shower? Put on a little make-up."

"Make-up? Why?

"I might need you to come down to the station." He looked at his pager again. "Sometimes, under questioning, new information comes out. I bet the team will want to see you. Hear it from your own mouth."

"Do you really think I'll remember more with a dozen men shooting questions at me?" I said. "This afternoon was bad enough and none of them said a word. They're a scary bunch."

"I'll tell them to be nice."

"Wonderful. That'll be even scarier."

His laugh sounded good, real. "Look, they'll probably wonder why I didn't bring you down right away," he said.

"Take a shower. Primp. Relax. I'll send someone to get you in about an hour."

"They'll think I'm insane."

"Imagine what they'll think about me when I tell them Mrs. Tan's story."

After LaSalle left, I called Bob for a dose of normalcy.

"Hi," I said.

"Hi, back at you."

"So, how are things in Albuquerque?"

"Windy." He paused to drink something; I heard him swallow. "Lonely." He took another sip. "Your message piqued my curiosity."

"What did I say?"

"Something about not butting into other people's business."

"Oh."

"Are you going to give me more? Or do I get to play twenty questions?"

"Oh, Bob. It's a long story. Suffice it to say that in less than a week, I've managed to piss off the police, get threatened with a felony, and step into the middle of the Twilight Zone."

"The Twilight Zone, huh?"

"Yeah. Space aliens, ghosts. The whole shebang."

"Wait a second, Sasha," he said. "What did you say about the police?"

I could picture him in his Eames chair, suddenly more alert.

"It's nothing important."

"No. You said something about a felony? About getting in trouble with the police?"

I didn't want to tell him everything. "I'll give you the quick version. Okay?"

"Okay."

By the time I finished, I knew he was scratching notes on a legal pad.

"Bob, you're not my lawyer. Don't worry about it."

"My new girlfriend is mixed up in a murder investigation and she doesn't want me to worry about it."

"I can do without the sarcasm."

"Look. Here's what I'll do. I think I know someone in Clovis. Someone dependable."

"I've talked to lots of dependable people here. It's okay. Really," I said.

"Let me see what I can do."

"Bob, that's not necessary."

"Of course, it's necessary. Let me do this for you, friend-to-friend."

"You really think I need a lawyer?"

"It couldn't hurt."

We talked some more, then said sappy good-byes. In the dating phase, relationships had such good energy. They vibrated with the thrill of getting to know another person, each moment a discovery. But after weeks or months, freedom gave way to possessiveness.

Would that happen with Bob, too? I frowned. Typical Sasha: in the middle of something fun, I started worrying. My history with men would depress Pollyanna. And I always felt so ambivalent—one minute in love, the next pulling away. Maybe I should just opt for celibacy; it'd be easier in the long run.

Get a grip, Sasha.

I shook the thoughts out of my head, then did a private, playful striptease in front of the bathroom mirror. Distressed by the dimples in my thighs, I hit the tub's spigot.

Before the bath water ran hot, LaSalle called to say he was sending someone to pick me up in twenty-five minutes.

TWENTY-SEVEN

IN THE LUXURY of the liquid, I swished my hair back and forth pretending to be a mermaid. Then showered. Squeaky clean, I donned slacks and a velour top. Just the thing for a date with a bunch of *federales*. With minutes ticking, I worked and waited for my prince to come.

When the phone rang again, I expected Josh or his uncle.

"Hello?" I said.

"Ms. Solomon?"

"Yes? Who is this?"

"Steve Cummings. Bob asked me to call."

"Oh. Thank you." *Wow, that was fast.*

"Bob said you've talked with the police," he said.

"Yeah. As a matter of fact, I'm going to the station in a couple of minutes."

"I'll be right there."

"That's not necessary. I'm just going to repeat something I've already told them."

"Ms. Solomon, it's always necessary to have a lawyer when you talk with the police." He sounded positively professorial. "A simple questioning can turn into an interrogation. And then where would you be?"

"Okay." I hadn't thought of it that way. "But my ride's gonna be here any second."

"Stall them. Don't leave without me."

Sure enough, a few minutes later a uniformed policeman tapped at my door. I told him we needed to stick around until

my attorney showed up. He borrowed my phone, told someone about the delay, and handed the receiver to me.

"What attorney?" said LaSalle.

"Steve Cummings."

"Why did you call an attorney? We just want to ask you a
couple of questions."

"I know. The guy I'm dating must have called him. Is it a
problem?"

"Nah, it's no problem at all. Bring Steve on down. Invite
the hotel manager. Why stop there? Bring a couple of people
from the bar. We can have a party." He paused for a breath.
"Let me talk to Officer Jamison."

I handed the phone back to the policeman.

"May I?" He pointed to a chair, then said, "Yessir," three
or four times and hung up.

I smiled at him.

He smiled back.

I crossed my legs.

"Ma'am, Detective LaSalle said to give Mr. Cummings five
minutes. If he hasn't arrived by then, we'll leave without him.
Mr. Cummings'll know where to go."

Milliseconds later, my attorney knocked at the door. Geeky,
thin and attractive in a lanky way, Cummings wore a gray suit,
maroon and green tie, tasseled loafers. He shook my hand,
greeted the policeman by name, and said he'd be driving me
down to the station.

That required another phone call. This time, LaSalle
wanted to speak with Cummings.

All I heard was, "Is she under arrest? I didn't think so." A
lot of *okays, uh huhs, you bets*. Then a smile as he handed the
receiver back to the policeman.

"You'll be more comfortable in my car, anyway," Cummings said. "Let's go."

As we walked through the lobby, people stared at my police escort. I yawned, tired by the circumstances, wanting to check out, to be in another reality.

"It shouldn't be bad. Henry will try to keep it civil." Cummings put his hand at the small of my back in a gesture of support.

I nodded, still seeking an out.

His black Jaguar had kid leather seats. I snuggled into one and said, "How much do you know about all of this?"

"Not much. That's why I wanted to drive you." He started the Jag. It purred. "The only thing Bob said was that you withheld evidence and that Henry was using a felony rap as leverage to coerce you into helping him."

"Huh." That didn't sound like Bob. We'd only dated a few weeks and I already knew he'd never use those words. Not like that.

"What?" he said.

"Bob said that? 'Coerced?'"

"He was very worried."

Something didn't feel right about this conversation. I couldn't pinpoint it. And I wasn't sure I liked or trusted Cummings.

"You've been seeing Bob long?" he said, stealing a look at me, evaluating.

This had happened before. Bob Kalco, successful and moneyed lawyer, went for stunning *señoritas*. He'd married and then divorced one of the most powerful women in New Mexico. Suzanne Kalco ran the biggest television station in the state. She was classy, gorgeous, and from what Bob said, a first-class shrew.

"I know, I know. I'm not Bob's normal type," I said.

"You're a lot more interesting." Cummings's smile was the kind that went down before it came up, a little too calculated. "And I've known you, what? All of four minutes?"

I started to like him more.

"How long have you known Bob?" I said.

"Twenty years, give or take. We drove to Harvard together, cross country." He hit the brakes hard when a car pulled in front of us. "Idiot," Cummings said, staring ahead. He squinted, as if he might recognize the driver who'd cut us off. "Bob and I lost touch. Tonight I get a call out of the blue asking me to help a close friend."

"A close friend," I said. "Tell me about his wife. I mean his former wife."

"You should really be telling me about what happened with the police."

"One word. Come on," I wheedled. "Give me something juicy."

"She has a small waist."

"That's it? A small waist?"

"Like a wasp's." He winked at me, a practiced gesture that cheapened our interaction. "Tell me everything that's happened since you saw the dead Chink."

Had he said it? A word as derogatory as *kike* or *spic?* I looked at him. His face betrayed no vileness. I must have heard him wrong. Unwilling to pursue it, I started talking about the night I saw Colonel Tan's body. Cummings wanted the minute details: my first impressions of the scene, verbatim snippets of remembered conversation. His interest perked up when I told him about my earlier encounter with the homicide team, the one where I'd told them about Charlene having lied. I didn't have time to tell him about Mrs. Tan's story.

"Why didn't you tell Henry about Mae King's abductions before?" he said.

"I didn't think it had anything to do with anything."

"Don't do that."

"What?"

"Editorialize," said Cummings. "God, I wish I had time to coach you." He slowed down. The policeman had already parked his car. "Look, only answer the questions they ask you.

Don't offer your opinion. Don't embellish. Give the facts. Short and sweet and to the point. Got it?"

"I guess," I said.

LaSalle claimed it wouldn't be a big deal. Cummings acted like this was going to be the next Inquisition.

I bit the inside of my cheeks, preparing for the worst.

The Detective Division looked quiet on the outside. Officer Jamison punched a code into a little black box, opened the door, and went to tell someone about our arrival. I watched the numbers, repeated them to myself.

We waited in the lobby. The sound of footsteps and voices carried beyond the closed doors. Detective LaSalle wasn't the one who came to get us. It was the man I'd seen at the chamber of commerce, spit-polished, anal. He flashed an ID, then spoke to Cummings.

"I'm Special Agent Frenth, FBI. Ms. Solomon has no need for an attorney." He turned to me and said, "Ms. Solomon, we just have a few questions. We should be done in no time."

My lawyer followed, but the agent stopped him.

"As I said, sir, she doesn't require the services of an attorney," said Frenth.

"Sasha, would you like me to come with you?" Cummings put his hand on my wrist, squeezed. "Are you requesting representation?"

"Yeah, I guess."

"You heard her," said Cummings.

"Well, then. We have a little problem. Don't we?" said Frenth.

TWENTY-EIGHT

MEET SASHADDY ANN, Raggeddy's sister. Cummings, LaSalle, Frenth, and the boys in back played tug of war and I was the rope. LaSalle would come into the lobby, tell us to follow him. Cummings would ask a question, not like the response, and tell me to sit down. With each interaction, I grew more nervous, sweaty, and irritable.

"Why are you making such a big deal out of this? They just want me to tell them what Mrs. Tan said," I whispered to my attorney during a quiet spell.

An expression flew across his face, hostility and something else. Fear? He spoke with disdain. "I thought you were smarter than that."

Seething, I turned my back on him.

"Okay, I'll spell it out," he said. "They have two potential felonies they can slap on you if you're coy, or if you don't answer a question, or if they don't like the color of your shirt." His patronizing voice had attracted my attention; I wanted to slap him. "Since you're not under arrest, you're in no-man's land. You don't have any protection under the law. They aren't obligated to record the session or even make it available to anyone else. You say LaSalle said he wanted you to talk about Mrs. Tan's story. That might be *his* intention. But any other guy in there can ask you things that are totally unrelated. If you don't want to answer, they arrest you on the felony counts. Simple as that. If you don't have any witnesses, it'll be your word against theirs and you know which side a judge will take. You won't have any proof of wrongdoing."

"All right. I see your point. But if they're getting this defensive with you here, doesn't that make matters worse for me?" I said.

"Maybe while they readjust their strategy. But I don't think you're in any worse trouble for it. And they'll think twice about trying to intimidate you."

Cummings watched the shadows beyond the windowed, locked door to the offices.

"Why would they try to intimidate me? I'm trying to help them," I said.

He shot me a look of pure exasperation. "Like I was saying. They know I'm paying attention to everything they say and do." He pinched his lip with one of his hands and played with the fat flap, then noticed me watching and stopped. "They know the felonies won't hold water if they keep dicking around. We can claim you thought the police were corrupt. You were scared to go to them."

"But that's not true."

"Neither was Mr. FBI's just-a-few-questions-out-in-no-time bullshit."

I don't know what surprised me more, the comment or the cussing. It didn't matter; LaSalle reappeared. He moved like he'd been erased, tired to his bones.

"Steve, what's your agenda here?" he said, sitting down in the chair across from me.

"Ms. Solomon's boyfriend called me. He's worried and wants her protected. You're the one who brought up the felony issues."

"Well, you can come on back with her, although I think you're antagonizing the wrong people." He addressed me, "You ready?"

"No."

That got a tiny smile.

"Ready or not, it's time," he said.

White walls. The conference room had been cleaned, cleared and rearranged. Gone were the working charts, papers, and graphs. What large sheets remained were taped face-in to the wall. The sterility of the place screamed of a padded cell. At least twelve men roosted around the table. Some acknowledged Cummings with a nod. Others didn't move. Flies frozen in amber.

LaSalle pulled out a chair for me between two men. Frenth frowned. I sensed the detective had defied him somehow. Cummings loomed behind me like a weeping willow, an iffy pillar of support. LaSalle went to the hot seat at the head of the table. Ah, that was it; I understood. Frenth had wanted me there, all the pressure, the focus head-on.

I tried to catch LaSalle's eye to thank him but he avoided my gaze. The detective straightened an already neat stack of papers and began.

"For the record, Ms. Solomon has been completely cooperative to this point," he said. "Once she realized her mistake about not mentioning the abductions, she tried to rectify it and gave us additional information. You have the notes she made from her interview with Mrs. Tan. Do you have any further questions?"

A clean-cut guy—I would have pegged him as FBI if I didn't know better—raised his chin, got a nod from LaSalle.

"Ms. Solomon, I'm Sergeant Koepke from OSI. You said Mrs. Tan sought you out. Can you tell us why she came to you in particular?"

I took a deep breath. "I guess it's because she knew I spoke Cantonese. She trusted me and figured I'd be sympathetic because I knew about Chinese culture and Buddhism."

"And because you're as crazy as she is," Frenth said. He gave us all a good-ol'-boy smile. "Ms. Solomon here has been seeing a therapist for months and there are reports of her excessive drinking."

"Hey!" I said.

"Wait one damn minute!" Cummings lurched forward.

I noticed a man who could have passed for a football player. He recoiled with obvious annoyance at Frenth's remarks. The man had a neck the size of both of my thighs. He saw me watching him and rolled his eyes in commiseration.

"Gentlemen, be civil," said LaSalle. "Let me remind you all that Ms. Solomon has come of her own free will. And she's free to leave at any time."

"Oh, she'll stay. If you don't slap her with a felony, I will," said Frenth.

His bluster evoked another response from the football player, who shook his head. When he was certain I was watching, he formed his hand into a mock gun and targeted the FBI man.

I cracked a smile, tried to see if anyone had noticed his gesture.

"Let's take this outside," LaSalle said, standing and looking in the FBI guy's direction.

He held the door for Frenth. Through the plaster, we heard muffled yelling. Those of us remaining in the room fidgeted, shifted in our chairs. We twiddled our thumbs, doodled. I played with a green spot on the table, making designs in the dry-erase ink.

"It was good of you to come," said Koepke.

I raised my head.

A couple of men nodded. The football player stayed quiet.

Someone else spoke up. "Ms. Solomon, how did Mrs. Tan seem to you? I know you trained as a therapist. Was she in her right mind?"

These guys had done their homework. I wondered what else they knew about me.

"Was she crazy? I don't think so," I said. "I think she acted pretty normal for someone whose husband was recently murdered."

"Sasha," said Cummings. He put a warning hand on my shoulder.

"You've got to understand, in her culture ghosts and ancestral spirits exist," I said. "There's a lot of latitude for the supernatural, especially in a philosophy like Buddhism." I warmed to my subject. "You add to that the fact that she believes her husband's soul doesn't have anyone to guide it. She's bound to feel…to feel desperate. It goes against all of her beliefs about what's right for him."

"And you know this because…" The speaker was older, bald, dressed in an ironed tee shirt. I would have placed him at one of the intelligence agencies.

"Because my undergrad degree is in Chinese. Because I lived in Hong Kong for a year. Because—as you must already know—I was trained as a cross-cultural therapist."

Cummings squeezed my shoulder. I squirmed away from his grip.

LaSalle walked in, red in the face. He sat down and straightened the neat pile of papers again.

"Do you think Mrs. Tan might have been on drugs?" said the bald guy.

"My client can't determine the mental state of—" said Cummings.

"No. I don't think she was on anything," I said, speaking over his objection. "If she was, it wasn't obvious. Her speech wasn't slurred, her story—weird as it was—made chronological sense. I think she really believes her husband is telling her about his murder."

I'd begun to think of the football player as a runningback, agile but big. He seemed pained at people's stupidity. I liked him and wished he'd say something.

"Excuse me," Cummings said. "I'd like to speak to my client in private, please."

I got up and followed him into the hallway.

"What's up?" I said.

"You're giving them extra information. You're not doing a thing I told you to do."

"This isn't a trial. They're asking innocent questions. I'm giving innocent answers."

Frenth emerged from LaSalle's office, noticed us and said, "Having a little tête-à-tête?"

"What's your problem?" Cummings puffed at the FBI guy.

"You." Frenth addressed me next. "Ms. Solomon, get rid of this clown. He's not doing you any favors."

I watched them, two dogs in a pissing match. The testosterone hung thick enough to hack with a machete. Unimpressed by their bravado, I went toward the conference room.

"We're not done," said Cummings.

"Yes, we are," I said.

"You don't know what you're doing," he spluttered.

"You're probably right," I said. "But from my perspective, you're making a bad situation worse. I'm sorry. I need you to leave." I continued toward the room, not waiting to see if he'd respect my request.

Cummings mumbled something. I heard a door click shut behind me.

Frenth followed me in with an expression of victory on his face.

"I know I don't have any control over you," I said to him. "But someone here does. And I'm making a formal request to be treated with respect."

The runningback fought a laugh; I could tell. I thought I saw LaSalle smile, too. But when I looked straight at him, his seamless expression held no trace of mirth.

"Is there any way I can answer everybody else's questions

without talking to him?" I pointed at Frenth but questioned LaSalle.

The detective did one better. He said, "Gentlemen, are we done here?"

"I might have more after I read this story again," said one of the men who'd been silent through the histrionics. "Henry, if it's okay, you can pass them on to Ms. Solomon."

"No problem, Lew." LaSalle paused. "Anyone else?"

After a moment more he turned to me and said, "You can go. I'll be in touch."

I got up to leave, purse in hand, then sat down again. I sighed and leaned my head against one hand and said, "Can anyone give me a ride back to the hotel?"

TWENTY-NINE

The FBI, OSI, CIA? What on earth was I doing?

Lew Mason, the state policeman, drove me back to the Holiday Inn. He claimed no one intended to arrest me. That the homicide team appreciated my help. I wanted to believe him but Frenth left more than a vile taste in my mouth. He scared me.

"Don't pay any attention to him," said Mason. "Some FBI guys are like that. They think they should be running the show." He turned into the hotel parking lot. "Jim just came back here from a stint in L.A. Maybe he had to be ruder out there."

"He's from here?" I said.

"Yeah, but he's been gone a long time." We sat in the car, listening to a train roar across the street. "You want my opinion? I think he's trying to prove himself. You know, big fish in a little pond. Only we're not so little here and he hasn't figured that out yet."

When I got out of the car, Mason said, "By the way, you were right to send Steve home."

"Yeah, he was really acting weird. I don't know *what* was up with him."

"Jim and Steve are peas in a pod. When Steve went away to Harvard and made it big in Boston, we all thought he'd never come back. Then he lost all that money." The policeman scratched his nose. "Steve says he had a corrupt financial consultant. And there's the lawsuit. But what a letdown, coming back to Clovis, living with his sister and her kids. And from what I've heard, he hates doing general practice."

"I thought he was a criminal lawyer."

"Is that what he told you?"

"No. I just assumed," I said.

Mason shook his head. "He was a big-wig intellectual-property lawyer."

"Really? He acted like a pit bull."

"I think the term is 'overcompensation'." He winked. "You have a good night. I'm sure Henry'll be in touch in the morning."

I meant to go straight to my room. Halfway there, I veered into the bar instead. It was smokier than before, the inside of a chimney. I had two no-name scotches, their rough, cheap taste mirroring my mood.

How did I get into this mess?

Mae's my friend, more than a friend.

Friends don't set friends up for felonies.

Why had Mae put me in this position? She should have known better, even if I didn't. Second-guessing her motives and feeling like a heel, I slammed down a third scotch before noticing its absence.

I chomped on the ice remaining in my glass, put money on the table, and went to my room. The message light glowed red again, my own private hunk of burning lava. Sitting in the dark, I picked up the receiver and punched in for messages. Abel King again. I looked at my watch; it was only 9:30. Bob had called, too.

My shoes thumped onto the floor when I wedged them off my sore feet. With a quick stab, I turned on the light over my bed. Had Mae set me up? The question nagged. Charlene was as double-faced as a fake penny. Was Mae? Maybe I'd idealized her too much and had been too blind to see her lies.

I let out a frustrated groan. Sixteen years was a long time to be wrong about a person.

I called Bob first. He'd be upset about the way I'd handled his buddy Steve Cummings; I wanted to get the apologies over with.

"Hey," I said.

"Hey, yourself," he said.

"How ya doin'?"

"Okay. How 'bout you?"

"Okay." I flexed my toes and pointed them before speaking again. "Bob, I fired Steve Cummings. I'm really sorry. I know you were trying to help but—"

"What are you talking about? Steve Cummings?"

I heard rustling in the background, like he'd been lying down but had sat up.

"He said you hired him tonight," I said.

"He did?" I heard Bob swallow. "That's odd. I talked with his sister tonight. She didn't mention Steve. I thought he was in Boston." Another swallow. "He's there?"

"You didn't hire Steve?"

"Sure didn't."

"Then why did he call me?"

"He may have been listening in while I talked to Judy."

"Oh, boy." My blood vessels tightened. I felt the color abandon my face.

"What a kook," Bob said. He couldn't see my reaction and hadn't paused to sense my change of mood. "I haven't talked with Steve in years. I mean, we see each other at alumni events." He sniffled. "He's in Clovis? What's he doing there?"

It was a rhetorical question. I answered it anyway.

"Odd. He told you I'd hired him?" Bob said.

"Pretty much. He went with me to the station." I didn't like the implications. "Isn't that illegal, to misrepresent yourself like that?"

"You bet." He sniffled again.

"You getting a cold?"

"It's nothing."

"Good," I said.

"Good, yourself." He teased me with a lowered, pompous voice, "Well, Ms. Solomon, is there anything else I can do for you? Given how I got you a lawyer without even trying?"

His tone reminded me of someone else. I fiddled with the phone cord and said, "As a matter of fact, would you do me a favor? Theodore King, Mae's oldest son, is a lawyer in Lubbock. Is there any way to find out about his reputation there?"

Bob agreed to make some calls. We said our *sayonaras*.

I leaned against the pillow thinking about Mae and her kids. I didn't have a handle on their family dynamics but did have theories: Josh loved Mae, Charlene hated her. Theo was a gaseous bag of snobbery.

I rose in search of a Guinness.

Mom's image drifted into my mind uninvited. She'd been so unhappy on Sunday, frustrated and vulnerable. I hadn't called her once since arriving in Clovis. How could I be such a lousy daughter? I pictured our lunch together and remembered Mary Stanford. Grateful for a distraction from self-recrimination, I searched through my wallet and found her daughter's phone number. Connie Womack. I'd give her a call on the morrow.

My neck felt stiff. I needed comfort food. In the depths of my purse, I found a squished miniature candy bar. It was pretty good in spite of the pieces of wrapper stuck to the caramel. I got up again and pulled the can of whipped cream from the cooler. Biting the nozzle, then bending it down, I filled my mouth. Of course, at that precise moment, the phone rang.

"Ms. Solomon?"

I swallowed.

"Hello?" he said.

"Mr. King. I was going to call you," I said.

"I can hardly hear you."

"Must be the connection."

His breathing was harsh, loud. I wondered if he had a pulmonary condition. He grunted, an old person's sound.

"You see what happened to Mae?" he said.

"Yeah. What do you think?" I sprayed whipped cream onto my hand and licked it.

"She's sane. Always has been."

"Mr. King, does Mae get along with her kids?"

"Why?"

"I think there's something wrong there," I said, knowing it was risky to trust him.

"You're sticking that pretty little nose into things that don't concern you."

"So, you're not going to answer?"

"You don't give up, do you?" He chuckled. The pause before he spoke again felt deep, heavy. "You've got to understand. Damon loved Mae more than anything. More than money, more than land, more than life itself. How do you think that made his children feel? To know they didn't matter one stitch?"

"But that's not Mae's fault," I said.

"You ever been in love?"

"Not really."

"Love's a slippery thing. You've got to work hard to hold onto it. Mae worked harder than most," he said.

"What do you mean?"

"I mean Mae cared more for Damon than her kids. That's what I mean. She never gave two cents about her kids. Now, how would that make you feel?"

"Rotten," I said.

"Yes, ma'am. And rotten is as rotten does."

THIRTY

I WOKE UP with a stomachache, popped four antacids, and tried to go back to sleep. No luck. The sun rested below the horizon. I flipped on the TV and watched powdered faces prattle about this miracle product, that emotional turmoil. What would space aliens make of our culture? Of infomercials and evangelists and talk shows?

Ah, yes. Space aliens.

In my earlier research, I'd opted for an overview of Internet sites and hadn't spent much time reading the testimonials or following the links. With hours to kill before daybreak, a trip into the ether tempted, then persuaded me to see what was really out there in UFO-land.

The varied approaches to "ufology" blew me away. There were the expected sites: MUFON, CUFOS, the museum in Roswell. Others popped up, too. Saucer Smear was written by an iconoclast whose perspective made me guffaw. Conspiracy Net and Cosmic Conspiracies offered such a broad range of information and references they could have been college texts. Conspiracies, military secrets, government cover-ups. Not everyone who wrote articles was nutso. Professors with *bona fides* penned responses in chat rooms, defended Carl Sagan, denounced faulty science.

My current PR plan reeked of sophomoric generalities. It was steeped in misconceptions. If Clovis wanted to participate in this community, it needed to respect the vital debate surrounding UFOs, space aliens, abductions, and encounters. As

I read, my assumptions lay debunked; these people weren't all fringe and fatuous. Although Sagan likened them to modern hysterics or witch believers in past centuries, it seemed to me true intellectual curiosity powered many of the discussions.

Even the big boys: Yahoo, Geocities, and About.com had UFO sites. At About.com, I found a map of New Mexico with a record of UFO sightings including two in Clovis and one near Cannon Air Force Base. Most of these were reported in the infamous *Blue Book,* the "definitive" governmental study about UFOs, which concluded that while unidentified flying objects did exist, no real alien encounters or crashes had ever occurred.

The potential to hit a mega-audience for Clovis from my office at home, sitting in my skivvies with a Guinness at hand, was stupendous. But in order to do justice to my PR plan, I'd have to rewrite, reorganize.

Fine with me. As long as I was working, I wasn't obsessing about money or Mae.

I reread the information on the recorded incidents around Clovis. On a whim, I looked in the local phone book. One name correlated. Edwin Gustafssen. Not a common spelling. The sun coaxed in the morning. I didn't have anything major planned for the day. I'd call this Gustafssen fellow, get a feel for what it was like to see a UFO. I also decided to call Connie Womack to say hello and invite her to lunch.

I headed for breakfast at 6:30. Hungry after all my thinking, I ordered three eggs, bacon, hash browns. When the waitress came with the food, I asked for hot sauce. I was pooped, no doubt about it. A teaspoon of pepper, a blob of catsup, and mucho shakes of Tabasco: that should wake my waning spirit.

Elbows on the table, I balanced my forehead against my hands, closed my eyes.

"Mind if I join you?" LaSalle looked as gray as a sidewalk.

"Only if you've got good news."

"I don't." He sat down anyway, said hi to the waitress who brought him coffee. He ordered the usual, then said, "You need a nap?"

"I didn't get much sleep last night." I pushed a clump of potatoes into a puddle of yolk. "You want to hear something funny?"

"Only if it's good news." His grin was lopsided, as if he didn't have the energy for more.

"The man I'm seeing didn't ask Steve Cummings to help me at all. Isn't that weird?"

LaSalle moaned.

"What?"

"Tell me you're joking," he said. "He's not your lawyer?"

"No. What's the matter?"

"A whole lot is the matter." Though he uttered his words softly, the detective's face had pinkened. An artery in his throat throbbed. "He misrepresented himself. He heard things last night that aren't public knowledge. And you've got to ask yourself why he used you as an excuse to hear them." LaSalle got up from the table. "Excuse me, I'll be right back."

Through the restaurant window, I saw him hurry to a dark car parked in front. He opened it, spoke into a mouthpiece. After he'd finished, he slammed the door. He noticed me observing him, pressed his lips together until they were white lines, and shook his head.

The waitress brought LaSalle's breakfast when he sat down at the table again.

"So what happens next?" I said.

"This is the craziest case I've worked in a long time," he whispered.

I whispered back, "That doesn't answer my question."

"Very astute." LaSalle cut his eggs. He looked at the mess on his plate, then dipped his toast in the goo.

"I don't want to get the guy in trouble."

"He got himself in trouble," he said.

"Do you think he might have something to do with the murder?"

"You know I can't answer that." LaSalle waved his hand. A piece of egg white fell to the tabletop. "Have you heard anything from Mrs. Tan?"

"Not a peep." I watched him eat. "Why? Have you?"

"I've got the next best thing. Mike Cho showed up at the station bright and early. He started with a yell and ended with a squall."

"Guys like him are pretty common in Asia. They expect their money and power to be enough to make the world kowtow."

"They're pretty common everywhere. But, in this case, there's a problem." LaSalle put his fork down. "You came up in the conversation. And Mr. Cho is not a nice boy."

"That's charming." My water glass made a popping sound when I picked it up.

"Don't treat this frivolously."

"You telling me you think he killed Colonel Tan?"

"No. He was in Singapore."

"So, what are you saying? You think he's coming to get me?"

"I hope not," LaSalle said. "But as a precaution, we've moved you into another room and registered you under a different name. Your calls will be forwarded automatically."

He resumed eating, not accepting eye contact.

"You know, I really resent being jerked around like this," I said. "You don't take Bud Johnson seriously. But Mike Cho comes in and scares the pants off everyone." I picked up a piece of bacon with my fingers.

"I understand why you might feel that way," LaSalle said.

"No, I don't think you do."

"Keep your voice down. Please." He followed his own advice. "Look, whatever Bud did or didn't do, it's not on the scale of a Mike Cho. In Singapore, he used his first wife for a punching bag. She had a frequent-flyer card at the local hospital. His second wife miscarried after one of his tantrums. They're divorced, too. I don't want you to get hurt."

"I'm touched. Really, I am."

"Sasha." He loaded his fork, stuffed the heap into his mouth. When he was done, he said, "Sasha, Cho is looking for a scapegoat. He thinks it's too much of a coincidence that you speak Cantonese and that you happened to be in the Coffee Connection that day. He thinks you're part of a bigger conspiracy."

"And I thought his sister was crazy," I said.

"Go ahead and laugh. But you'd better take this seriously."

"I am," I said. "I'll do whatever you want me to do. I'll move into another room, dye my hair blonde. But I'm not going to hide."

"I'm not asking you to."

"Okay," I said.

"Okay," he said.

"So, what have you done about Charlene?"

He moved his plate away, the bitten toast remnants stuck to the congealed yolk.

"You did do something," I said. "Didn't you?"

With his middle finger, he drew an X in a small bit of water on the table.

"Nothing's going to happen to her? Nothing at all?" I said.

"We're keeping an eye on her. It's complicated," he said. "She's a friend of Agent Frenth's, coached both of the chief's daughters in basketball."

"And I thought justice was blind." The sarcasm in my voice made me flinch. "She lied. She set Mae up."

"Maybe yes, maybe no," he said.

"What's that mean?"

"What I said." LaSalle threw a twenty on the table. "My treat." He frowned. "Let's get you settled in your new room."

"I'm not going to stay in there all day. I've got interviews planned. I need to work."

"I'm not asking you to be a hothouse flower," he said. "Just pay attention. Use your intuition. You're one of my best sources and I want you to stay that way."

"Intuition, huh? Do you buy Mrs. Tan's story now?"

"There's a big difference between a hunch and seeing ghosts," LaSalle said.

"But you're open to the possibility there's something there. Right?"

"Let's say I'm not as closed as I was."

We climbed the stairs to the second floor and he handed me a keycard. My suitcase, work papers, and laptop were arranged in an approximation of where they'd been in the other room.

"Marvy," I said.

"You don't like the room?"

It took me a second to realize LaSalle had made a funny.

"Do you know Mae was paying for my room here? What's she going to think when she gets a bill for two?" I said.

"She's not. You can thank the City of Clovis for your current domicile."

"Why?"

"You're helping with an investigation. I want to know where you are. I want to know you're safe and reachable at all times," he said, fiddling with his pack of cigarettes.

"I'm not sure I like that."

"I'm not sure you've got a choice," he said. "I understand you recently lost your job."

"How do you know that? Oh, never mind," I said. "I sure hope you don't tell anybody."

"It's nobody's business."

"It's none of yours, either."

"Sasha. Don't worry. Your secret's safe with me."

"Oh, great."

"And the homicide team." LaSalle patted my shoulder. "Don't worry."

"Be happy," I said, kicking the door closed when he left.

THIRTY-ONE

LIFE AT A COMPUTER isn't what it's cracked up to be.

My fingers felt as brittle as last year's dried aspen leaves. I yawned, stretched, and made some calls. By ten, I'd set up lunch with Connie Womack and an afternoon appointment with retired Lieutenant Colonel Edwin Gustafssen.

The more I thought about Mike Cho, the more worried I became. I decided to fight the victim mentality, to take action. First on the agenda: find Mae's farm and scope out the lair Charlene guarded like a Doberman.

"King Enterprises? Follow the highway out of Clovis back toward Fort Sumner. Right past the Putt Putt turn left onto the dirt road. Cross the tracks and go until you see the sign. You can't miss it," said Carlos at the front desk.

"So, it's like, what? A half-hour from here?" I said.

"More like five minutes. Really, it's five, six miles at the most."

My smile shattered.

"Are you all right?"

"I'm fine," I said.

If I'd known how easy it was to find, I would have gone to see Mae days ago. I could have seen her before she'd been hauled off.

Troubadours would have written songs about this spring day. The land burgeoned with life, sea-green fields of emerging wheat, alfalfa, and millet. Cows and calves, horses and colts, sheep and lambs, the whole world around Clovis had reproduced. The place teemed with newness, expectation and innocence. Difficult to believe how cold it had been, how the snow had hit the ground less than a week before.

I rolled down the window, breathed in the cool, healthy air. No scent of trains for the moment. Sun on my skin, birds singing. I felt like I was in a Disney flick—traipsing around with talking animals in the minutes preceding the bad moment when the music turns discordant and Evil makes his entrance.

And then there was the turnoff, minutes after I'd started my drive.

Over the bumpity bump of the train tracks, I rode through oceans of sweet-smelling crops. If Clovis could bottle and market this, it'd be wealthy. The Chamber should bus in loads of city folk, stick them in the middle of all this non-human life, and watch them blossom. Of course, some people might get lost in all the openness.

A weathered wooden sign announced King Enterprises. I drove past and strained to see if I could find the place where Mae had turned off the road the other night. Why had that journey seemed so long if the farm was so close? Nothing looked familiar.

As I continued, I began to grasp the size of Mae's holdings. A wire fence delineating her land ran from the train tracks past the farm entrance, and miles beyond, before cutting to the west. Where were the cows? I smelled them. But all I saw were long, white, plastic bags resembling mammoth worms, sleeping in clusters, lumpy and shining in the morning sun.

I turned the car around and pulled into the farm's driveway. Two structures stood in front, a large construction site trailer and a house. Dogs barked, heard not seen. Crickets chirruped. Other insects clicked and hummed. I stepped onto the dirt and headed toward the temporary building. A new white truck was parked out front. I peered in the trailer's windows and saw three desks, computers on each, and phones. The furniture must have been bought at auction. It was cheap, metal, the cushions torn. I pressed the buzzer. No response.

Next, I went to the house. Along the way, newly planted posies trembled in the slight breeze. Purple and white crocuses bloomed near the front door. Tulips and daffodils pushed leaves through the damp ground. Mae's home stood, a plain two-story affair, somber in its maroon brick façade. Not a single interesting design element. This dwelling existed for sleeping and eating, period. I rang the doorbell and heard chimes, a carillon. Dogs yelped from within. I rang again. Dog nails scratched on the other side of the door.

I meandered around the high-walled perimeter of the building and jumped several times to peep into the backyard. It was grassy, carelessly landscaped. A decrepit swimming pool needed repainting. Sun-bleached lawn chairs lay willy-nilly on the ground. Upturned plastic tricycles added color. A custom brick doghouse with four arched entrances hunkered in a corner.

I'd imagined Mae in a palace, New Mexican style. I'd visualized her drinking fine scotch in a rambling adobe mansion with soft angles, skylights, chili ristras hanging on either side of a carved pine front door. The reality disappointed. My friend lived in a drab, ordinary home.

A burgundy truck with tinted windows pulled up the driveway and blocked my car. The door opened, releasing a tall, trim man in cowboy boots, hat, and sunglasses. He wore jeans and a flannel shirt.

"Can I help you?" His voice had a slight drawl, more Texan than Deep South.

"I'm looking for Mae," I ad-libbed.

"Are you a reporter?"

"No. I'm a friend of hers from Albuquerque."

"Albuquerque, huh?" He reassessed me. "You must be the famous Sasha Solomon."

Bowing, I said, "The one and only."

"And a good thing, too." Not quite smiling, he held out his hand. "Travis Simpson, Charly's better half."

"Oh. Nice to meet you." I hadn't expected it to be him. My fortune. His strong grip reassured me we weren't enemies yet.

He brought the hat farther down on his head. "I don't know what you've been saying to my wife but I'd sure appreciate it if you'd leave her alone. She's got enough to deal with, with Mae's troubles and our kids."

"Mr. Simpson, believe it or not, I don't really want to talk to your wife," I said. "She just happens to pick up the phone every time I call."

"Yeah, she's pretty protective." He took off his sunglasses to expose hazel eyes. "You know she's in Albuquerque?"

Mae or *Charlene?*

"How's she doing?" I said.

"I dunno. Charly's been up there trying to see her, but it's pretty hard. No visitors. Nothing. Thank goodness my mom can take care of the kids until this blows over," he said.

"I sure hope it blows over."

"It will." He put his glasses back on. "Mae couldn't kill a man if her life depended on it. And she's no crazier than I am."

"Did you say that to the police?"

"Sure."

"And what happened?"

"Henry just sat there and took it all in." Travis looked up at the sky. "He heard me."

"What do you think about those abductions Mae's claiming?"

"Ma'am, I work alone at night a lot. I've seen things I can't explain, that didn't look natural. No one chucked me into a nut farm."

"Don't you think it's weird the abductions came up all of a sudden? It's like someone wants to make Mae look bad." Okay, okay. I wasn't being totally honorable here.

Placid as a cow, he said, "From what I heard, you're the one who did that."

"No way would I do that to Mae."

"Well, I don't know anything about anything. I'm on the road a lot." He held his open hand out to the west. "King Enterprises is a big business, Ms. Solomon—the farm, ranches, and other concerns. I run it, though Mae's technically my boss. We have a lot of other holdings throughout the state. Most of last week I was in Estancia checking on calves. Then I had to fix fences near Springer. I've hardly seen Charly and the kids in a month."

My theory about Charlene and Bud Johnson having an affair might not be so farfetched. Though why she'd choose that lump of flesh over this taut, tanned man was beyond me.

"You want me to tell Charly you stopped by?" he said, sounding bored with the chitchat.

"I don't think that'd be a good idea. Do you?"

A smile touched his lips and faded.

We walked behind the trailer. There were several buildings in the distance. I eyed the horizon, searching for a familiar landmark. I still hadn't seen any cows.

"You ever been to a dairy farm before?" Travis said.

"Never."

He glanced at his watch.

"Hop in the truck. I can give you a quick tour before I get back to work," he said.

"Really?"

"Sure, why not? One hour out of twenty-four isn't going to make much difference."

"May I use the bathroom? I really thought someone would be home." I pointed to the house, wanting to see how Mae and her kids lived.

"Charly's got the keys to Mae's place. I'll take you over to our little *hacienda*." He butchered the Spanish word. "I need to check my messages anyway."

Another assumption shot down; I thought Mae lived with Charlene and her family. If she didn't, why was Charlene there every single time I called?

"…and we've got three circles of our own," said Travis.

"Circles?" Wow! There were crop circles in Clovis? This could be another UFO tie-in.

He sighed, realizing I knew less than nothing when it came to agriculture. "A circle has to do with irrigation, how the water from our sprinklers hits the crops. It's about one hundred and thirty-two acres."

"And you've got three of them," I said.

"Yeah, but that's nothing." He took off his hat, scratched the black and gray hair underneath. "Like I said, King Enterprises is much bigger than that. Mae owns a couple hundred sections in New Mexico alone."

It sounded big.

"More than a hundred-fifty thousand acres," he said.

"Cool," I said. "So, she owns land as far as my eyes can see?"

"Not exactly. There're six circles here. Then, we've got stud ranches and beef production in other parts of the state. Damon bought a couple sections between Santa Fe and Taos as straight real estate investments back in the sixties." Travis stopped, shrugged. "Come on, you look like you're about to explode."

I'd forgotten the whole potty ploy. Scrambling into the high cab, I was glad to be wearing pants rather than a skirt. Travis had the engine on before I fastened the seatbelt. We drove five miles down the road.

The Simpson house was functional. Not much to distinguish it either. A vegetable bed had been prepared in a gated area to the right of the entrance. Travis strode past it and unlocked the front door. The place screamed country precious— dried flowers, porcelain dolls in wood cases with glass fronts, and kid mess. Tee shirts, tennis shoes, socks, and shorts covered the floor, overstuffed couch, chairs at the kitchen table. Making no apology for the disarray, my host directed me to the bathroom.

A framed poster of a cow with a digitally created smile hung on the back of the door. She was hooked up to a milking machine. I read the reflected caption in the mirror, *Mooowhee! That feels good!* Guest towels not intended for use dangled dusty on a little brass holder. The soap was shell-shaped and scented. I rinsed my hands, wiped them on my pants. Emerged and found Travis in the kitchen.

"Want a cup of coffee?" He'd already poured two.

"Thanks."

"Take it with you," he said, moving toward the door.

As we drove, I asked about the plastic worm things.

"Ag bags," Travis said. He kept his eyes on the dirt road, avoiding potholes. "They're cheaper than silos and they let the grain breathe. We grow most of our own corn, wheat, and milo. It's cheaper and we have more control over the quality that way."

We pulled onto Mae's property again and drove past the house and office.

He pointed to a high and wide metal structure partitioned into five separate areas filled with what looked like sand.

"To the left, there, is the grain," he said. "We change the feed mix depending on how the cows are milking. That's milo, cottonseed, corn. Over here's the calf barn."

We got out of the truck and stepped into another metal building. Its large sliding wood doors stood open. The smell overwhelmed me, sour and medicinal and manure-y. Two long rows of pens lined the sides of the building with two more back-to-back in the middle. Every one held a calf. The floor was concrete. There was a contraption on a trailer that the workers filled with a watery, milky substance. It had cow-sized versions of baby bottles and mammoth rubber nipples suspended outward. Fifteen or twenty calves could eat at once. Two more trailers were parked at the other end of the barn.

A thin tabby cat rubbed against my legs.

"That's Tiffany and her new litter," said Travis. He gestured toward a bed of towels. The tiny kittens blinked at the combination of natural and florescent light.

He walked down one of the rows. "This is where we keep the babies, up to two weeks. We feed 'em colostrums—just like their mothers would, and keep a close eye on 'em."

"How many are in here?"

"About a hundred and ten."

We got in the truck again. This was all fine and dandy, but I wanted to see something familiar like the trough where Colonel Tan had been. We drove by rows and rows of pens, small wooden slated things with fences. Then more rows of tan plastic doghouses.

"This is where we keep the calves from two weeks to three months," Travis said.

"They don't have much room."

"They don't need it. Cows don't need exercise. They're for milking." Travis shook his head. "You sound like Josh. He says we're cruel to keep 'em like this. But we need to be able to watch 'em carefully without spending time running around trying to catch 'em. We've got to know if they're eating, drinking enough, how much they weigh. Don't forget, this is a business."

"Oh, I know that. I've just never been on a dairy farm before," I said.

"Over here are the milking cows." Travis turned down a clean dirt alley between two large corrals. "Here's something you don't see every day." He slowed the truck. "Damon knew a lot about dairy farming. When he bought the place, he had all the corrals built on slopes. That way the water runs downhill and our cows don't have to lie in mud and muck."

He sped up. "This alley is where we put the food for the cows. They stick their heads out and eat. Then a trailer comes along and shoves the food back for them—since they don't have hands to grab it themselves—so they can keep on eating." Travis slowed down yet again. "Believe it or not, the average cow eats the equivalent of three hundred and sixty-five hamburgers a day."

"Really?" I said, thinking two things: it was funny he'd mention hamburgers in relation to what cows ate, and, this was a colossal waste of time.

"Look at this." He stopped the truck on a bridge. "This is how the cows get into the milk house. They don't walk through their own muck and food. Instead they go in these nice, clean tunnels before they get showered off. Keeps them healthier and the milk house cleaner."

We drove into another alley, startling a flock of black birds with bright gold markings. Ahead was the biggest building yet.

"This is the milk house," he said, turning off the ignition and unlocking our doors.

Before entering, we toured the "maternity ward," the cows swollen with unborn babies. We saw the dry-cow area where the lucky gals got to rest before being bred again.

Travis led me to the machine room. It was filled with air compressors, portable generators, ice chillers, vacuum pumps, and six big stainless steel storage tanks. He shouted over the noise, saying the milk house was modeled on large California operations.

We walked outside and through the main entrance. Someone had taken the time to tile the walls white with two bands of red and sky blue in a step-like design, making the hallways pretty—an unexpected touch given the drab dwellings of the humans who ran the business. The floors were tiled, too.

The medicine room stank. The milking area gleamed, wet, busy, and mechanized.

I could see how Josh was offended by all of this. The cows had my sympathy, too. But without dairy farms, I wouldn't have low-fat milk for my skinny lattes, cheddar cheese, or brie.

The tour over, we sauntered back to the truck.

"Tell me about totally integrated farming. What do you think of it?" I said.

"There's a place for it. It's a major investment of time and money though." Travis used a remote to unlock the vehicle again.

"Do you think Mae's crazy to think about it?"

"She mention it you?"

I gave a half-nod he could interpret any way he wanted.

"Well. I guess I'm with Josh on this one. It's Mae's money, her farm." He slammed his door. "I've told her I'd help find the people to manage the cheese production and distribution part of it. But with what's happening now, I don't know."

"You said yourself it'll blow over."

"People have got to trust you when you're borrowing money, Ms. Solomon. Murder doesn't exactly instill trust."

"People have got to know she didn't do anything wrong," I said.

"People believe what they want to believe."

Travis parked in front of my car, jumped out and opened the door for me. His first burst of chivalry.

"Where was the body found, anyway?" I said, putting my hand to my forehead for a last view of the land we'd traveled. "Nothing looks familiar from the other night."

"That's because it wasn't here. It was near our peanut farm outside Portales. We let some of our moms dry up out there."

"Thanks for showing me around," I said, disappointed. I shook his hand.

"Anytime." Travis held my hand a second too long. "You know, Ms. Solomon, this whole thing with Charly and Mae. It goes back a long way. I've never been able to figure it out.

Sort of a love-hate thing." He frowned. "The worst part of it is, they're both good women. But they've forgotten how to talk with each other. They talk at each other instead."

I nodded, got into the car and rolled down the window.

Travis leaned against it, cleared his throat and said, "All I can say is, cows are a lot more forgiving than any woman I've ever met." A rueful smile. He stroked the doorframe, turned away, then toward me again. "You take care."

"Thanks. I will," I said, looking into his handsome hazels.

If Charlene was having an affair, she was a fool.

THIRTY-TWO

As sober as if I'd never had a drink in my life, I motored back to town. A couple of things didn't sit right. Everyone made it sound like Charlene ran the farm. Travis claimed he was the brawn behind the bucks. And why had he talked about how Charly and Mae related? Had I overlooked something obvious? He presented so well, so trustworthy and hardworking. The absolute stereotype of a man of the land. In my experience as a PR pro, when things look too good, there's probable cause to doubt them.

Was Travis behind Mae's troubles? I didn't like how that felt. Didn't like the idea I could be that gullible. But why had he spent an hour showing me the farm? What if he was really a greedy, conniving man who knew a dupe when he saw one? Could be he and Charly were in cahoots, trying to wrestle the farm away from Mae. He'd sure been complacent about the cheese factory concept.

I shook my head against the flood of suspicions. How did policemen do it, living with a baseline suspicion all the time? No wonder LaSalle had a thick line of pale flesh where a wedding ring should have been. He'd doubtless alienated his wife with the emotional detritus from years of murder investigations.

In an instant, something changed. Goosebumps rose on the back of my neck and scurried down my arms. Someone was watching, following me. I looked in the rearview mirror. There was no one there. Still, the feeling remained. Had Mike Cho spotted my car?

I had forty-five minutes before my lunch with Connie. To pass the time in the safety of a public place, I went to Denny's. I bought a newspaper and ordered a large OJ. Mae's story wasn't front-page fodder any more. The lead article concerned Clovis city politics and the resignation of the city manager. I glanced at the story, uninterested until I saw Bud's name.

"The man is leaving us in the lurch," Dr. Bud Johnson said. "He doesn't have Clovis's best interest at heart any more. We should fire him and cut our losses."

I scanned the beginning of the article and found the place where the reporter justified quoting the dentist. In addition to being a member of the Chamber, Johnson served as chairman of the budget committee. The reference to his two unsuccessful bids for mayor made me grin. I recognized the dig. Bud's mayoral failures were old news. That meant the reporter didn't like him one bit. If my weasely friend kept bugging me, I'd seek out the news hound. Compare notes.

I looked around the near-empty restaurant, scanning for Mike Cho in disguise. Reassured, I read on. Page two announced openings in the next session of the People's Police Academy. There was a brief history of the program. The Chief of Police had started it to encourage local businessmen to become better citizens and to educate them about how to spot and deal with a variety of crimes. Among the list of graduates were Jan Cisneros, Judy Cummings Slant, Charlene and Travis Simpson—that was interesting—Theodore King, and Bud Johnson. The boy sure got around. I stored that crumb of info for my next conversation with LaSalle, wondering if graduates of the "academy" received preferential treatment or used their knowledge to thwart investigations.

Also on page two, *Cannon High on List for Closing*. Mr. Lester Donry, a Clovis 25 member, was the main talking head.

He was good with sound bites. The astute reporter asked if Colonel Tan's murder was having a bad effect on the base. Donry responded that, of course, morale was low.

"I assure you, the community of Clovis has united to offer support to the widow and her family," he said. "We've promised the Singaporean government swift and severe punishment for whomever committed this heinous crime."

The murder investigation merited page-three treatment, including a summary of a press conference where the Chief of Police—his face coarse and cementy in the black-and-white photo—played point person. He stood flanked by LaSalle, Frenth, and Mason, none of them looking happy. There were the standard responses and pleas: *we're making solid progress, please come forward if you have information, we expect to make an arrest soon.*

I didn't buy it.

When asked about Mae, the chief said she was still under psychiatric observation.

Letters to the editor focused on the murder. Violent crime wasn't common in Clovis. There was a sense of distress, of disbelief that Mae could be a murderer. Many of the writers used biblical references; the old cast-the-first-stone parable featured prominently.

What struck me was the general feeling of sorrow about the incident. In most bigger-city papers, Albuquerque's among them, Mae would be portrayed as guilty. An uncomplimentary photo of her avoiding the camera or being led away in cuffs would make the front page. The writing would be filled with "alleged," and "she claimed," and "no comment." But not in Clovis. Even the reporter was downhearted about writing the story, spending an extra paragraph describing Mae's many contributions to the city.

Something dropped at my feet. My knee hit the table when I bolted, excitable as a lizard. I looked up, then down. My napkin had slipped under the table and landed on my foot. I kicked it away, angry to be nervous about Cho. I took a deep breath, realizing I hadn't done so for a long time. The good news: No hallucination hounded me yet.

I finished my juice, folded the newspaper back to the piece about the murder, and went to the register. The cashier was a young, bulky woman with short brown hair. She noticed the article when I laid the paper on the counter to get my money.

"Sure is a shame about that man. Isn't it?" Her concern seemed more than casual.

"Sure is."

"It doesn't make any sense. Mrs. King's a good lady," she said.

"Do you know her?"

"Everybody does. I went to school with Josh. I was always over at their house. Mrs. King's as good as they come."

"I know. She's a friend of mine," I said.

"Yeah?" She handed me the change. "Well, what I don't understand is why she did it. She must have cracked or something."

"She didn't do it." Annoyance rippled in my voice.

Her eyes met mine, prepared for a confrontation. "Well, if she didn't, then who did?"

THIRTY-THREE

DID I MENTION that Clovis is flat? Totally flat without even a hill? For a poor kid like me, who usually used Albuquerque's mountains and volcanoes to figure out what direction I traveled in, the town didn't offer a clue. Though small and straight-streeted, my marketing project could've been a maze.

I'd made a wrong turn somewhere and dead-ended at a farm.

Bidding adieu to a mare and her foal scampering in the brisk spring air, I turned the car around and hunted for my missed turnoff into Jonquil Estates.

The landscaping around Connie Womack's house was fresh and scanty. From the street, I could see the lines where sod would be laid. Cutting from sidewalk to front door was a golden brick path that matched the building's façade. I closed the car door and noted the over-tall entryway with its over-large windows framing a nine-foot portal. A brass and crystal chandelier sparkled through the semi-circle of glass at the top.

Then, I got to the door.

Right above the button for the bell was a small brass gargoyle, the kind you'd find gazing down at you from Notre Dame. His expression was half grimace, half grin. I chuckled and pushed the bell. It chimed the first few bars of the William Tell Overture. I laughed out loud.

The woman who answered was in her mid-thirties, dressed in torn jeans and a lime-green sweatshirt. Unruly black hair licked her face like flames, highlighting blue eyes. She wore plastic orange fish earrings and purple tennis shoes flecked with white paint.

"Sasha?" She held out her hand, opened the door wide. "Boy, I sure lost track of time."

"Do you want me to come back later?"

"Of course not," Connie said. "Unless you're a neatnik."

"Don't worry about that."

From the minute I entered the house, I felt Lilliputian. The entrance was the size of my casita in Albuquerque. The furniture was dwarfed by spaciousness, a dollhouse couch, a miniature reclining chair and ottoman. I knew the rugs were large, but they didn't make a dent on the expanse of peach-colored *saltillo* tiles. Only the paintings were on a giant's scale, murals filled with multihued flowers, brilliant petals as large as my torso.

"Wow," I said.

"Yeah, I like to work big." She grinned. "Those were part of my rainbow phase."

"You painted these?" Celebrities don't mean a thing to me. However, I'm always a bit in awe of fine artists. "They're wonderful."

"Thanks." Her pleasure in bringing pleasure was genuine. "Come on, I'll show you my latest experiments."

I loved the feel of the place, like being wrapped in an immense goose-down blanket on a cold day. We walked through her kitchen. She'd decorated it in simulated jungle with vines and lemurs painted on the walls. A banana tree light fixture hung over the ten-chair table.

Connie noticed me turning this way and that, trying to take it all in at once.

"Clovis may not be a cultural hotspot, but it does have lots of land—and you can get it cheap," she said. "I'm not going to tell you how much this place cost new. You'd cry for a week." She stopped at a door. "I don't usually apologize for my messes. But today, well, the studio's not pretty."

"Don't worry," I said, convinced I'd found a kindred spirit.

"If you care about your shoes, take them off. We're about to enter Creativity Central and there's plenty of paint underfoot."

She opened the door and I forgot everything but the view: a full wall of windows at one end, round and square skylights, drop cloths gorgeous enough to sell. Canvases the size of VWs stood stacked against a series of shelves laden with bottles, tubes, and jars of paint. I felt a powerful urge to take up a brush, strip down to my undies, and splash those colors everywhere.

"Your mom didn't tell me you were a painter," I said.

"She likes to surprise people. Pretty perverse if you ask me." Her impish face reminded me of Mary when we'd been in the lunch line at the rehab hospital.

Connie checked under a covered canvas, dropped the cloth back over it and said, "By the way, Mom's going home later today."

"Did they find out what was wrong?"

"Nah. But who cares? As long as she's almost back to a hundred percent."

"Wish I could say the same for mine," I said.

She nodded.

"Do you like these?" She paused next to a series of landscapes. Their colors reached out from the canvases with a giddy joy: forest-green mountains, Beaujolais-red rivers, brandy-amber trees. The sheer audacity of her vision evoked exuberance. The kind of feeling a kid has when school's done for the year and the freezer is full of chocolate ice cream.

Connie concluded the art show. We meandered into the kitchen where she spread out a meal of crusty bread, baba ganoush, hummus, and stuffed grape leaves. Easily the most interesting meal I'd had since arriving in Clovis.

"I don't mean to be ungrateful but where's the Retsina?" I said.

"I've got the next best thing. Hold on." She left the room. Seconds later, she came back, a bottle of Barolo Chianti in hand.

"Yum," I said.

While the bottle emptied, our conversation moved from superficialities to more meaningful, private topics. Finally, we settled on moms. It was obvious Connie got a real kick out of hers. I envied their relationship.

As I swirled my fourth glass of Chianti, I felt an uncomfortable sensation, similar to being bitten by fifty mosquitoes at once. I imagined welts popping out on my legs, progressing to my stomach, the back of my neck. Within minutes, I wanted to rip off my skin and start over. Excusing myself, I went to the bathroom, pulled up my shirt, and gasped. Chest to pelvis, red bumps the size of nickels splotched my torso.

"Sasha, are you all right?" Connie knocked on the bathroom door.

"Um. No. Not exactly."

I came out, showed her my belly.

"Oh my!" Her eyes widened half in dismay, half in amusement. "That's one impressive case of hives. What are you allergic to?"

"Nothing. I'm not allergic to anything," I said.

"Well, it's probably the wine. The sulfites, you know. Some people react to them."

"I'm not allergic to wine."

Connie opened the cabinet behind the mirror, exposing a cornucopia of medicine. She handed me a foiled sheet with white pills. "Here, take an antihistamine. It'll help."

"Are you sure they're hives?"

"My whole family gets them from one thing or another. Yes, I'm sure." She filled a glass from the faucet. "The trick is to drink lots of water and get that wine out of your system."

"I'm not allergic to wine." I pocketed the rest of the pills, just in case.

"Well, they could be stress-related. Some people break into hives before they give speeches, that sort of thing. Are you stressed out about something?"

My laughter sounded desperate. We alighted back at the kitchen table. I swigged more water, then told her about Mae. I talked about doubting our years-long friendship because of what had happened. Connie was a good listener and didn't interrupt. I finished my sorry monologue.

"My husband, Rick, is commander of the public information office at Cannon," she said. "He grew up here and knows the King kids real well. You want to talk with him? Get some background on them?" She tore a piece of pita, dipped it in the baba ganoush. "I know he was a friend of Theo's for a while."

"I'm not sure what he could tell me. I bet most of his information is privileged anyway."

"Privileged, schmivileged," she said. "He's not a lawyer. He's in PR, like you."

"I suppose it might be worth it." I frowned, thinking of Mike Cho and wondering if he'd try to follow me onto the base.

"Don't be so pessimistic," Connie said. "I'm sure Rick can fill in some of the blanks. He knows everybody who's anybody in Clovis."

"Okay, sure." I still didn't believe he'd be much help. If he were a friend of Theo's, he'd sketch a positive picture. If I asked about Colonel Tan, he wouldn't be able to say squat.

"Connie, I have a question," I said. "How do you survive here in Clovis? I mean, it's not a cultural Mecca—"

"Yeah, sometimes I'm surprised by how happy I am here," she said. "Would I choose to live in Clovis if Rick weren't at Cannon? Probably not. But there's a lot of good here. People are friendly, sincere. It's a wonderful place to raise kids." She looked at me. "Do you have any?"

I shook my head.

"Well. Rick and I aren't particularly religious but we go to church here and have a lot of acquaintances. Our kids are safe. The air is clean."

"What about *real* friends?" I said.

"That's what phones and computers are for." Another sip of wine, a finger dipped in the hummus. "There's something to be said for a place where you know most of the people in town. Rick always says that if we ever suffered a real crisis, Clovis would be the only place to be. People come out of the woodwork to help in a pinch."

A train whistled in the distance. Connie listened, then continued, "And I travel for my shows. So, I get the best of both worlds." She stood up. "Let me call Rick. I'm sure he'll have something useful."

"Okay."

While she spoke with him, I thought about Connie's life. If I got the job in Clovis, would I rent an apartment or a house? Would I like spending a lot of time here? Would I make friends?

"Rick said to come after three," Connie said. "He'll leave your name at the gate."

With another afternoon appointment, I had reason to avoid the hotel even longer. At this rate, Mike Cho wouldn't have a chance to get near me.

By the time Connie brought out the whiskey for our coffee after lunch, my hives weren't bothering me anymore. We dollopped real whipped cream on top of our drinks and talked more about family. Connie said her mother was wonderful but had chosen a prick for a husband.

"You know, Sasha, when Dad was dying, I learned something important. There's a point in anger when you have a choice. You can release it or let it spread like a malignant cancer. Compassion wasn't easy for me. I wanted him to change, to transform into a loving, accepting father. But that wasn't who he was. I worked hard on loving him, warts and all."

She stared into the mug for a minute, scooped whipped cream with her little finger. "In the end, it wasn't about anger anymore. And now I don't have to carry around any of that awful baggage. I guarantee your mom has a lot more kindness in her than Dad ever did. When she acts crazy or hurtful, remember her good moments, the loving ones. Focus on that."

"That's the problem," I said. "I search and search but can't find them. It's all bitterness inside and blame. I know there's got to be more, but it's like a computer file I can't access."

"Sasha, honey, that's bull. I've only known you for a couple of hours but I can say absolutely that you wouldn't be the interesting, intelligent, and caring person you are, without a mother's love. Stop feeling sorry for yourself, and look, really look, inside. You'll find those moments of grace."

THIRTY-FOUR

CONNIE'S WORDS ADHERED to me like syrup, rich flavor, annoying stickiness. I'd spent a lifetime blaming Mom for my problems and most of my adult years searching for her good points. How could Connie say I hadn't done enough? When I turned down a street toward Lieutenant Colonel Gustafssen's house, a realization stuck me. I stopped the car to process it.

All these years, I'd been blundering, bumping into this emotional crisis, that traumatic experience. I needed to approach this mother thing in a new way. Public relations taught me to find meaningful hooks, useful angles for touting my clients' strengths. Why not apply the same know-how to Mom?

More food for thought than I wanted to eat right then. I stowed the concept away, hoping I'd remember it when next I spoke with my therapist or had time to reflect.

Gustafssen's house was one story and shipshape with budding crocuses all in a row. The porch was swept and the chairs didn't dare show a speck of dust. The cleanliness spurred me to inspect the bottoms of my shoes, to make sure no paint from Connie's would mar its precision. The doorbell sang the song of my youth, a simple ding-dong that caught my attention after the ostentatious chimes of other places I'd visited in Clovis. The lacy curtain by the front door moved a fraction before I heard locks unlatch.

Mrs. Gustafssen's expression said she'd grown accustomed to people and things knowing their place. Eyes narrowing at my outfit—slacks, tennis shoes, and long-sleeved tee shirt—

she greeted me with a firm handshake and invited me to follow her. Something wasn't quite right about her gait. Each step held a second's hesitation. A kettle wailed in another room, loud in this quiet house.

"The colonel and I take our tea at two. Will you join us?" I'd never heard a woman refer to her husband by a title. That odd fact, compounded with Mrs. Gustafssen's careful, exact enunciation, made me wonder if she'd learned to speak anew or had a hearing problem.

I accompanied her into a bright yellow kitchen. She pointed to the chair she wanted me to use. Lieutenant Colonel Gustafssen sat at the formica table, his head shaking in a constant small arc. He held out his hand, his grip strong in spite of the quivering.

Mrs. Gustafssen pulled the kettle off the stove with two hands and transferred the hot water into a raku teapot. Her concentration was intense, as if a moment's inattention would be disastrous. The danger averted, she centered the pot on a trivet at the table and set out small matching cups, no saucers, no spoons and no sugar.

"I hope you don't mind green tea. We've been in the habit for nearly fifty years." I would have thought her rude but for the smile touching her colorless lips. There was a way to do things in the Gustafssen house. Guests were expected to respect it.

"I love green tea. Thank you."

She poured, again double-fisted, filling my cup first. Then on to her husband who got much less, and the same for her. Lieutenant Colonel Gustafssen's hands were in continuous motion. I understood his wife's caution with the hot liquid.

"Old age is the pits." His first words to me, said without bitterness. A simple statement of fact.

"That's what I hear," I said.

"Parkinson's for me, two strokes for Mrs. Gustafssen here.

But we're managing. Don't plan to move until we have to."
His defiance hinted of a life's habit of command.

I didn't know him well enough for platitudes or denials. Mrs.
Gustafssen sipped her tea, put a hand on his to still the shaking. She looked at him with what only could be a warning. He
stared straight back at her. Something passed between them.

"I understand you want to talk with the colonel about his
experiences in the Air Force. I'll leave you to your conversation," she said, emitting an involuntary groan when she rose.
She stopped at the door leading out from the kitchen. "I'll be
in the sitting room if you need me."

Gustafssen watched his wife leave, grunted once, and
drank the tea. I felt like I'd blundered into a Tennessee
Williams play—the formal language, the confusing but potent subtext—and I'd missed a cue.

"Thank you for agreeing to speak with me, sir," I said.

"That's the way it should be. In my home for less than five
minutes and you're practically ready to salute." His wry smile
surprised me. "Don't let Mrs. Gustafssen's 'the colonel this
and the colonel that' intimidate you. I retired as a lieutenant
colonel, almost the real McCoy, but not quite. Mrs.
Gustafssen's never forgiven the Air Force. Years ago, she got
it into her head that calling me 'the colonel' would garner
more respect. I haven't the heart to disabuse her of the notion."
He lifted his cup an inch off the table. "The Japanese would
wince at my crudeness, but would you pour me some more
tea? Not too full or I'll bathe in it."

When I had served him, he said, "Remind me. How did you
get my name?"

I told him about my computer search.

"Pardon my ignorance. Don't you have an account of my
experience already?"

For some reason, I got the feeling his question wasn't for
my benefit.

"Only a four-line summary. I'd like to hear it in your own words," I said.

"And this is for?"

"A project I'm bidding on with the chamber of commerce."

We'd gone over everything when I had made the appointment. He glanced at the doorway Mrs. Gustafssen had used.

"Speak up. I can barely hear you," he said, bending his head toward the door. I could picture his wife sitting rock-still listening in. "So, this story might go out into the world, into an article or a book, or on that Internet everyone talks about?"

"Yes, sir. That's my plan. To publicize these incidents. Especially ones with credible sources." I pulled out my notebook and a good pen to write with.

"I'm honored." It rang with sarcasm.

"Sir?"

"Never you mind."

I cleared my throat.

"Would you tell me what happened that night, sir?" I said.

Mrs. Gustafssen came into the room, poured tea for us, and left.

He whispered, "She doesn't approve. People's mocking and scorn can be a painful thing." Then loudly, "Well, let me see. It was in the spring of '55. I was a fighter pilot and had just completed a mission at the gunnery range at Fort Hood. In Texas, you know. I was on my way home. It was late, near midnight, and I had the whole sky to myself."

He grasped the teacup in both hands, watched them fight for a moment.

"Have you ever been in the cockpit of a fighter, Ms. Solomon?"

"No. Never."

His face reflected such pleasure from the memory. I felt envy for the first time since I'd met him.

"It's amazing. Just you, a machine that responds to your

slightest touch, and the sky. Endless sky. I loved it. Especially flying at night with millions of stars as my only company. The beauty of it. Well, it's indescribable." He grabbed the table until his fingertips turned white.

"I haven't been able to fly a jet for decades. Lord, I miss it." Gustafssen arched his eyebrows, sighed. "That's not what you're here for, memories of an old man."

"I'm here to hear your story, sir." I liked him.

"Well, as I was saying, it was near midnight. I was tired but felt good. Glad to be coming home, to see the children. We had eight, you know. And the littlest, Felicia, was less than a month old." An internal smile touched the surface of his mouth. "So, my mind was on pleasant things when I noticed a flash out of the corner of my right eye, far off on the horizon. I turned my head and saw a spot of brilliant light. Much brighter than any star. And it looked like it was moving. But I wasn't sure. Not then."

He squinted and said, "As quickly as I'd seen it, it disappeared.

"At first I was curious. What in the world was it?" Gustafssen scratched his balding head. "I scanned the sky but it was gone. I'd just written the whole thing off as fatigue-induced when, boom, there it was again. But instead of the one light, there were five of the things flying together in definite formation." He returned to that distant moment, excited, unaware of me.

"I'd never seen anything like them before. They broke formation with staggering speed and went in all directions. Just crazy. Up and down, sideways, turning in ways—steep drops, near-right angles—ways fighters simply can't go. I pulled up and rolled into a ninety-degree turn to lose 'em. The things tagged me. I did a one-eighty and they were still with me."

Gustafssen skidded to reality. He yanked his emotions in check.

"You need to understand that in 1955, I'd already been in

the mouth of the cat twice. Once in the big war and again in Korea. I'd had rounds come right through the cockpit both times and survived. I knew what fear was. And I can tell you, I was scared by what those lights were doing."

He picked up the teacup, put it down. "Well, I pulled up again as fast and hard as I could and it didn't matter a bit. They surrounded my plane like gnats. Whenever I changed position, altitude, speed, no matter what I did, they were with me."

Mrs. Gustafssen returned and sat down next to her husband. She didn't say a word but took one of his hands in hers. Their gaze locked onto each other, the battle apparent. The fierce silence of it evinced an ancient disagreement. One they must have waged for decades.

Gustafssen coughed, rotated his body away from the conflict.

"By this time I was preparing for descent and wondering what on earth I'd tell my ops commander." He scratched his head again. "Now, like I said, I wasn't some wet-behind-the-ears youngster. I was high up enough in the Air Force that I pretty much knew what aircraft were being developed and what the future held for fighter jets. This wasn't a question of the Russkies having some kind of new technology. No machine known to man could do what these craft were doing, toying with me like a bunch of cats with a mouse. Hell—"

Mrs. Gustafssen cleared her throat in obvious displeasure.

"Well," he said. "Well, I couldn't shoot 'em. Couldn't catch 'em. And they could do whatever they wanted to me, to the base, and to the United States.

"I can tell you, I felt a real conflict in here." He tapped his chest. "Should I land and bring these babies in? Or should I keep flying, run out of fuel, crash, and leave my family with no one to look after them? I took the selfish route, figuring if they came in after me, at least someone else would see them."

He rested his head on his hands. Their trembling diminished with the pressure. "I think I need to explain something here. I was on the fast track, a junior major already, headed toward a good career. I'd enlisted when I was eighteen. That night I saw them I was twenty-eight. I had a lot of seniority, a lot of flying experience." His eyes lit up. "And I can tell you I'd heard it all by then. New pilots, kids really, would see strange lights during flights and go off about aliens like there was no tomorrow. Of course, with Roswell, they were spooked anyway."

He smacked his lips. "Before that night, I believed there was always a logical explanation for those anomalies, be it northern lights, weather balloons, lack of oxygen. Whatever. So I could predict how my commanders would respond to my report." Gustafssen looked at me, shook his head once. "Believe me, the temptation was great to ignore it all and go home. But I believed our national security was at risk. Even though I knew it would tarnish my record, the right thing, the only honorable thing to do was to wake up my ops and squadron commanders and tell them what I'd seen." Another glance passed between the two, pain on both their faces.

"I knew my story would sound crazy. But it was my responsibility as a pilot, as a defender of my country, to make that report." He pursed his lips. "At about six hundred feet before I touched down, the lights shot straight up into the sky, and there seemed to be even more than five, eight maybe. They were so bright I couldn't get a good handle on their shapes."

He drank the rest of his now-cold tea before speaking again. "My immediate superiors believed me. But they were obliged to report the incident to their superiors. Then came the psych eval. When I heard they'd ordered a Type A physical, well, I knew I had a problem. Turned out no one else had seen a thing. Not even a pilot who'd landed at about the same time I did." His cup docked loudly on the table. "He must have been blind not to see them."

His rage hovered in the air.

"You don't need to hear the details of the next few months. The ridicule nearly ruined our marriage. My flight status was in jeopardy for a while. Finally they realized I was too good a pilot and too strong an instructor to let go," he said. "To keep me away from the reporters, they threw me a bone. Station in Japan. Me and the family. It ended up being a good thing for all of us."

Mrs. Gustafssen patted his hand. Cleared our cups and began washing them.

"Of course, both times I came up for colonel, they found a reason to deny me," Gustafssen said, staring at her back. "Even though I'd never had a complaint. My commendation folder bulged with praise."

A teacup clattered to the floor and broke.

"Oh, tarnation!" said Mrs. Gustafssen, who rushed to a pantry and retrieved a broom.

"Here, let me help," I said.

"No, no. I may be unsteady, but I can do my own cleaning, thank you," she said.

I sat back down. "Sir, what do you think those lights were?"

"I have no idea," he said.

"Do you think they could have been beings with intelligence?"

"They acted intelligently," he said. "I won't bore you with speculation."

"But that's exactly what I'm asking you to do."

"Don't you think I've tried to figure it out? One blasted report and my earning power and retirement were cut by hundreds of thousands of dollars. I haven't come up with a thing that makes sense."

Mrs. Gustafssen stopped sweeping. Her lips tightened into thin, straight strips.

"Pardon my outburst, Ms. Solomon. Bitterness is an ugly emotion," he said. "Ms. Solomon, I know you want me to say it was space aliens out there controlling those ships. But I can't do it. I can't say anything definite except what I saw with my own eyes. Beyond that is conjecture and I'm not prone to flights of fantasy."

So, that was it; he refused to give me more. No problem. I had time to work on him. If the Chamber bought my PR plan, I'd approach him again. Charlene's pesky resistance notwithstanding, when it came to my work, I could persuade a tree to shed its bark. I knew Gustafssen would change his mind.

For now, he'd addressed me by name enough during the last few minutes to indicate the interview was over.

"I'm sorry, Ms. Solomon, but I'm tired now. It's time I take a little rest." The sadness in his voice made me want to cry. "Used to be, 'rest' was a four-letter word."

Mrs. Gustafssen walked me to the porch and paused, her hand light on my arm. The physical contact surprised me.

In a restrained voice, she confided, "The colonel suffered a great deal for a great many years because of making that report. People can be very cruel." She frowned. "He's worked hard not to be resentful." Then she said, "My own efforts have been much less successful."

"What do you think, Mrs. Gustafssen? Were they aliens?" I said.

She looked beyond me to the street before answering.

"Why, of course they were." Her voice had dwindled to near nothingness. "They've visited us regularly ever since."

THIRTY-FIVE

MRS. GUSTAFSSEN'S ZINGER reverberated through thoughts muddied by the antihistamine, wine, and whiskey. Was everybody in Clovis mad? I buried my head in my hands to stave off a headache nudging my brain.

Oh, my kingdom for a nap. Alas, it was after four. If I wanted to catch Rick Womack, I'd have to defer the numbing release of sleep. I started the car and drove past a park—a monument really—with a real B-27 airplane mounted in its center.

Was Mrs. Gustafssen nuts? Did aliens really visit them? Most likely one of Mrs. Gustafssen's strokes was the culprit. After all the hurt of years past, something deep in her psyche must have cracked and surfaced, uncovered like a buried penny after a rainstorm.

I let the afternoon heat distract me and opened my windows to the smell of coming rain. With a flick of the wheel and a small press on the gas pedal, I zoomed into rural New Mexico again. Animals frolicked, bugs popped through the air and crickets chirruped with vigor. A person could fall in love with this place. Connie's embracing of it was understandable in this instant of beauty, although she hadn't spoken about any love of the land.

I zoomed by the Putt Putt and wondered if Mae was in her padded cell blaming me for the incarceration. A police car passed me going the opposite direction. Were the police somehow tied into Tan's murder? They sure were letting Charlene off easy.

What I knew about the People's Police Academy made me queasy. Clovis's movers and shakers partied hardy with the Chief of Police. I didn't question LaSalle's honesty but his ability to solve the crime might be hindered by relationships that had been a lifetime in the making.

For a kooky moment, I thought about pressing the accelerator and heading straight home. I could ask the hotel to pack up my things, send them to me via one of the trains that invaded the town like maggots in a felled apricot. I'd find work in some other small New Mexico town; I didn't have to depend on this bid, this job.

Who was I fooling? I'd spent money like an idiot since I'd been fired. If I didn't land the job here, I'd be hurting for sure. Nevertheless, the daydream had a very real appeal. I missed my exit and had to make a U-turn in the middle of the blue highway.

From where I sat, there appeared to be only one way in and one way out of Cannon Air Force Base. At the checkpoint, two close-shaven young men, no older than puppies, asked for my driver's license, registration, and proof of insurance. They verified my appointment.

I didn't even try to shoot the breeze with them; their faces said they hadn't laughed in a week. After a few minutes, they returned my things, along with an ID and a map with directions to Womack's office highlighted in yellow marker.

Captain Womack greeted me at the door. Movie-star handsome, chiseled chin. You know, the whole nine yards. He stood dressed in blue, his hair short, his name badge gleaming.

"Glad you caught me," he said. "I was about to leave."

"Sorry I'm late. I had an interview with Lieutenant Colonel Gustafssen. Do you know him?"

"Ed? He's a legend around here. Good man, great flier. How's he doing?" Womack led me to a fake wood-paneled room that offered nary a clue about the man who spent hours there each day.

"He seems okay given the Parkinson's," I said.

"Horrible disease. Especially for a pilot. To lose control like that after being in such fine shape." The captain went to his desk, picked up a piece of paper. "I'm supposed to ask you about your hives."

"I guess they're gone. I haven't checked," I said.

"You'd know if they were still there."

Once forgotten itchiness nudged at my back, down my legs anew. I shifted in my seat.

"What can I do for you, Sasha?" He exuded reserved interest and a warm edge of anticipated amusement.

"According to an excellent source, you grew up here and know everyone who's anyone."

"The president of my fan club surely exaggerates." He laughed. "There're a couple of newborns I haven't met yet."

We both smiled.

If you've been in the business as long as I have, you recognize the confidence and ability of a pro. He was as smooth and restrained as a dry martini. The opposite of Connie. She'd been as spicy and frank as new scotch.

"Would you mind telling me a little about the King kids? I'd like to get a feel for Theodore and Charlene," I said.

His face relaxed a speck. I'd missed the important question, asking a too-easy one in its place.

"Theo and Charly? Not much to tell, really," he said. "I dated Charly in high school. She was okay. Ambitious."

"Why did you break up?"

"Why do kids break up? Charly wasn't much for anything besides dairy farming and beauty queening. She didn't have plans for college and wasn't a serious student," he said. "I guess I got tired of her. I wanted more from a girlfriend."

"Do you stay in touch at all?"

"Not really. We bump into each other at plays at the community college, Chamber events, concerts here on base." His eyes lightened. "You've met Connie. Would you bother staying in touch with old girlfriends if you had her to come home to?"

"Not on your life."

He nodded.

"How about Theo? Connie said you'd been close," I said.

Womack pushed back from the desk, relaxed even more. "Theo and I go back to elementary school. He was always at my house or I was over at his. Plus, I loved Mae's cookies. They were works of art."

Here was a new image: Mae, the hard-core rural journalist, standing with a cookie tray and a splash of flour across her nose.

"Are you two still friends?" I said.

"Never had one of her chocolate chips, huh?" He shook his head in mock pity. "You're missing out on one of life's true pleasures."

I waited for him to stop avoiding my question.

He caught my expression. Leaning forward, he rested his elbows on his knees and took a deep breath.

"Okay, here it is. Theo's a bright guy but his head's screwed on wrong. He's greedy and mean-spirited and rotten to his very core," he said.

"That's pretty harsh."

Womack opened both his hands in a short upward wave as if releasing attachment to his words. "Theo's nastiness shows up in a thousand little ways. When I'm feeling compassionate, I figure he's insecure and manifests it in competitiveness against everyone and for everything."

He scooted his chair back farther, got comfortable again. "Here's a small example. He came on to Connie the first time I brought her home. Another example. He bid on a house I told him I wanted to buy. The deal fell through. He didn't have enough money when push came to shove. But by then, I'd given up and gone in search of another one. Another example. He deliberately tripped my son at a soccer match. One of Charly's kids just happened to get the ball and score."

"You're kidding. What did the ref do?" I said.

"What could he do? He hadn't seen it, although other parents did. Do you want more?"

"No, I think that's enough. What about Josh?"

"He's always been a real sweet kid. I don't know him well. He was quiet, involved in geeky stuff." Womack looked at his watch. "I can tell you I was glad he went to California. He needed to get away from his siblings, to find his own voice."

"That verges on poetic," I said.

"If you can't hear your own voice, you're in trouble." He peeked at his watch again.

"I've got four other people you might know about. You game?"

"Depends on who."

"Bud Johnson, Steve Cummings, Travis Simpson, and Abel King."

His laugh was genuine, tickled. "I've never heard those four mentioned in the same breath. It's like ordering two corn dogs, an ounce of Beluga caviar, and fifty-year-old scotch at the same restaurant."

"Three of them went to the People's Police Academy."

"No, they didn't. Steve's sister, Judy, attended. Not Steve."

I acknowledged the correction. "Okay. So, who's the caviar?"

"Travis Simpson. The man's word is better than gold." Another glance at his watch. "He spends real time with his kids when he's not on the road, works hard, and is basically one of the most admirable people I know," said Womack. "Charly lucked out. Travis's family moved here in his senior year of high school. She knew a good thing when she saw it. Poured on the charm and got pregnant." He smiled. "She was showing under that black gown.

"Bud Johnson and Steve Cummings, those two are something else. Bud's a decent dentist but he thinks he knows absolutely everything about everything and then some. I guess that's why he keeps running for mayor and losing." The captain stopped, acknowledging my body language. "Oh, you know about that? Well, did you know that he's got a serious gambling addiction? His parents have spent good money on treatment. Nothing works for very long. The sad thing is he's a pretty smart guy but his impulse control is nil."

"What about Steve Cummings? I heard he's a lawyer." Play dumb, get more information.

"Strange case, that one. He's bright but has no horse sense. People say he made bad investments and lost all his money. I've heard he might go into practice with Theo in Lubbock."

Bingo.

"Was Cummings part of your high school crowd, too?" I said.

"I was in class with both of them. By high school, Theo and Steve were inseparable. They laughed at me for postponing college to enlist in the service." He looked me in the eye. "I wouldn't trade my life for theirs. Not for all the money in the world."

"You sound bitter."

"Do I? I guess I am, a bit." Womack shook his head. "I think I'm more mystified. They were really popular in high school, the crème de la crème." He seemed to be thinking about it. When he spoke again, his voice had deepened. "I don't think I'm bitter. Not exactly. It's more that I'm astounded at how people who everybody believed in—excluding me and a couple of my friends—how they could turn out to be such bad apples."

"What about Abel King? He's the scotch?"

"Have you met him?"

I nodded.

"If you've met him, you know he's an ornery old cuss. But I'd put my life in his hands in a second. You can trust Abel. Always."

"I understand he and his brother had some conflicts." That $20 bill wasn't evidence of deep love.

"Not that I know of." Womack looked at his watch.

"I know you need to go. I only have a couple more questions," I said.

"Shoot."

"Can you tell me what they're saying here on base about the murder?"

"Only in general terms." In an instant, he'd transformed from informal to professional. "Colonel Tan was well respected, above reproach in Singapore. No one understands why this happened. We're all working hard to reassure the 428th that this was not a hate crime. That's about all I can say."

"What about you, personally? Do you think Mae's involved somehow?"

"No. No way," he said. "I can't see a single connection between Mae and Colonel Tan. Except that he was found on her land."

Womack didn't know about Mae's nightie and diary. Those details hadn't been released to the public. I simply hadn't realized it until he'd spoken. What an easy and quick way to find out who knew more than they should. I felt like Nancy Drew finally coming up with a good clue. I tried to remember Becky Tan's exact words. Had she mentioned them? Thinking of her reminded me of LaSalle.

"Do you know Detective LaSalle?"

"Baby face Henry?"

I spluttered into a smile, then nodded.

"He's some policeman, I can tell you that," said Womack.

"I've had some interaction with him." I realized only a few people in Clovis knew I'd seen Colonel Tan's body that night.

"Well, then you know he's a straight-shooter." The momentary mirth downshifted back to PR mode. "Ever since I've known him, Henry's wanted to be a cop. Even as a kid, he'd

hang out at the police station. Graduated from New Mexico
State with a degree in criminology. Then went into the service for years. He could have been the Chief of Police several times over, but he hates administration and loves solving
crimes."

"Is he married?" Why had I asked that? *Stupid, stupid,
stupid.*

"Are you?"

"Oh, no. No. I—"

"I'm teasing," Womack said. "Henry was married for
twenty-four years. All that time, his work was first, his wife
second. The week after their last kid graduated from college,
they got divorced. That was last June."

"How old is he?"

"You'll have to ask *him.*" He saw my embarrassment. "I'm
kidding. Henry's forty-eight." His eyes gleamed. "Why all the
interest in his personal life?"

"Just curious. That's all."

"He inspires that in a lot of women. He's got this intoxi-
cating mix of the boy next door and that guy Mel Gibson
played in all those *Lethal Weapon* movies."

Womack checked his watch for the tenth time. "You know,
I really ought to get going. I like to spend time with my kids
before dinner. Is there anything else?"

I wanted to ask about Mrs. Gustafssen, but said, "Not really."

"Well, you know where to find me." He walked me to
the door.

We shook hands. I left.

Driving got in the way of thinking. I turned onto a road
edged by greening fields and stopped the car to focus. Womack had given me two gifts: insight into people's personali-
ties and the realization I'd been wearing mental blinders.
Crucial details about the murder had been kept from the public and I knew what they were.

Bud Johnson was up to something. Charlene, Theo, and Steve Cummings were a bunch of sleaze bags. Theo and Steve were linked by the law practice. Bud, Theo, and Steve all had money problems. And Charlene. What was her gig? Maybe she was sleeping with Bud and Steve. The image made me cringe but it explained a lot. If true, all of them had reasons to get Mae out of the way.

But how in the world did a Singaporean colonel fit into their scheme?

THIRTY-SIX

OVERSTUFFED BRAIN, understuffed tummy, and sluggish body to boot. I went straight to the hotel restaurant for an early dinner. After an undistinguished burger and undercooked fries, I thought about grabbing a scotch in the bar but refrained; I had too much work to do.

Back in the room, the message light glared. I glared back, then turned off the phone's ringer. Putting my still-shod feet on the bed, I thought about the day. Too many conversations, too many people. I needed silence, stillness to regroup. I closed my eyes.

Wham, wham, wham. The giant woodpecker assaulted the tree. Its muffled voice called, "Sasha! Sasha!"

I awoke to the click of an electronic key in the door. Lying motionless in the dark, I prayed the sound was a remnant from my dream.

As my eyes adjusted to the light he'd switched on, I saw Detective LaSalle. His grim face had several extra wrinkles tonight.

"Good evening. Glad to find you all comfy." The sarcasm didn't fit his face. Then he noticed the red message light. "Why didn't you call back? What's wrong with you?"

I gave him a look he didn't like.

He sat down at my makeshift office, pushed the laptop away from his elbows, and shook his head.

"I always intend to come on like Barney Fife with you and end up sounding like Tommie Lee Jones in The Fugitive," he said. He yawned to give us both time to settle down. "Tell me where you've been. Please."

"Around."

"Sasha, I'm sorry I scared you. Please tell me where you were from noon until four."

"Why? What's happened? Is Mae all right?" I sat up.

"Why do you ask about Mae?"

"Who else would I ask about?"

We were both way too tense.

He nodded.

"Right. So, tell me where you've been. Then I'll tell you what I can," he said.

"Okay," I said.

"So?"

"At noon, I was probably in Connie Womack's bathroom. I stayed there until around one-thirty."

"In the bathroom?"

"Let me talk," I said. "After Connie's, I drove to Lieutenant Colonel Edwin Gustafssen's house for an interview." I ticked off the items on my fingers. "From there I went to Cannon to talk with your friend and mine, Rick Womack. I left at about five-fifteen, came here, had dinner in the restaurant. Accidentally took a nap." I folded my arms across my chest. "Your turn."

"My, my, my. Busy, busy." LaSalle's raised shoulders descended to normal position as I recounted my movements.

"Well?" I said.

"Someone shot out the windows at Mae's place. Hurt one of her dogs."

"Don't tell me you thought I did it."

"Not seriously. But if you had it in for Charly, you might be mad enough to take some kind of stupid action. We had to consider the possibility," he said.

"She doesn't even live in Mae's house," I said.

"You get the grand prize." He smiled. "But how do you know that if you've never been there before?"

"Ah, but I have. You didn't ask me about this morning."

"Tell me about this morning."

"I went to Mae's after breakfast. Travis Simpson himself gave me a tour of the place." I thought for a moment. "Why do you think the bullets were directed at Charlene anyway? Was there a note or something?"

"Wouldn't that be nice?" He picked up one of my work papers, realized what he was doing and put it down. "You're right though. They were probably meant to scare Mae."

"That doesn't make any sense. She's not even here," I said. "Could it be a fluke?"

"That's unlikely." He looked at the phone, pointed at it. "Would you do me a favor and listen to your messages?"

"No problemo." I picked up the receiver. "Remind me to tell you about my research today. I learned some interesting stuff."

There weren't many messages. Two from LaSalle, one from Laura at Bob's office telling me to call her if I got in before five. One from the hotel manager asking about my new accommodations and apologizing because he still didn't have an explanation about the box left in my room. No Becky Tan. No Abel King. No Josh.

"Did I ever tell you about my lunch with Josh King?" I put down the receiver.

"Excuse me? What lunch?" LaSalle wrote something in a notepad.

"It must have been Wednesday. I feel like I've lived weeks in the past couple of days."

"I know the feeling. For me, it's years instead of weeks," the detective said.

I reached for the alien mask, fiddled with the elastic band on the back.

"The lunch," he prompted.

Feeling goofy, I began the monologue with a twang, stroking my chin as if I had a beard. "We went to Poor Boys. I got some pickled okra to start, mighty fine, mighty fine. Then I moved on to the tomatoes."

"Spare me the menu and tell me why you brought this up," he said.

"Did you know Mae wants to do something called 'totally integrated farming'?"

"Everybody and their brother knows that."

"Does everyone know how Charlene and Theo feel about it?"

LaSalle perked up. "Why don't you tell me?"

I had him and it felt good. "Well, according to Josh, both his sibs are vehemently against the plan."

"'Vehemently.' That was his word?"

Caught in the embellishment, I backtracked. "No. But he implied both of them were really opposed to it. And he said Mae was planning to sell some prime property to finance it. And, there was something else…"

LaSalle doodled in his notepad while I thought.

"Josh said Theo had expected to take over the farm when his dad died," I said. "Apparently, when Mae inherited the whole shebang, it came as a total shock."

"That's it?"

Not the reaction nor the gratitude I expected. "Well, yeah."

"What does any of this have to do with the murder?"

Dumbfounded by his response, I said, "A lot. Charlene and Theo are in cahoots with people like Bud Johnson and Steve Cummings. They want to prevent Mae from doing the totally integrated thing." I spoke fast, certain about the scenario. "So, Charlene gets you to do her dirty work for her, gets Mae declared mentally incompetent, and then takes over the farm."

"Where do Bud and Steve fit in?"

"For starters, they're both losers and make lousy decisions."

"Don't we all?"

I waved off his interruption. "Let's say Charlene and Theo offered them money."

"For what?"

"I don't know—you're the policeman," I said. "Okay. I've got it, at least for Cummings. He's involved because he's going into practice with Theo."

"And you're basing this on what?" he said.

"Rick Womack told me."

"Go on."

"Johnson's a little more difficult. I think he and Charlene are involved somehow. They might be having an affair."

"You've gotta be kidding." LaSalle burst out laughing. "You've seen Bud. And Travis. You've met Travis. That's the most ridiculous thing I've ever heard."

"No, it isn't. There's no explaining attraction," I said. "And if Travis is out of town a lot, Charlene must get lonely out there in the middle of nowhere."

"Why are you bent on blaming Charlene? Is there more here than I know about? Some old animosity?"

"I only met her this week," I said.

He squinted at me. "So why do you think she should be a suspect?"

"Because Mae treats her like she's still in diapers—that's fodder for resentment—and she lied and got you to take her mom into protective custody."

"And?" he said.

"And what? Isn't that enough?"

"No. Especially if she did it to prevent Mae from hurting herself." He rubbed his eyes then trained his blues on my hazels. "Sasha, you're not even considering the obvious."

"What's that?"

"That Mae is crazy and committed murder," he said.

"Impossible."

"Nothing's impossible." He pulled out his pack of cigarettes. Its foil remained unbroken. "Okay, let's say Charlene is trying to get the farm from Mae. It still doesn't explain the murder."

"How about this?" I said. "Charlene and Theo stumbled across Colonel Tan—he was dead already—and they put Mae's things in his hands. See? Or, they could have killed him to get Mae out of the way and then framed her to make sure she'd *stay* out of the way."

"Listen to yourself." He twirled the pack of cigarettes, tapping it end-on-end on the table. "Why would Charly and Theo be out, miles from both of their homes, walking around with Mae's nightie and diary? And what are the chances they'd stumble on Colonel Tan?"

LaSalle pulled out a business card and used it to pick at his fingernails.

"You're so intent on clearing Mae, you're making incredible leaps of logic with nothing to base them on," he said. "Why would Charly and Theo, two successful business people, kill an innocent man? If they really wanted to get rid of Mae, why not just kill her?"

"They could, but then they'd be suspects. This way, there's nothing to tie them to the crime," I said.

"But why Colonel Tan? Why not someone who worked at the farm?"

"Because he was convenient," I said. "Or he saw something he shouldn't have. That's the explanation Mrs. Tan gave." I sat on the edge of the bed, hands raised with excitement, an idea forming. "Okay, here's what happened. Mrs. Tan talked about people who looked wrong. I've got it! They took turns dressing up like space aliens. In that case, Bud wasn't following me to Roswell—he was buying more masks like the one I've got."

This felt so right.

"I bet it's Theo and Steve. They're the ones who killed Tan. And Charlene is lying to protect them," I said. "When Theo and I talked for the first time, he introduced himself as Charlene's brother, not Mae's son. No love lost there." I lowered my voice, caught my breath. "Mae hasn't been abducted by aliens at all. Her own children are dressing up like space aliens and have been tricking her for months. Theo's a lawyer. He'd know how to have her declared incompetent. Have you thought of that? Huh? Have you?"

"Ah, what tangled webs," LaSalle said, yawning.

I wanted to slug him but the thoughts were coming too fast.

"What if Colonel Tan saw them carrying Mae into some kind of fake spaceship?" I said. "That would jive with Mrs. Tan's story. He confronted them. They panicked and shot him. See? Then they realized they could get rid of Mae, destroy her credibility, everything." I leaned forward. "You've got to admit it makes sense."

LaSalle sighed and didn't write any of my ideas in his notebook. He yawned again.

"I'm boring you?" I said.

"No, not at all. You're great with fiction. I guess you have to do a lot of that in public relations." He grinned at his joke.

"That was low," I said. "Low and rude."

"I'm sorry I offended your professional pride." LaSalle put the pack of cigarettes back in his shirt pocket. "How's this? You should write mysteries. Scheming kids, space aliens. You've got a great imagination."

I shook my head.

"Problem is, there's not a shred of evidence for anything you've said." He got up, stretched. "Well, thanks for the story, but I'd better get back to work. Do me a favor, call me if Becky Tan contacts you or if Mike Cho shows up."

"Wait a minute. You're going to ignore my theory?"

"Sasha, I never ignore anything you say."

"Who do you think shot out the windows at Mae's place?" I said, wanting to kick him so hard he couldn't smile for a week.

"I've got a couple of ideas."

"Would you mind sharing them?"

"Yes."

With that, he opened the door, tossed a half-salute my way, and left.

My thrown shoe missed its mark, thudding when it hit the curtained window.

THIRTY-SEVEN

IN THE SHOWER, the more I scrubbed with soap, the more I coated myself with fury. My sudsy monologue took direct aim at Detective Know-It-All LaSalle. While I hadn't spent years as a cop, that deficit might make me more objective. The homicide team wasn't making progress in this investigation. Otherwise LaSalle wouldn't be spending so much time with me. How dare he ignore my theory? It held merit and made better sense than accusing Mae.

I turned off the water and shook myself like a dog. The clock radio's red numerals glowered, eight o'clock. Swathed in a flimsy towel, I settled in for work. By ten-thirty, I'd finished a solid draft of the PR plan. Tomorrow, I'd edit and polish my masterpiece. I had Sunday to add any last-minute touches. And poof! On Monday, I'd hand the beauty in.

With the phone's ring, I remembered why LaSalle had transferred me to this new room. I answered with caution, "Hello."

"Sasha?"

"Bob?"

"Are you okay?" Weariness laced his joviality.

"How about you?"

"I've been better," he said. "I didn't call for sympathy. I wanted to let you know what Laura found out about Theodore King." He sniffled.

"Anything interesting?"

"I don't know." Papers rustled in the background. "Here it

is. He's a plaintiff's lawyer in Lubbock. Makes decent money, has a reputation for ambulance chasing and class action suits. He's not married and never has been. Rumor has it he's unethical but there've never been any complaints registered with the Texas Bar." Another bit of shuffling. "Laura has something here. Let's see. It's something about racial discrimination. I can't make it out. Sorry. Does any of that help?"

"I was hoping for major dirt," I said.

"Sorry I can't oblige." Bob paused to take a drink, then he sniffled again. "This is funny, she's got something here, 'full of self, colleagues dislike.'" He laughed. "Welcome to the wonderful world of lawyers."

"Is there anything about money troubles or gambling?"

"Not that I can see. If he's got problems, it's not for lack of work. Maybe the money goes up his nose."

"Oooh. That'd be something. Is there anything like that?"

"Nope. Only the racial discrimination thing," he said.

"That could mean anything," I said. "Oh well, thanks for trying."

"Anytime." He sniffled again. "So, when are you coming home?"

"Monday, I think."

"How about we go out and celebrate? Do something special?"

"I'd like that," I said.

"Me, too."

We smooched our sappy so-longs. I thought about Bob. I didn't like all his sniffling. Was it a cold or cocaine? I didn't know him well enough to say.

To rid myself of the icky suspicion, I stretched. It felt good. I got up and touched my toes, did a few forward lunges. When the phone rang, I expected it to be Bob again.

"Howdy do," I said.

"Hello? Is this room two-forty-eight?" A raspy bark, an older man's dry voice.

"Colonel Gustafssen?"

"Is this Ms. Sasha Solomon?"

"Who is this?"

"Roc Johnson. Is this Ms. Solomon?"

"Yes?"

"Ms. Solomon, I believe you've met my son, Bud."

Another cough, a paper crackling. When he spoke again, I could hear the click of a hard candy or throat lozenge as it hit his teeth—or dentures.

"Ms. Solomon, I'd like to speak with you."

"Mr. Johnson, it's very late. Would you mind calling back in the morning?"

"I can do you one better. How would you like breakfast? My treat?"

"That's a nice offer but—"

"I'm available at six forty-five," he said.

Sunrise on a Saturday? No way, José. The prospect of meeting Papa Bear first thing in the morning and listening to him defend Baby Bear didn't appeal at all.

"Ms. Solomon? I know it's early, but I've got a full day tomorrow. I need to fly to D.C. before noon and still have a briefing to prepare tonight. I'm afraid six forty-five is all I've got."

"Mr. Johnson, it sounds like you're very busy," I said. "Is this about Bud? Because if it is, I'd like to invite Detective LaSalle."

"Goodness gracious. What does Henry have to do with this?"

Nah. Papa Bear's tone played as sincere as a prostitute pleading virginity. To let him know he wasn't talking to a fool, I enumerated Bud's activities to date.

"Blasted idiot," said Papa Bear.

"Excuse me?"

"Not you. Bud. Excuse me a moment, please." On his side, the phone whacked hard and made me jump. I heard his muffled yell, "Mabel, dammit! Get in here!"

I imagined the scene: Johnson scolding his wife, blaming her for Bud's embarrassing behavior, saying, "Why can't you control your son?" He'd get back on the line and plead with me to let Bud be, or offer me money, or say he could smooth it over with LaSalle.

"Ms. Solomon?" he said. "Whatever Bud may have done has nothing to do with our meeting tomorrow. If you'd like to invite Henry, he's welcome."

There was a quiet knock at my door. Probably the wind.

"All right, I'll meet you at a quarter to seven. Where would you like to eat?"

"How about your hotel?"

"That'd be fine," I said. "Mr. Johnson, if this isn't about Bud, what is it about?"

"Are you familiar with The Clovis 25?"

"Yes, indeed," I said, distracted by another soft knock.

"I've been asked to speak with you."

"Why?"

"All in good time, Ms. Solomon." A rustle on his end. "I know it's late. I look forward to meeting you." He hung up.

Outside, someone tapped on my window. I went to the door. The peephole granted a fish-eye view of the world with Mike Cho at its center.

I ducked down, knees bent. Rummaging through my purse, I found LaSalle's home number.

The soft rapping on the glass continued.

Come on. Answer the phone.

I wanted LaSalle to show up with a SWAT team.

"LaSalle," said the detective, his voice sleepy.

"It's Sasha. Mike Cho is here," I whispered.

"Where?"

"On the other side of my door."

"Don't turn on your lights," he said.

"They're already on. I haven't gone to sleep yet."

"You're sure it's him?"

"Of course I am."

"Listen to me. Go into your bathroom. Take a book or something. Don't come out until you get the go-ahead."

"What are you going to do?"

"I'll send someone out right away. And when I get there, I'll knock three times, stop, then knock three times more. Got it?"

"Yeah."

"You do what I tell you, okay? No Wonder Woman stuff, okay?"

"Yeah," I said.

"You sure?"

"I said 'yes,'" I snapped, feeling afraid.

"Okay. I'll see you soon."

Cho tapped on the window, a slow metronome beat. It sounded metallic, like he was using a key. How had he found my room? I sank to the floor and crawled to the bathroom.

The toilet lid cracked when I sat down. I moved to the floor. Hysteria nibbled at my psyche. I told myself Cho wasn't a murderer. He was just a violent maniac and a misogynist.

The knocking stopped. I heard yells across the open courtyard, footsteps skittering along the outdoor walkway, others on the roof. Then silence. I waited, clutching the book, scarcely breathing. Afraid to move.

Three knocks, a pause, three more.

LaSalle wore a rumpled black sweat suit, his short hair spiky from recent sleep. He shook his head, looked me in the eye and said, "We lost him."

THIRTY-EIGHT

LASALLE'S ASSURANCES before he left gave no solace in the long night hours. Not when weighed against the fact that Mike Cho had an inside source at the hotel. How else could he have tracked down my new room? Maybe I'd been wrong. Maybe he was the author of those notes. If so, they'd morph from amusing to ominous.

Lousy night, lousier morning. The sun was too bright, the sky too blue. I emerged from my burrow, photophobic with fatigue. Hives, red and abundant, forced me to pop two of Connie's antihistamines on the way downstairs to my meeting. I arrived at the restaurant clean-clothed and scraggly with distress and settled at the table in time to see a man in a wheelchair roll in. One of the waitresses welcomed him with an enthusiasm reserved for regular customers. He spoke to her. She blushed with a giggle and then pointed at me.

He wheeled my way. I felt compelled to rise in greeting.

"Do sit down," Roc Johnson said, scudding his most charming smile my way. "It makes me feel even shorter when people are courteous enough to stand."

I stared at him, impolite as a star-struck teen. He was handsome—Gregory Peck *redux* even though he'd long passed sixty. His gray hair, tanned skin, even the wrinkles on his forehead and around his eyes, all spoke of an adventurous, fully lived life. Before it became awkward, our waitress moved a chair out of the way. Johnson parked across from me.

"Millie, I'm expecting two more here," he told her. "I'd

love some coffee while we wait, though. Ms. Solomon?" He exuded self-assured class. I remembered his yelling at his wife last night. The rudeness, the tone. They couldn't have come from this man.

"That'd be nice." I felt enveloped in powerful energy, a buoy caught in his wake.

"Will Henry be joining us?" he asked.

"Not today."

We appraised each other and liked what we saw. The smile lines near his eyes said humor was one of his default emotions.

"Well. We meet." Johnson launched the smile again. "You're an amazing woman, Ms. Solomon. Seems everyone I talk to mentions your name. You've got a real talent for meeting people."

"Why, thank you."

Part of this game we were playing had to do with finding out the rules.

"Do call me Roc. It's only appropriate," he said.

"Really? Why's that?"

"For one thing, I plan to call you 'Sasha.' For another, I've seen your work. That grand opening campaign for TrueHealth was a thing of beauty. Very effective. I'd rather you consider me a colleague than a father figure."

"Believe me, I'd never make that mistake."

"Father figure or colleague?"

"Both."

"Ah, a wise woman. Don't ever reveal all your cards." He actually winked.

I wasn't sure what we were talking about but it was fun, unexpected. Bob and I had clicked in the same way when we'd met. I'd loved it. The verbal sparring, the toying with innuendo. But already, on this trip, the giddiness had begun to subside.

Two men came into the restaurant, dressed Saturday-casual although their body language screamed for suits. Both as old, or older, than Roc. That's where the similarity ended. Fidgety, slope-backed, they didn't act as though they were easy in their skins. Roc watched me observe them before he raised a hand to invite them over.

They scuttled toward us, human hermit crabs, swift and nervous.

"Sasha, this is Sam Hodgins and Pat Quirt," said Johnson.

They took their places, bookends to our seats at each end of the table. Coffee was poured. Breakfast ordered.

"Correct me if I'm wrong," Roc said. "You mentioned you've heard of The Clovis 25?"

"Yes. It's an impressive group," I said.

"Thank you. Sam and Pat are some of our main backers. I'm one of the traveling squad, one of the representatives who hobnobs with the powers that be."

"Interesting organization," I said, thinking it sounded paramilitaristic. "How many people per squad?"

"Five. Five squads. In my group, all of us are free to get away at a moment's notice, and all of us have good military credentials." Roc patted the arm of his wheelchair. "In case you're wondering, my current mode of transportation is testament to an injury in Korea."

What should I say? *Congratulations for losing the ability to walk in service to your country?* I thought not.

"Sasha, it's come to our attention you may have gotten the wrong idea about us—that you perceive us as meddling in a criminal investigation, for example. Or perhaps you think we would resort to petty threats to force you to give up your attempts to help Mae King." His feigned concern did little to instill confidence.

"Both thoughts crossed my mind. As a matter of fact, I think I mentioned them to Jan Cisneros over at the Chamber. Did she happen to tell you?" Gossip and little towns. Yet another example.

"You'd make a good detective," he said. "Jan called me. As did Rick Womack, Henry LaSalle, Ed Gustafssen. You see, we all have a vested interest in the quick resolution of this murder and the preservation of Cannon."

"At any cost?" It shot out of my mouth before I could harness it, the suspicion in my voice coarse, rude.

Ol' Quirt and Hodgins shuffled and huffed in indignation. Roc smiled and addressed them, ignoring me for the moment.

"You see how she's gotten the wrong impression?" he said, tsk-tsking. "How could she reasonably believe a group with our clout would stoop to breaking the law?"

I wanted to answer along the lines of, *the government does it all the time.*

"Well, Sasha, we can't afford to do that," Roc said. "We're known for honesty, hard work, and delivering the goods. I'll admit, I'd love to find the murderer. But do you think for a minute we'd try to make Mae King the fall guy?" He didn't stop for an answer. "She's a stalwart member of our community. Why would anyone want to railroad her?"

"I don't know. I've been asking myself the same question." I stopped, regrouped. "Why are we having this meeting? Why do you care one way or the other about what I think? I'm just a little PR gal from Albuquerque."

"Good question," said Hodgins. "Pure and simple, Ms. Solomon. We can't have anyone thinking ill of us. And, when we hear that someone who has numerous media contacts might suspect us of wrongdoing, well, we need to nip those rumors in the bud. You need to understand what's at stake."

"What is at stake?"

"I assume you know the Senate Armed Forces Committee is considering base closures again." Vexation tugged at Roc's mouth as he spoke. "If you've done your homework, you also know all the low-hanging fruit has already been picked. Cannon is mid-to-high on the list—especially with the Melrose

Bombing Range close by—but we can't rest on our laurels and we can't be too vigilant. We certainly can't afford bad PR."

I scooted back from the table to include all of them in my range of vision. "Gentlemen, I'm not planning to badmouth Cannon or The Clovis 25. Frankly, those are the farthest things from my mind."

"That's very good to hear, Sasha." Roc placed both hands on the table on either side of his plate. "But we still have a problem."

"Oh?"

"Who killed Colonel Tan?"

"I'm leaving the investigation to the experts." I sipped my coffee. "The only thing I know for sure is Mae didn't kill anyone."

"From my understanding, she remains the most reasonable suspect."

"That's not true. What about Mike Cho?"

"Colonel Tan's brother-in-law? Not even an option," Roc said.

"Why not?"

"To begin with, there's no history of conflict between the two. And he wasn't anywhere near here when the murder happened."

"He has a history of violence and spousal abuse."

Roc waved his hand, dismissing my last comment. "Not the same thing."

"Well, then we're back to square one, Roc, my friend." I'd had enough of the cat-and-mouse. "It sounds to me like you'd love for Mae to be guilty."

"Not true," he said. "But none of us, including you, can afford to have blinders on." Underneath his plain words snarled ugliness. "We're anxious to resolve this situation. You're anxious for Mae to be found innocent. I hope the two aren't in conflict."

He took the check and said, "Oh, I'd like to correct you on a little item. Last night, on the phone, when you thought I was

Lieutenant Colonel Gustafssen, you said, *'colonel.'*" Roc's smile was conspiratorial. It echoed in Hodgins's and Quirt's smirks. "I wouldn't expect you to know this. But there's quite a difference between a full colonel and a lieutenant colonel."

"Yes, the *colonel* told me," I said.

"I see."

"I hope you do."

He flinched, then recovered. "Oh, I do."

"Good."

"Well, as long as that's quite clear, there's no problem." He turned to his cronies. "Gentlemen, I'm sure Sasha has a lot to do on her proposal for the Chamber. We wouldn't want to impede her progress. Would we?" He held out his hand, gave mine a firm shake.

I pulled it away before he squeezed it harder.

"I understand you recently lost your job. Such a shame," he said. "And with your poor mother in a rehab hospital, too." He shook his head in pseudo sympathy. "That must make landing this job even more important to you."

I didn't like where this was going.

"I bet you're going to work on your proposal all weekend long. Probably won't have time for anything else," he said.

Our eyes met and both pairs held rancor. The instant passed. Roc flashed his quick Hollywood smile, then wheeled out of the restaurant. Quirt and Hodgins tailed him like well-behaved puppies.

Without another glance at my breakfast, I hustled back to the room. More messages on the machine. One from Josh, one from Abel King. Josh's return number was out-of-state.

Concentration would be difficult but Roc Johnson was right; I needed this job. What had he meant by mentioning Mom?

All noise in my room hushed. I hugged myself against the sudden silence.

Breath shallow, hands unsteady, I turned on the computer.

THIRTY-NINE

THE KNOCK AT MY DOOR caused me to vault from my chair, bang both elbows, and let out a string of choleric epithets rarely, if ever, heard in the town of Clovis. Massaging both elbows and still cussing, I looked out the peephole. Abel King stood there, dressed in overalls and a faded plaid shirt. His shoes were muddy.

"Mr. King?" I said, letting him in. "How did you find me?"

He lowered his chin as if the question were plumb stupid. "Are we playing hide and seek, Missy?"

"No. That's not what I meant."

"I know." King patted my shoulder and walked past me into the room. "Henry told me where to find you. I called him when you didn't return my second call."

"He gave you my room number?"

King slapped his hands on his thighs.

"No, a little bird told me," he said, making sure I was looking at him. "Of course he gave me your room number. You're acting mighty jittery."

"It's been a rough morning," I said.

"Sorry to hear it. You want some breakfast?"

"I've already eaten. With Roc Johnson, no less."

If I could have caught the expression of shock on Abel King's face, I would have used it for a horror film.

"What did Roc want with *you?*" he said.

"Roc, Pat Quirt, and Sam Hodgins wanted to threaten me not to make any more waves about Mae. At least that's what I think they wanted."

"Oh, heavens to Betsy!" said King. "Of all the hare-brained ideas. I don't believe it." From the depths of one of his denim pockets, he pulled out an ultra-modern cell phone. A miniature jobbie. He punched in a number.

"Hello, Mabel. Is Roc there?" He went to my window and stared though a crack in the curtain. "He did? Well, you tell him as soon as he calls that if I don't hear from him by the end of the day, he's going to have real trouble on his hands." He listened for a minute. "That's right. Yes, he did. I know. I'll see you at church tomorrow."

I watched him, wondering who he was to be calling Roc Johnson to task.

Meanwhile, King dialed another number. "Tom, it's Abel. You hear what Squad Three did?" He looked at me. "I can't talk. I'll call you later."

"Mr. King, what do you know about all of this?" I said.

"Missy, I started The Clovis 25. And I certainly won't have anyone jeopardize our good name by going off like vigilantes and making threats. I won't have it."

"You started The Clovis 25?"

"I need to make some calls." He stood. "I'll be back in an hour. Think you'll be here?"

"You started The Clovis 25." I sat down.

"Good. I should have this straightened out by then," he said, hand on the doorknob. "In the meantime, let me apologize on behalf of the entire group. This should not have happened."

The minute King left, I called Henry LaSalle. After he calmed me down, he said, "Of course I gave Abel your room number. I trust him implicitly."

"Why?"

"He saved my life, Sasha. Literally."

"How?"

"That's neither here nor there."

I groaned in exasperation.

"What?" said LaSalle.

"No one wants to tell me anything about the man but I'm supposed to think he walks on water."

The detective laughed. "Have you seen all the Pump-n-Snaks around New Mexico? You ever wonder who owns them?"

"Abel King," I said.

"Don't let his down-on-the-farm act fool you. He's Harvard educated, a multi-decorated veteran, and one of the wealthiest men in the state. And do you know what he does with most of his money?"

"No," I said, feeling small.

"Turns right around and gives it to charity. New Mexican charities. He never, ever takes credit for it. You know those *anonymouses* you see on banquet programs and annual reports and everywhere else?"

"Yeah?"

"Chances are, they're all Abel," said LaSalle.

"He's rich, honest, and you trust him. Okay. I got it. Okay."

"You sound shell-shocked," he said. "You all right?"

"Oh, I'm fine. My intuition just took a major blow. That's all."

"Happens to the best of us."

I hung up the phone, feeling like a dope. I should have sensed there was something more to Abel King.

To pass the time until his return, I worked on the plan.

The future stumped me. What if I got the job in Clovis? Would I live here or could I telecommute? Would I be able to avoid Charlene, Steve, Bud, and Roc? Would things deteriorate further for Mae? Would there be a trial? Would I have to testify? Would my testimony help or slam Mae into jail for a crime she didn't commit? My mind spun in an interrogatory inferno.

I brewed the lousy hotel coffee for distraction. It didn't work.

Back to the computer and more angst.

What if Charlene was telling the truth? Mae could have assumed a different persona the few times we saw each other every year. I wouldn't have known. And when your main mode of communication is email, you can project whatever image of yourself you want. Especially if you're an accomplished writer like Mae. I could have been misled from the start. But could she really have killed Colonel Tan?

Stretching my arms over my head, I inhaled deeply three times and then snookered down to work again. Come what may, I needed this job. A success here would catapult my career in the direction I wanted. Through the Chamber network, Jan Cisneros could help me get jobs in other parts of the state.

I began proofing the outline, the plan itself, added finishing touches to the cover letter. Engrossed, I jerked when the phone rang.

"Ms. Solomon, I want you to stay put," said Abel King without preamble.

"Excuse me?"

"Stay right there. I'll come by in a few minutes." And that was that.

Forget about work. I paced the room, drank rank coffee and took deep breaths with the hope of avoiding hives or worse, another hallucination with Colonel Tan as the star of my own psychotic mental video.

King hadn't lied. It took him under five minutes to get to the hotel. He held a finger to his lips when he entered, signaling me to be quiet.

"What?" I mouthed the word.

He shook his head. Held up his finger again and began searching my room. First, he gently ran his hands along the wall closest to the window. Then the sill. Then he progressed to the wall next to the headboards of the beds. As I watched him, my emotions ping-ponged between curiosity and trepidation. King stood, stared, moved back from the wall then forward again. He cocked his head this way and that, gauging something.

Consternation won. I felt sick to my stomach.

After he'd finished the first inspection, he proceeded to lift my worktable, open dresser drawers, crawl on his hands and knees to look under the beds. He lifted my suitcase, the television, the clock radio. He unscrewed the telephone receiver. After that, he concentrated on two stationary overhead lamps, one above each bed.

"Well, well, well," he said, softly.

"What? What is it?"

He held up his finger again.

With too much gusto, he said, "Do you like sports, Ms. Solomon? I love sports. Let's see what's on TV." As he spoke, he shook his silencing finger and head. I still had to keep quiet.

King pressed the remote, found a college basketball game, and hit the volume, up, up, up. He unscrewed the lamp above my bed and placed the loose components on the mattress. With a wry smile, he pulled something out of the wall wiring.

I opened my mouth, but he shook his head.

He reattached the light, made sure it worked, then moved to the other one, and went through the same process.

Putting the thing he'd found into his pocket, King unlocked the door to the room and said, "Sports always make me hungry. Let's get something to eat."

"I'm not—"

His eyes widened and he mouthed, "Now."

I followed him downstairs, out of the hotel and to my car. "Mr. King, what is it?"

"I'm starving. How about a nice big steak?"

"Tell me what you found."

He retrieved a small, round, metal device, no larger than a baby ring.

"What am I looking at?" I said.

"A bug. Someone's been listening in on you. The good

news is that I didn't see evidence of video surveillance—but a lot has changed since I was in the service."

"Oh, God." I searched the parking lot to see if anyone was watching us. "Oh, God."

"He had nothing to do with it," King said. "Calm down, Ms. Solomon. It's all right."

"But who'd do this to me?"

"I have my suspicions." He whipped out his cell phone again, dialed a number, asked the person on the line to meet us at Poor Boys.

"Oh, God," I said. "What have I been saying?"

The rape of my privacy pierced my spirit more powerfully than any physical assault. I fingered the tiny tapping device, turning it over and over in my hand. It was smaller than a Chiclet and so much bigger than I wanted it to be.

FORTY

SWEAT FLOWERED ON each side of my face. Whether its origin stemmed from the hot wings or Abel King's discovery, I couldn't say. King ate his bacon-encircled filet mignon with the same precision I'd noticed in Mae. I, on the other hand, quivered through the spiciness, dropping my fork more than once.

My misery curled in on itself, laced with a sleazy feeling. The horrid sensation of being watched, of a voyeur catching me in acts I couldn't remember, tarnished each of my thoughts with crud. What stupid comments had I made talking to myself as I worked or muttering when I hung up the phone? Had I somehow jeopardized the murder investigation with a snotty remark? Had I put Mae further at risk?

LaSalle stopped at our booth, his scowl titanic. King laid down his silverware and frowned. I couldn't decipher the look that passed between them.

The detective jutted his chin to greet me and said, "Let me see it."

I handed the device to him. He turned it over and over, as I had done. His concentration finally broke when a waitress stepped on his toe as she tried to inch past him.

"Have a seat," said King, his invitation loaded with command.

"Where did you find it?" LaSalle squeezed in next to me, exuding ire. The swollen artery in his neck throbbed. He placed the device on the table in plain view, then picked it up again.

"Overhead lamp above her bed." King spoke as he resumed his meal. "Someone did a pretty good job of concealing it." He paused, steak midway to his mouth. "I think it's the only one, but I could be wrong."

"Abel, this is unacceptable," said the detective.

Our waitress came and took LaSalle's order.

"Don't I know it," King said.

"It's not one of ours," said LaSalle.

"I know that, too." King's hands held the fork and knife in position. "I'm working on it."

"Hello," I said, feeling ignored. They stared at me as if I'd just materialized—kerplop—on the seat. "Would you mind telling me what's going on?"

"I can't do that," said King.

"Abel," said LaSalle.

"Gentlemen," I said. "Someone bugged my room. I have a right to know what's going on."

LaSalle winced, closed his eyes and rubbed his temples. "Sasha, if Abel says he's working on it, he's working on it."

I turned to King. "It was Roc Johnson, wasn't it?"

"He's saying 'no.'"

"You believe him?" I said, stabbing at a pea and shuffling the corn and red pepper salad from one side of my plate to the other.

Johnson had become evil incarnate to me. The clincher had been his parting shot about Gustafssen. He'd left no doubt that he'd had something to do with the man's humiliation. As if he'd personally flamed Gustafssen's suffering for years.

No. I take that back. The clincher had been when he brought Mom into the conversation.

"Roc has never lied to me before," said King.

"There's a first time for everything," I said, smashing a piece of baked potato with my fork until LaSalle stayed my hand with his own.

"Abel's working on it," he said.

"If it wasn't Johnson or his mutant son, it was his cronies. The Pat and Sam show," I said.

King's microscopic smile met LaSalle's.

"What's so funny?"

"Not a thing, Sasha," said LaSalle.

Silverware clinked against china in the background. Our waitress served LaSalle a dinner salad.

"Did you ever find who blasted out Mae's windows?" I said.

"Not yet." LaSalle gored cherry tomatoes with his fork.

King picked up the bug. "You know, Henry, there're a couple of possibilities about this. That Mike Cho for example. He has military experience."

"Oh, sweet Jesus," I said.

"Sasha, please," said LaSalle.

"What?" said King.

"Cho and Johnson. They both knew about my new room. Cho came right there. And Johnson. When he called me, he asked if it was room two-forty-eight." I crunched on a carrot stick for emphasis. The sweetness turned corrosive in my mouth. "They're in cahoots."

"You're being ridiculous," said LaSalle, his alertness sizzling, then fizzling. "You know, my life was a lot easier before you came to town."

"It's not my fault things happen," I said.

"No. But it's your fault you attract trouble like lint."

The hush at our table prompted a visit from the waitress. "Y'all need something else? Coffee? Milk? More water?"

"I'll have a martini," I said.

"Beg your pardon?"

"Some more water would be nice," I said, responding to King's stern gaze.

"No need to take out your problems on an innocent girl," he said when she'd left.

"I had no need to be bugged either."

King sighed, looked at LaSalle. "She like this all the time?"

"Pretty much." LaSalle passed his hand over his forehead, stroked the stubble on his chin "So, what now?"

"Do I have to move again?" I said, shifting in my seat. I scratched my arm. Quarter-sized, red welts re-pocked my skin.

"Probably not," said the detective. "We need to do a sweep. Shouldn't take more than an hour or two."

"Ms. Solomon, how'd you like to see some more UFO artifacts?" said King.

"You're kidding, right?" I opened my purse, liberated two more antihistamines from their protective foil.

"Absolutely not." King watched me swallow the pills. "I've collected the stuff for years. Have a regular museum at my house."

I looked at LaSalle for confirmation.

"I'd jump at the chance, Sasha," he said.

I scrutinized the two of them, back and forth, back and forth, for several seconds. They weren't joking.

"Okay," I said. "I'll get my trampoline."

FORTY-ONE

YOU CAN'T JUDGE a book by its cover. At least not the book of Abel King.

We rode in his dirty brown Land Rover, its seats lambskin soft. McCoy Tyner's rendition of *Blue Dolphin Street* caressed in the background, the car's sound system a higher quality than the ones in most theaters. Our path arrowed down Norris Street and zigzagged into Sandzen. We turned onto a long paved driveway. On the way, the obligatory Ten Commandments, painted in gold on a sign, graced King's front lawn and sparkled in the sunlight.

My elderly escort opened the car door and led me under a wisteria gable shooting out its first fuzzy gray-green buds. We walked to a carved wooden entrance. He keyed in a code and I heard the click of locks releasing.

"Since Helen died, I've gotten into the habit of coming in the back way," King said, entering.

We passed through a laundry room and came to a large, open kitchen done in chestnut brown. Beneath my feet lay a mosaic of new-penny copper and gold tiles. A russet dinette set stood in a corner of the room surrounded by a floor-to-ceiling mural featuring the cartoon character Pogo and his buddies from the Okefenokee Swamp.

King noticed me looking at the mural.

"Walt Kelly himself did that when he came for a visit. Helen just loved it. I've never had the heart to paint over it," he said.

My jaw opened, shut again.

"How'd you like a good cup of coffee? The stuff they serve in restaurants tastes like the roasted dandelion root my parents favored," he said.

"That'd be great."

A fancy espresso machine rested on the nine-foot stainless steel island in the middle of the room. Its counter sported neither blemish nor scratch. The fridge was a Jenn-Air subzero, the stove one of those custom Viking brands.

"Do you like to cook?" I said.

"Not much sense in it now that Helen's gone." King steamed milk for our lattes.

He brought over the drinks. With a sharp paring knife, he shaved chocolate from a bar onto the froth, then used an electric grinder for the cinnamon and nutmeg.

Talk about cognitive dissonance.

"Mr. King, what keeps you in Clovis?"

"Family mostly." He sat across from me, took a draught from his oversized mug. "I split my time between here and a couple of other places. But traveling is lonely without someone to share it."

"How long were you married?"

I toyed with the idea of a wealthy, elderly boyfriend.

"Sixty blessed years." King leaned back in his chair, comfortable in his home.

"My God."

"He had a lot to with it. Hard work, love, forgiveness, and faith." Another sip. "You married?"

"Not yet."

"Didn't think so."

"Why not?"

"Don't be offended," he said. "You don't act married. You're too independent. There's not enough bend in you."

"It's always up to the woman to bend."

"Not in a marriage that endures, it's not. Don't speak about what you don't know, Missy."

To preempt a lecture I said, "What was your brother like?"

"Which one?"

"You're playing with me, Mr. King. Damon."

"Stubborn, brilliant, a bit of a scoundrel." King smiled. "Despite what anyone says, marrying Mae was the best thing that ever happened to him."

"Rumor has it he left you a pretty unique bequest."

"You sure do get your nose into everything. Don't you?"

"I can't help it," I said.

"Of course you can."

Our conversation swerved to a halt; I could smell the tires burning. I drank the dregs of what had been a truly excellent caffe latte. King cleared my cup along with his own and sat down again.

"Ms. Solomon, I know you're dying to hear some dirt. About my brother, me, Mae. I'm sorry, but I'm not going to give it to you." He twirled the gold wedding band on his finger. "That bequest you refer to, it's really a simple story. A last little gift of love."

"A twenty-dollar bill from a multimillionaire?"

"All you see is the money. It's deeper than that," he said.

"Tell me."

"You're not going give me any peace about this, are you?"

"Nope."

King heaved a dramatic sigh, stage-worthy in its plaint.

"Back before you were a twinkle in your mother's eye, I landed on an idea so crazy I could hardly believe it." He became youthful with the memory. "What if there were little stores filled with the items people wanted and needed most as they traveled from town to town?" King looked at me. "What if the stores were located all along main roads and highways and were so convenient, so easy to use, that people would pay higher prices for that convenience?"

"You're talking about your Pump-n-Snaks," I said.

"You're a perceptive little thing, aren't you?"

I nodded. So did he.

"Well, you see, I didn't have much money of my own when I came up with the idea. So, I asked Damon for a loan," he said, smiling again. "He refused. Said the whole idea was nuts. I had to go to the bank and borrow my first five hundred dollars from total strangers. When I got the loan, I went to Damon's place and waved that money right in front of my big brother's stubborn face." King's smile morphed into a sheepish grin. "We made a bet right then and there. If the stores worked, I'd get the money. If not, Damon would."

"The twenty-dollar bill?" I said.

"You know, Ms. Solomon, I'd completely forgotten that bet until he left me the money."

"Amazing."

"But that's not all. Hold on a minute." King went into another room. When he returned, he held an envelope. It had turned ivory with age. On the front in flowing calligraphy was written: *Abel Abraham King.*

"Go on, open it," said my host.

Inside was a page from a newspaper and inside that, a piece of paper with a note written in the same script. And a $20 bill.

I've always believed in you, little brother. The date on the simple message and the newspaper was August 10, 1943.

"Wow," I said.

"I checked. That was the day I got my money from the bank. Damon must have gone straight to his office and written that note. He kept it all those years." King tilted his head. "So, you tell me. What kind of man was my brother?" Then he winked, slapped his thighs as he got up, and said, "Come on. Let's go see some space alien bones."

FORTY-TWO

BEHIND KING'S HOUSE was a glassed-in building with a cathedral-tall ceiling. Similar to a conservatory. He punched in another key code and my nose flew to heaven. Vanilla mingled with more exotic fragrances from hundreds of orchids on tables, in chrome racks, on rows and rows of wooden, waist-high cabinets. It felt as if the air was richer in here, as if the oxygen levels were supplemented.

King reached around one of the chests and I heard the familiar *ca-chunk* of a lock releasing. He opened a drawer, pulled out a long something wrapped in black velvet, and handed it to me.

"What is it?" I said.

"Look and see."

I leaned against another cabinet and slowly unrolled the fabric. Inside was what looked like a femur. At the top, where there should have been a rounded end, the bone made a sharp right-angle turn. And it was serrated.

"An alien bone?" I said, my skepticism evident.

"Yep."

"Come on. What is it?"

"An alien bone."

"Get real."

"Well, if you know so much, Missy, you tell me."

I turned it over in my hands. "It's got to be some kind of animal."

"Yep. An alien animal." He'd removed another velvet-encased object to show me a flat, triangular bone with the same kind of serration. "What do you think this is?"

"Part of a pelvis, maybe, or a piece of bone that broke off something else."

"Then how come there's no evidence of breakage?"

I shook my head. "You're creeping me out here. Come on, tell me what they really are."

King unwrapped other bones.

I went to the table where he was laying them out. "Where did you get these?"

"I've collected them all around here," he said.

"What are they?"

"Alien bones. I kid you not."

Then he handed me a jagged flesh-colored piece of fabric. It appeared as if it had been ripped or torn off of a bigger portion. The texture was unlike anything I'd ever felt before, part plastic wrap and part living skin.

"What is it?" I said.

"Alien skin."

"Ewwww!" I dropped it.

"Sissy," he said, bowing to pick it up. "These things are too valuable for you to go dropping them. Do you want to see more or have you had enough?"

"You're pulling my leg, aren't you?" I searched his expression, waiting for him to fess up to the joke.

"Ms. Solomon, why would I do that?"

"I have no idea."

King came over to me. In his hand lay a circular beaded bracelet. He jiggled it and I heard music, bell-choir clear, an almost Asian melody with half- and quartertones. I touched it and the music stopped.

"It's beautiful," I said. "These really are real. Aren't they?"

"Yep."

"How many people know about them?"

"Not many. A couple of scientist friends," King said. "And Henry."

"Amazing. What are you going to do with all of this?"

"I was thinking of loaning them to the City of Clovis. I hear they're thinking of hiring you to get this UFO initiative going." He stared me in the eyes. "You want them?"

"You're serious?"

"I can't take them to heaven with me."

"Do you have the documentation on them? The scientific results, the tests?"

"You don't ask for much." He motioned to the cabinets. "It's all there."

"My God."

"He's glorious, isn't He?" said King.

I heard a small chirrup. King answered his cell phone, listened and said, "I'll tell her." He punched it closed and began to wrap up the artifacts. "Henry says they're done with your room."

"But what about all of this?" I said.

"It's been here for years, Missy, waiting for a nosy woman like you. And it'll be here still when you're ready for it."

FORTY-THREE

IF YOU'VE EVER COME HOME to a burglary, your dressers open, clothing strewn on the floor, you'll know what it felt like to walk into my hotel room. Violated. The room felt violated. Though nothing was out of place, I wanted to be somewhere else.

The message light on the phone seared red but I didn't have the energy to listen. I sat on the bed, thinking. King's collection of alien-alia would catapult Clovis into the big time. I turned on the laptop and revised my PR plan to include a grand opening event with national and international media in attendance. I had to be vague, since not many people knew about the artifacts. If they really were real, they'd create the kind of attention Clovis couldn't even dream of. And I'd orchestrate it.

But why was King offering me this opportunity? I batted away the thought. There'd be plenty of time to question his motives once I had my first paycheck from the Chamber.

A couple of hours later, I realized with a start that I'd never reconnected with Josh. Usually I could juggle ninety balls at once. Zoe would say my current forgetfulness emerged from spending too much time avoiding thoughts about something specific. Typical Psych 101 analysis.

Gee, I wonder what I might not want to think about? Could it be the murder? Or Mae blaming me for the leak that got her thrown into a padded cell? Was it possible I was avoiding the idea that someone had been listening to all my phone conversations, or worse, watching me alone in the room? Nah, there wasn't a thing in the world I wanted to avoid thinking about!

I got up and searched for the number Josh had left most recently. I couldn't find the scrap of paper anywhere and I didn't want to listen to any more messages. I noticed a business card with LaSalle's name on the dresser near the television.

On the back was a note. The tight, all capital letters read,

WE GOT EVERYTHING. I'LL BE IN TOUCH TONIGHT. HENRY.

My fruitless search forced me to listen to the messages again. Two new and seven old. I replayed the old ones first, determined not to forget Josh again. Fiddling with one of my floating alien-head pens, I waited until his voice came up and wrote down the out-of-state number. I'd retrieve the new messages after returning his call.

A woman's low voice, swathed in a Caribbean accent, answered, "Good afternoon to you."

"Hi. Is Josh King there?"

"And who are you?"

"Sasha Solomon. I'm returning his call."

She laughed, a deep rich sound, reminding me of milk chocolate and piña coladas. "Ah, the famous Sasha Solomon. Joshua has told me all about you."

"Is he there?"

"You are in Clovis, right?" she said.

"Yes. Can I talk to him, please?" I doubted the City of Clovis would be crazy about a major long-distance charge on my bill.

The receiver on her end thudded as it hit a hard surface. "Pardon me. The phone slipped."

"Ma'am, may I please speak with Josh?" Was this another runaround?

"I'm sorry. He's not available."

"Where is he?" My exasperation and impatience flew through the phone line. "And who are you anyway?"

"I'm Marguerite Thomas. Joshua's older, wiser, and wealthier lover."

I closed my eyes, my imagination running full force. Josh as a gigolo, a kept man. What if he'd been lying all along? Instead of a forthright defender of his mother's innocence, he could be a spitball living off his rich lover's money until he could get hold of his inheritance. Maybe the whole environmentalist act was a sham. Josh could have had lunch with me that day to steer me in the wrong direction—away from his greed and toward his siblings. It had worked.

"But, Ms. Solomon, Josh is in Clovis." Worry seeped through her words.

"No, he's not. He's there. He left your number."

"But he said he was going there. Yesterday when he left, he said he was flying to Lubbock to meet his brother." Her voice twanged taut with anxiety. "The two of them were going to drive to Clovis."

"Maybe they did and I don't know about it yet." I wanted to soothe her. "I've been busy with other things."

"Something's wrong." Her certainty disturbed me.

I glanced down at the message light.

"Excuse me, Ms. Thomas? Let me check on something before you get worried. I'll call you back in a few minutes," I said.

"Fine. I'll wait right here."

I disconnected, punched the button to listen to my new messages. Josh's voice asked me to call him at Mae's, saying it was important. The second missive was Connie Womack inviting me to lunch. Too late for that.

I dialed the long-distance number again. Marguerite Thomas answered on the first ring.

"I was wrong. He's here," I assured Josh's paramour. "Sorry for the false alarm."

"Oh, thank goodness." She exhaled as if she'd been hold-ing her breath for a long time. The warm island tones resur-faced. "This thing with his mother has me spooked, I guess."

"You and me both."

"Watch him for me, Ms. Solomon. He's naïve when it comes to people."

"I'll try."

"That's all any of us can do." She bid me adieu.

I dialed Mae's number. Got the answering machine for the umpteenth time. "Josh, this is Sasha returning your call. You know, you really should change the tape, it's garbled. I'll—"

"Hello? Sasha?" It was Josh, his breathing hard, as if he'd run to pick up the phone. I heard another click. Someone else's breathing, deliberate, slow.

"Whoever is on the line, please get off," I said.

"No one else is here, Sasha," Josh said.

"You're sure?"

"Of course I'm sure."

I didn't believe him.

"So," I said. "What can I do for you?"

"Can we meet somewhere? I'd really like to talk about Mom some more."

"I've got a lot of work to do, Josh. Can't we do this by phone?" I'd finished the basic PR plan but didn't have the oomph to meet with another King that afternoon.

"I really need to see you." The urgency in his voice changed my mind.

"Okay. What time?"

"Seven. Can you meet me at Mom's at seven?"

"How about a little earlier?" I wanted a quiet night in front of the TV.

"No." His voice was frantic. "No, I don't think that would be a good idea."

"Josh, are you okay? Is something wrong?"

"No, no, no. Nothing's wrong." He cleared his throat. "So will you come?"

"You know what? I'd rather meet at a restaurant." My intuition screamed for caution. "Let's go somewhere and have coffee."

"Okay, Sasha. Whatever you say. Just, come alone. Okay? It's really important."

FORTY-FOUR

"WELL, GUESS I'D BETTER get going," I said to the television at a quarter to seven. I took a last, long, edifying drag on the can of whipped cream I'd purchased after my conversation with Josh. Then I walked to the door, unlocked it. Before going out, I turned around, grabbed the sweet stuff again and took another last, long, and edifying drag. Rather than leaving it to molder in the room, I took the can with me for comfort. This nighttime meeting with the youngest King had an odd odor; I could sense the wrongness of it even though the specifics were yet to be discovered.

Well, if he got too weird, I could whack him over the head with the metal container.

Josh waited outside the entrance to the Denny's, skittish. Gone was the poster boy for health and happiness; in his place an imposter. Rawness marked his face. Distress pulsed beneath the handsome veneer.

He came toward me, halting with a jerk at the curb. Without a handshake, he said, "Glad you could come."

"Me, too." I hoped my voice conveyed neutrality.

The sky deepened into cobalt blue. We stood in the cool evening, watching the remnants of the sunset, wisps of orange, yellow, and pink clouds.

"What have you heard from your mom?" I said, scrutinizing Josh's face for clues to his extreme discomfort.

"That's what I need to talk to you about."

He used his thumb to scratch the bridge of his nose. The

motion didn't look natural, a single downward sweep. For all I knew it could have been some kind of signal. I shook my head, told myself to get a grip.

The rumble of trains hummed, predictable and strong. The air was a mixture of fumes from car exhaust and fresh growing grass. And then, with unexpected speed, it became chilly. The slight breeze turned into wind, more definite and cold.

I held myself against the change and said, "Let's get out of this. Come on, I'll buy you a chocolate sundae."

"Actually, I was thinking you might want to see Mom." What a lousy attempt at spontaneity. The rehearsed quality to the words hung between us.

"I thought Mae was in Albuquerque," I said, prolonging the sentence to show my skepticism.

He didn't respond.

"Josh, I don't know what's going on," I said. My shoulders sank; I didn't want to play this game anymore. "I feel like you're dicking me around. And I don't know why. And I don't care." I headed toward my car.

"Wait! Please!" He reached out, snatched at my wrist.

"What?" I looked at his hand on my arm, then up to his eyes.

"Shhh. I don't want to attract attention." He spoke as if it hurt. In a whisper he said, "Mom's out. We got her out early. The police don't know yet." His glance darted across the lot and back to me. "She's not home. We've got her someplace safe. She wants to see you."

Holy cow. Had the King kids rigged an escape? I didn't think Mae was technically under arrest but didn't know for sure. If she were, this little caper wouldn't help.

"Are you messing with me, Josh?" I tried again to read his face, to gauge the truth.

He shook his head, his expression so blank it looked painted on. "I can drive you there."

"Okay," I said. "But I need to make a phone call."

"Why?" he asked, panic replacing the strain.

"Because I had something else planned for later."

"Oh," he said.

"Look, it'll be okay. I won't mention your mom."

His nervousness spurred me to comfort him even as I tried to remember LaSalle's office and home numbers. I patted him on the shoulder, then walked to the pay phone in the restaurant's foyer. The bottom of my purse yielded a quarter and a dime. Through the glass door, I watched Josh stand in the parking lot, looking from left to right, right to left. I thumbed through the phone book. With the meager change, I could make only one call. I opted for LaSalle's home.

"Hello?" A woman answered.

What do you know? Henry had a honey.

"Is Detective LaSalle there?" I said.

"This isn't a police department."

"I know. I was calling for Henry LaSalle."

Josh had begun to pace outside the restaurant's door.

"You've got the wrong number," she said.

He came in. "We've got to go."

I put my hand over the mouthpiece. "What's the hurry, Josh?"

"Do you want to see her or not?"

I hung up.

We left the building's warmth and shivered in the night wind.

"Boy, it's really kicking up," I said.

"Yeah." He crossed the lot, leading me to Mae's mondo truck.

I stopped, unable to move forward, the nausea hitting me hard.

A car started up behind us, its lights bright. Josh watched it pull out of the lot and continued staring until it was out of sight. Then he looked at me. "What's wrong?"

"Your mom's truck. The one from that night. The night she took me to see Colonel Tan."

"I'm sorry. I didn't think—"

"It's okay. I can do this. Give me a minute." I breathed

deeply, wondering if I'd hallucinate again. Another breath and then I touched the door handle, seized it, and hoisted myself into the cab. I felt pale, dizzy.

Josh watched me settle in.

"See, good as gold." I smiled, faking it.

"I brought some coffee. Would you like some?" He held out a thermos.

Coffee sounded good. I wanted to be very awake for whatever was coming. I poured a cup for myself. "You want some?"

"In a while."

We drove out of the parking lot, me sipping coffee to calm my nerves. Josh remained as wound up as a spring toy. He headed toward Prince Street and over the bridge. The coffee was good. I praised it out loud. Josh made a quick, strange sound, a cross between a whimper and squeak. But when I turned toward his face, its passivity convinced me I'd had an aural hallucination. My imagination was on overdrive tonight.

I took a long draught of coffee and an even longer breath. If I started hallucinating now, it would ruin everything. I needed distraction.

"Is Mae in Portales?" I asked to stimulate conversation, and refocus my mind.

"Past it a bit."

That'd be out of LaSalle's jurisdiction. Smart move. "So, how's she doing?"

"Okay," he said.

"Did I tell you I spoke with Marguerite?"

"Is she all right?" His voice cracked.

"She was really worried about you."

"I'm okay."

"No, you're not, Josh."

"What makes you say that?"

I yawned, snuggled down in the big seat. The heater blew

softly. The stars shimmered in the silken blackness of a sky far from light pollution.

I leaned my head against the window. "What did you say?"

"Nothing."

"Okay."

"Sasha, will you ever be able to forgive me for getting you into this mess? Do you understand I had no choice?"

"Josh, you didn't get me into anything." I stretched, yawned again. My eyes closed for a moment, then opened. Exhaustion licked my neck, massaged my shoulders. "Your mom and I go way back. This isn't anyone's fault."

He shook his head, misery evident in the motion. His despair suggested too strong a reaction for this moment. My mind muddled, I vaguely remembered the coffee, took a sloppy swig and stared out into the shadowy level land past Portales. My body floated, no longer tethered to the inside of the truck. The world swirled. My head throbbed. The coffee slipped out of my hands, drenching my thighs.

As I slid into a drugged sleep, I had enough time for one last thought.

Help me.

FORTY-FIVE

THERE IS A WHITE so bright it stings. My eyes opened to it, and to Arctic cold. Inert, I lay on a hard surface solid as wood but too icy to ever have been animate. A distant sound—harsh and removed—a crash. Grogginess enveloped me, my mind thick with sluggish half-thoughts. My body wanted sleep, to hide until my brain could catch up. I shivered, tried to roll over, to curl up against the frigid air. Only my shoulder moved; my arms remained anchored. I tried again and realized my wrists were strapped down. I fought the restraints, then paused to force cogent thought through my viscous consciousness.

Instincts prevailed. My legs tensed against more straps. I moved my face to one side. The intense light lessened. Adrenaline nudged my mental wooziness aside for a moment. I forced my head into an even more awkward position. The table upon which I lay shone metal gray. A new sound overtook the others. The whirring, buzzing hum came nearer. A needle pricked my arm.

I closed my eyes against a possibility too outrageous to believe. Opened them again to the brightness, and knew. Mae's aliens had found me.

Muffled voices modulated beyond my sight. A being floated toward me, tall, thin. Its wet eyes gleamed the size of golden kiwi fruits, but black, unfathomable. It spoke to me, its voice melodic, though I couldn't understand the words. The inflection tickled my memory, then like a miniscule dust mote, flitted away. I concentrated, waiting for a telepathic message but sensed only my fear. Sheathed in a white shapeless garment, the entity moved with feminine fluidity, sinuous. It raised an instrument, long and metallic, capped with a needle as wide as a crochet hook. The skewer spun like a drill. The being placed the instrument, still turning, next to my head.

Another alien—shorter, heavier—joined the first one. Its voice was lower, masculine. And again, I had a feeling of familiarity, though it turned to gossamer when I tried to grasp it. Heads together, they conferred. The short one glided toward me, holding a tool that looked too much like a scalpel. Its sharp edge reflected brutal light. A putrid odor emanated from the alien.

The tall creature wafted around the table to the other side. I stared at the knife that might cut me. The being cradled my head, plugged my nose and forced my mouth open. Liquid poured down my gagging throat. Coffee! Josh! I struggled against the straps, pulled with as much strength as I could, then sank into dreamless sleep once more.

Sometime later, I awoke.

Darkness.

Blessed darkness.

I breathed a silent prayer of relief. Still strapped to the table, I took inventory. My extremities cramped with the cold. I heard a thump and waited, motionless, for more. Body rigid, I listened with the same intense focus as I have at night with my windows open after hearing a single scream outside, waiting to hear one more before calling the police.

When no sound came, I concentrated on motion, prepared to feel the spaceship soaring through the galaxies, pulling me away from everyone I loved, everything I cared for. I realized I'd been holding my breath and forced air into unwilling lungs. Strange. I felt no movement, not a bump or dip. If we were hurtling through space, it was a very smooth ride. When my eyes adjusted to the darkness, I saw strips of lighter gray in every direction, as if the walls of the spaceship had gaps.

My heavy body yearned for more sleep. With great will, I forced an aching head from side to side. I tensed stomach muscles to lift my torso for a better look around. The thirty-degree angle gave me enough information for thought. Panting with the effort and newfound fury, I lay down once more.

Anger renewed my energy and shoved the toxins from my brain. With that more complete look, I understood my stupidity. Every inch of my being howled with indignity.

Poor, poor Mae. This wasn't a ship! It was a cabin or shed, painted white. I struggled against the straps and although they were looser, I couldn't wriggle out of their grasp. After another semi-sit-up, I rolled onto most of my left hip, my legs pulled tight at the clumsy position. My right shoulder bent forward stretching my hand until it felt like the restraint would sever it from my wrist. I felt a pop but didn't let it distract me from the attempt. Holding my breath for strength, I strained my head toward the strap on my left hand. Just a tad more, a little more, and—contact. I started to saw with my teeth, back and forth.

Saw, saw, saw, rest. Saw, saw, rest.

Hours must have passed. Chewing at the leather, I felt like an old, tired dog. My jaw ached. While I worked, the shed grew light and warm with the morning sun. During one of my many breaks, I noticed an orange trouble light, its long cord dangling. Someone—definitely *not* alien—had strung it from a rafter and angled it to shine directly in my eyes. I bellowed a string of obscenities.

Josh had to be involved in this hoax. Hell, he'd kidnapped me. What more proof could there be? Stupid, stupid me; I'd thought of him as Mae's good kid. Like a fool, I'd trusted Josh. And I'd earned a fool's reward.

Pure rage washed over me in waves, providing the willpower to continue gnawing in spite of my full-body agony. My teeth hurt. They'd probably fall out before I could sever the restraint. I wriggled my wrist to and fro, bending it full back upon itself and tried to inch it out of its hold. More time, more incising, and then finally, my bloodied left hand slipped free. I fumbled with the buckle on the strap constraining my right hand. Unsuccessful and dizzy, I lay back and stared at the ceiling.

Stupid, stupid, stupid. How could I have been such an idiot? I should have known better than to trust a handsome, soft-spoken man. I'd fallen for his act entirely, gulped it right down because of those deep dimples. But why? Why was Josh—and whoever was helping him—staging these abductions? And why include me in the fun?

Suppose he had taken me to lunch to sound out my sympathies? Finding I was on his mom's side might have made me the enemy. Could be he didn't lust after Mae's money as much as he wanted to disgrace her, to torture her because of long-nursed resentments. Instead of his professed love for her and happiness with her being "emotionally there," maybe he was furious with her for having a career, for abandoning him to siblings and a father he couldn't or didn't want to understand. Or, he could just be your run-of-the-mill psychopath.

I set to work again.

After what seemed like another couple of lifetimes, I could control my left-hand fingers well enough to work the buckle on my right. I sat up puffing and braced myself with one arm to stay a backward collapse. My eyes closed. I willed them open. When the room stopped spinning, I undid the leg buckles. I listened for a minute, alert, and unafraid. Then I took stock of my surroundings.

The small structure consisted of a single room with no windows. Light leaked in through the old weather-shrunken siding on the walls and a hole in the ceiling that might have once accommodated a pipe from a wood-burning stove. I shook my head, exhaled loudly, and muttered things that would have made a biker blush. Who cared? No one was around to hear me.

I stood, unsteady from whatever drug had been administered, and held onto the table. It was an old hospital gurney, minus the bedding. Suddenly angry at the dim light, I went to the door and kicked it open onto a dazzling, bright day. My eyes closed again; the drug must have made them photosensitive. I pulled them open with my fingers, held them that way as tears flowed.

I went outside, surveyed the brown-gray structure. Letting go of my eyes, I grabbed hold of a loose board and yanked it down. Walked two steps to the left and ripped off another, wanting for one crazed moment to pull the whole building down.

Inside again, I noticed the cheap tools of Josh and his partner's deceit. They must have felt pretty cocky to leave everything here. Must have been certain no one would ever find this place. But what they didn't know was that I was a survivor. No way on earth I'd let some punks pull this kind of crap on me or my friend Mae.

I walked over to the thing that looked like a drill in the blinding light. Surprise, surprise. It was a drill. Alien-head masks, twins to my own, lay on the floor. Their black cloth backings were tan with dust. Next to them lay a cookie sheet with instruments to instill fear: scalpels, pliers, ice picks, large sewing needles and syringes. I checked my arm. A red bump with a thin dot in its center pocked my pale flesh. It hurt to the touch. Someone had used one of those syringes to puncture my arm last night. Working my toe underneath the tray, I kicked it over. Then I kicked the drill.

A pile of clothes huddled in the corner. I went to it, picked up one, then another, nightgowns. Each one reminding me of the gown Colonel Tan clutched in his hand that night. Moving the entire wad, I uncovered something I hoped never to see. A telescope. Tan's telescope.

Oh, God.

A part of my world unraveled with the discovery. I sank to the ground, staring at it. I wanted to retreat into a ball, to roll away from this place. I yearned to be rescued. But no one and nothing could save me from what I knew I needed to do.

Time oozed, gelatinous, undefined. After minutes or maybe hours, I exited the shack. Becky Tan's story echoed in my memory, her descriptions horribly accurate. I walked around the shed first, found the generator at the back. I kicked it over. Screamed and kicked it again, hurting my foot this time.

Limping, I returned to the front of the building. A yard or two from the door, I noticed a flattened clump of brown wild grass. On one knee, I eyed the sun-baked dirt next to it and found faint indentations from truck tires. Following them down, I came to the place and stopped. I'd almost stepped on the blood-darkened earth. My low moan pierced the silence. Then I looked right at the sun, hoping to sear the vision away. Instead, I got very dizzy and nearly fell down.

Deep breaths, tears. I kneeled by the wide dry stain on the dirt, searching for answers to impossible questions. Nausea caught me by surprise. I threw up pure bile, the burn cleansing away a microscopic bit of the horror.

I expected a hallucination then, settled onto the ground, asking for one.

Colonel Tan, who did this to you? Tell me. I want to know. What did they say? Why did they kill you? Please, please talk to me.

I waited.

"Please, I know you can hear me. Let me help you, Colonel Tan. Let me help Mae," I said out loud.

Nothing came.

How could Josh—it had to be Josh—have done it? Killed an innocent man whose only crime was to look at the stars? Becky Tan said there'd been two at the murder and there were two last night. The one I'd taken for a female must have been Josh; he had the height for it. I shook my head, trying to dislodge the stubborn muddled remnants of the drug. The little pudgy alien—could it have been Bud Johnson? The tall one might have been Steve Cummings. So, Josh was in cahoots with him *and* Bud. Maybe those two had been waiting for me in the simulated spaceship last night. All Josh had to do was deliver the goods. With three of them, Josh would have an alibi in California though he may have masterminded the whole thing.

The sun was low, afternoon for sure. I welcomed the heat of this early spring day. Were they coming back for me? Had they left me to starve to death? I went back into the building and grabbed a wad of nightgowns and ripped them into big strips.

I placed the first piece of cloth under a rock near Tan's murder site, then followed the dirt road at the bottom of the hill, careful to side-step the faint tire imprints that hadn't yet been completely erased by the spring winds. A single black stinkbug sunned on a rock. My feet thunked and skidded on the gravely terrain. I focused on the ground to keep from falling. At intervals, I stooped to place a strip of cloth. Each one would serve as a marker to guide LaSalle and his team back, even though a part of me wanted to lose the place, to never see it again.

I halted frequently to wipe the sweat from my face. The sky was a brazen blue, endless, cloudless. For a brief stretch of grace, my thoughts hung in stasis, so jumbled none swayed singly into consciousness. After I found the highway, they nudged their way to the surface. Between marveling at the beauty of this solitary land with its desert colors—forty shades of brown, rust red, yellow, granite white—and reliving the stupidity of having trusted Josh, I thought about other people who'd been terribly wrong. True-crime writer Ann Rule had

worked alongside a nice young man at a crisis center. Ted
Bundy. She'd been wrong.

Josh had convinced me of Theo and Charlene's guilt. I
hadn't even considered the possibility that he could be the
criminal. No wonder his sibs treated me with such indignation. I merited their rudeness. I'd be livid if they'd treated me
the way I'd treated them.

I walked along the paved road, almost recognizing it. My
skin hurt as if raw from an acid wash. Cars and semis passed
me, some honking in greeting. Idiots. Couldn't they see I
needed help? The remnants of cloth in my hand flapped in
their gusty trails like kite tails.

Then, in the distance, I saw a clump of buildings and trees.
A few minutes more and I came upon a green sign with white
lettering. I'd arrived in Elida. There was a run-down storefront
that looked like a good bet, the swamp cooler already clunk-
ing to fend off the heat. The door was locked. Unwilling to
take one step farther, I vowed to break into the place if I had
to. What was one more felony compared with murder? I
pounded on the frame.

I heard the click of a lock. A woman opened the wooden
door, then the screen. Intelligent, practical eyes resided in her
thin sun-damaged face. She looked at me, sucked in her lips
until they disappeared.

"You don't need to wake the dead. I'm the only one here,"
she said, her voice rough but not mean.

I stared at her, unable to speak. Relief and exhaustion
caused my legs to shake, my stomach to turn. I clutched the
flimsy handle on the screen door to steady myself.

She took in the messy, wild sight of me and shook her head.
Then moved to let me in.

FORTY-SIX

My STOMACH SLOSHED with water. Still, the woman plied me with more. She pushed platefuls of homemade chocolate pudding pie in front of me. I ate and drank first from hunger and thirst, then from politeness, and finally to avoid talking. She seemed to understand. She sat across from me, watching.

"Miss, I've fed and watered you. How about you giving me your name?" she said.

"I'm sorry. I didn't think…. My name's Sasha Solomon."

"Ida Thompson," she said with a single nod. "And there's nothing to be sorry about."

"You've brought me into your home. I could have at least introduced myself."

"You going to tell me why you look like something the cat dragged in?"

Ida frowned when I began to speak. A few minutes into my edited story, she excused herself. While she was gone, I relaxed in the stiff-backed chair, sheltered in this stranger's kitchen. She returned wearing a flowered Sunday frock in place of the faded robe in which she'd answered my insistent knocking.

"We'll need to go on down to Kenna to make a call," she said, pushing the pie pan toward me. "Go on. Eat."

"It was great. Really. Thank you." My wrists hurt. Swollen rings encircled them like bloody bracelets. My ankles ached as well, the friction burns apparent through my once-white socks. I felt my body buzzing from the sugar and caffeine combo. Tremors ran through me. Was I in shock?

"I tell you, people today," Ida said, shaking her head. "Kidnapped, huh? People are just low-down crazy nowadays."

"Only some of them," I said.

She took my glass and refilled it. The water tasted like minerals—arsenic, lead, copper—but it was cool.

"The little girls' room is down the hall," she said, pointing in answer to my unasked question.

The tidy bathroom was worn just like Ida and the rest of her house. It reminded me of an old couch, the stuffing intact but so compressed from years of use you could feel the springs. The medicine cabinet mirror had a small chip on the lower right side. A rust-colored trail, years in the making, traced where water had flowed from the faucet down the sink drain. My reflection showed the reason for the painful, raw heat from my face. My vermilion skin blistered as I watched. I splashed cold water on it, but the real burning, the pain, came from within.

Ida's Buick Electra harkened back to a time when gas-guzzlers sang of status. My chauffeur wore a hand-knitted sweater and blasted the air conditioning, silently offering me what comfort she could. The ride was no more than twenty minutes. Ida drove to a house slightly better tended than her own. Her knock at the door was definite, strong. We waited. After a while, she bent down, snorting with the effort, and removed a key from underneath the thick, bristled doormat.

"We share the cost of a phone out here. Tim works in Roswell. He leaves the key when he's gone." I wondered why she wanted to assure me she wasn't breaking in. I didn't care as long as a hot bath, a can of whipped cream, and a bottle of scotch were the end result.

The dark house smelled of old man. A woman's touch tempered the masculine with a doily on the dining room table, plastic flowers in a vase near the sink. The phone was an old black rotary model, beautiful in a way I'd remember from this day forward. Ida dialed a number, spoke for a minute, and handed the barbell receiver to me.

"It's the police in Roswell. Go on, tell 'em your story," she said.

I told them some, kept more to myself. Mentioned I'd been kidnapped from Clovis and that I thought Detective LaSalle might be interested in hearing about it.

"Henry LaSalle?" said the man on the other end.

"Yes. He's probably worried about me." I could imagine LaSalle's reaction when he got the call from Roswell. He'd be furious I'd gone off alone with Josh.

"Where are you?"

"Kenna."

Ida took the phone away from me before I could say more. "The girl's confused," she said. "We're in Elida. Yessir."

"Isn't this Kenna?"

"I live right in the center of town. In Elida," she said, staring at me. "On the main road in an old converted store. There's a sign on my house. It says, 'Rick's General Store.'"

On the way back to the car, I said, "Why couldn't the police come here?"

"And cause trouble for Tim? No, sir." Ida unlocked the doors, opened mine first.

"Tell me why you still live in Elida," I said.

"Where else would I go?"

"That's not what I meant." I looked out the window as we drove. "I guess I wonder what it'd be like to live in such a small town. Doesn't it get lonely?"

"First of all, I never get lonely." She cracked her window open in spite of the air conditioning. "Haven't much cared for most people most of my life. I've got a couple of friends in Roswell. Tim in Kenna. That's enough."

"What about family? Do you have children?"

"You raise your children right, they go away. I've got three girls and four boys. They're all older than you."

"Do they help you out?" Ida's current life stood in contrast to Mom's. Where she lived alone, talking to no one, Mom was surrounded by caregivers, friends.

"They send me money, if that's what you mean. But they've got their own lives. I've got mine." The wrinkles in Ida's face merged into a scowling sort of smile. "Once you've lived long enough, the sound of your own thoughts is more interesting than most anything you come across in conversation," she said. "I talk with the Lord and He gives me peace. That's enough."

We bump-bumped up her driveway. The house that had seemed old and tattered before held coziness now. I wanted to snuggle down on her musty couch and stay for a while. Ida tried to stuff me with more food, water, tea. Tired and in pain, I didn't want more to eat; I wanted to stop everything for a minute. Ida must've known. We sat at her Formica-topped kitchen table, not talking, not needing to.

Beyond the clank of the swamp cooler, I thought I heard a different pitch to the hum of the traffic passing through Elida. My hostess looked up, alert as a prairie dog. She left the room and opened her front door before anyone knocked. I heard car doors slam, the descending tones of a siren.

I didn't move but listened for LaSalle's voice. He'd ream me out for sure. I'd been irresponsible; he'd be pissed.

"Sasha?" he said, more softly than I'd ever thought possible. His face held such compassion, such concern, that it yanked my reserve from under me.

I reached out for him, shaking my head, willing my tears back.

He embraced me hard, the sweet smell of unsmoked cigarettes permeating the hug.

"You okay?"

"I will be," I said.

FORTY-SEVEN

THE PARAMEDICS WANTED to take me to the hospital. I didn't want to go. We settled for gauzy bandages over ointmented wrists and ankles. They frowned and cleaned the place where I'd been pricked with the needle. LaSalle watched, not saying a word. Ida stood by him framed in the kitchen doorway.

My unwillingness to succumb to tests at the hospital frustrated the medical pros. They left, dissatisfied after issuing final instructions about the care of my friction burns. One of them stopped to repeat the instructions to LaSalle and then again to the crowd in the front room.

"Are you ready to talk, Sasha? Or do you need a few more minutes?" LaSalle said.

I got up, feeling unsteady, but brazened it through, not wanting Ida—or anyone—to worry about me.

She saw through the bravado, nodded at my thank you, and patted my shoulder with a bony hand. "You're a strong girl. You'll do fine."

"Thank you so much. For everything," I said, again.

A smile, unfamiliar to her normally downturned mouth, touched her eyes. "Don't mention it. I'd do it for a sick skunk. Probably drive all the way to Roswell to the hospital if I had to."

"Excuse me?"

Ida laughed, the sound as brittle as dried grass crunching underfoot. "Go on, git out of here."

I crossed through the living room, sensing rather than seeing all the people there. Outside, the dusky sky darkened as

I sat on one of the cars. Clouds turned from light pink to fuchsia, the last hurrah of the day. LaSalle's unmarked Ford, two police cars, a crime scene van, and two others crowded the street, parked haphazardly. No traffic would be inconvenienced, no tickets dispensed on Elida's main drag. In the cooling, fresh air, I gave LaSalle the short version of the story: meeting Josh, drinking the coffee, waking up in the shed, escape, Tan's telescope and blood, the walk to Elida. He didn't interrupt once.

The gush of words left me stunned, as if I had nothing left inside me.

LaSalle scratched his ear. "Well, we know where Colonel Tan was dumped to die. Thanks to you, we'll finally see where he was shot."

"That poor man."

"Think you're up to pointing out the turnoff?" His mild voice unnerved me again.

I breathed deep, controlled breaths, forcing myself back from emotional wreckage. "I think I need to do more than that. I need to take you there. To the shed."

"If you think you're up to it."

My sunburn stung, my wrists and ankles pulsed with pain. We got in his car. "I need to apologize," I said.

"What for?" LaSalle held the key an inch from the ignition.

"A lot of things. For haranguing you about Charlene, for jumping to conclusions, for not giving you enough information through my self-editing. And that's just the tip of the iceberg."

He smiled and started the car.

"What? You think this is funny?"

"Absolutely not. I'm not laughing at you or your apology. It's accepted, okay?" He turned to make sure I'd heard. "But you've got to know how important this is. You found where he was killed. You found the telescope. Anything you've done up to this point is forgiven and forgotten." He checked his rearview mirror. Our law enforcement parade traveled well below the speed limit. "I should thank you, Sasha. Yes. Thank you."

"I'm glad I could help."

"Do me a favor next time. Don't get yourself kidnapped to solve my case. Okay?"

"You got it."

A half-hour later, LaSalle spotted the first long strip of cloth and turned onto the dirt road. From there it was a rough ride. I looked at the sky while we drove. Soon, we ran out of visible road. I asked LaSalle to stop and got out of the car. Turning around, I searched for the correct horizon. My eyes adjusted to the minimal light as I walked forward and climbed a short mesa. Squinting, I saw another piece of Mae's nightgown fluttering in the wind.

"It's beyond that hill," I said to LaSalle, who had joined me, his body so close, I could feel its heat.

He nodded then went down the hill. In a single breath, all the vehicles extinguished their headlights and cut their engines. No noise but the soft closing of car doors. Three men, dressed entirely in camouflage, ran past me, a slight breeze following their quiet steps. I realized they had semi-automatic weapons in their hands.

I started after them when quick footsteps came from behind me and LaSalle whispered. "You need to stay here."

"What are they doing?"

"That's the S.R.T., the special response team. They secure the area, make sure no one is waiting for us."

"No one's there. I know it."

"We don't," he said, gazing in their direction. "Sasha, this is going to take some time. Why don't you go back to the car and get some sleep?"

"I want to be here."

"Suit yourself. But please, stay out of my way."

I stepped back, the next hill still in view. What I wanted

more than anything else was to get back into that shed, to re-live the experience and let LaSalle help me exorcise it—to prevent some lurking phobia from taking root.

After awhile, the S.R.T. returned, then two men from the crime scene van went to the shed. They carried a video camera, another camera, and bags of equipment I couldn't identify.

Again, we waited. At one point, I did lie down in the car. But sleep didn't come and I gave up.

Finally, LaSalle said, "Sasha, you ready?"

"I think so."

"Okay, you and Frank come with me."

Frank turned out to be my runningback from the homicide team. I hadn't even noticed him until LaSalle mentioned his name. He nodded a greeting and I wondered if he ever spoke.

We walked slowly, dislodging a few pebbles, their journey downward the only noise save our breathing. The air's brisk caresses felt welcome on my face, clearing my head anew. I thought I smelled something fragrant, caught a wisp of white, but when I focused on it, nothing was there.

Up the hill that had hidden all of us, and beyond it. The shed stood small and ratty in the quivering flashlight beams. I showed LaSalle where Tan's blood had first colored the ground. The detective didn't say a word. We approached the building.

The shed was dark, its door open. The hand-held lights lent a strange, evil quality to the structure. LaSalle and Frank put on latex gloves.

"That's where they tied me up." I pointed to the gurney.

"Hold on a second," said LaSalle. He pulled a hand-held tape recorder out of his pocket. "Do you mind speaking into this?"

I took it from him, pushed the ON button and said, "Over here are the instruments they threatened me with. They spoke in gibberish to make me think they were aliens."

The concentration on the two men's faces reminded me of

surgeons. They stood at the door, their eyes scouring the structure and noting details of crimes infected with hatred.

"Can you imagine what Mae must have gone through in here?" I said. "And Josh, her own son, doing it to her?"

"Why do you think it was Josh?" said LaSalle, entering.

"Get real. The man kidnapped me!"

"I know he did. But did you actually see him put on the mask or are you making an assumption?"

"He's been kidnapping Mae, too," I said. "Isn't that enough?"

"I can't jump to conclusions."

"Henry." Frank held up a rag smudged with almost-brown stains. Dried blood. Going to his knees, he focused his flashlight on the floor, turned off the light. A greenish glow came from a pile there. He lifted one of the space-alien masks, then put it back carefully.

A glance passed between Frank and LaSalle, then the detective swiveled his attention back to me. "Sasha, I'm not saying Josh wasn't involved. But you mentioned two people. It's possible Josh drove you here and met up with others. Are you absolutely certain it was Josh behind that mask?"

"No." It had to be Josh. Who else *could* it be?

"Hey, it's okay," said LaSalle. "I have to make sure I'm not overlooking anything." He laid a hand on my shoulder. "We'll find whoever did this to you. And to Mae and Colonel Tan."

"I hope so."

"Believe it." LaSalle stooped to pick up something shiny. "If you weren't such a pain, Sasha, I'd hire you to work for me."

"PR'd be a great cover," Frank said, his voice velvety smooth, Cole Porter incarnate. No wonder he rationed it.

LaSalle grinned, "Yeah, you oughtta know."

That evoked a grunt.

I surveyed the one-room structure, imagining how terrible it must have been for Mae. And how terrible it would be—when she learned that her own son had been behind the scam.

"You know that theory I told you the other night? It's not that farfetched," I said.

"Humm?" LaSalle shone his light on the stainless steel instruments as Frank picked up and then replaced each one where it belonged.

"I was wrong to think Charlene was involved. But doesn't it look like Josh might be trying to get Mae declared incompetent?" My voice sounded girlish to me, shrill. "If the psychiatrists in Albuquerque hear her talking about the abductions and she's able to give them minute details, what do you think they'll do? And if she wasn't depressed before, I bet she is now. Can you imagine trying to convince people with that kind of power over you that you're not bonkers?" I spoke as a way to steel myself against the discomfort of being in the small, windowless room.

It didn't matter. No one paid attention to me anyway. LaSalle lifted an ice pick.

"Look at this," he said to Frank.

"The bastards."

"What?" I was afraid of the answer.

LaSalle brought it over for me to see. In minimal light, it was difficult to distinguish anything special about it, other than its sharpness.

"Look at the tip," he said, shining a beam on it. The last half-inch had flecks of dried blood. He returned it to its place near another metal tray.

The tiny wound in my arm throbbed. "Oh, God, was that what they used on me?"

"We'll have to see," said the detective.

"Hey, Henry, look what I found," said Frank. He held out a scalpel covered with old blood.

"Oh, God. Was that what he used on Mae?" Indignation sprouted from my discomfort. "He tortured his own mother?"

"People torture people everywhere," Frank's gorgeous voice rendered the words even creepier.

"Yeah, but this? And Josh?" I said. "The guy's a vegetarian. He's worried about how they treat the cows on his mother's farm."

That got nasty laughs from both of them.

"Some animal activists care more for ferrets than people," LaSalle murmured. "Sasha, why don't you look around for a few more minutes, see if anything jolts your memory. Just speak into the recorder so we have it for later. Okay?"

"Sure." I did as he asked, but nothing new came, or at least nothing of which I was aware.

I stood, now silent, by the gurney.

LaSalle noticed me, cleared his throat and spoke with a tenderness that hinted at something else. "Well, I think you've gone through enough for one day." He stroked my hair with a parent's gentleness. "How about I stop by the hotel later? We can talk then."

Glad to be released, I agreed.

LaSalle spoke into a microphone. A short time later an officer appeared at the door.

"I'll take you back to Clovis," he said, eyeing me with concern.

"Hey, Sasha, could you do me a favor?" LaSalle said.

"What?"

"Stay in your room. Just for tonight."

"That shouldn't be a problem." I wanted to be done with this. "Tell me why."

"Think about it. Whoever did this has no idea you've led us here. They have no idea you're even free. Those are powerful little secrets."

"Okay, I'll hide."

"Consider it police work," he said. "I'll call you later. Three rings, stop, one ring, stop and then you answer."

"Do we really need a code?" I shook my head. "I feel like Nancy Drew."

"It fits. You're an unofficial detective," he said.

"Henry, this classy lady deserves better than that," said Frank. "She should be deputized your right-hand man."

FORTY-EIGHT

ALTHOUGH I'D SPENT the past twenty-four hours mostly alone, it hadn't felt that way. My thoughts had been crowded with demons of despair, fear, and fury. Though my body ached, my soul was sicker. I filled the tub, then remembered I wasn't supposed to get my wounds wet until they stopped oozing. But I needed to be clean, to strip away the physical and metaphysical grime of my experience.

I tried to maneuver myself into the hot water without wetting my ankles or wrists. It didn't work. And, I wanted soap anyway. Lots and lots of soap.

After the bath, I showered. My face screamed with the heat of the water. The blisters popped, leaving raw skin underneath. With each stab of pain and inconvenience, I vowed to get even with Josh. Dressing was difficult. I chose the easiest outfit, a grungy sweat suit.

Three knocks at my door, stop. One knock, stop.

I opened it, expecting LaSalle. Abel King stood in his place, holding a Blake's bag.

"Don't stand in the light," he said.

"I suppose Detective LaSalle told you what happened."

"Yep." He unpacked the food. French fries, green chile cheeseburgers, chocolate milkshakes. It smelled magnificent.

"Thanks," I said, picking up a handful of fries.

"My pleasure."

I ate. He watched. I ate some more.

"What do you think about all of this?" I said. "Everything that's happened?"

"It's a mess," he said, his voice crestfallen. "No matter what, people I love are going to get hurt. There's no way to avoid it."

"Why would Josh do this?"

"I have no idea. Up until he kidnapped you, I would've sworn he wasn't capable of it. Never in a million years."

"You didn't have a clue? Nothing?"

"Like I said, it's a mess." King got up. "I'd best get going."

"You just came by to drop off the food?"

"That. And to make sure you're all right." He looked at my unmanaged wrists. "You need anything else?"

"I don't think so."

He went to the door.

"Mr. King, I'm sorry," I said.

"Whatever for?"

"For all of this."

He nodded. "Me, too, Ms. Solomon. Me, too."

I finished dinner, then slumped onto the bed, television remote in hand. Twenty minutes later, the phone rang its coded jingle.

"Hello?"

"Sasha? This is Henry. Are you up for a visit?"

"I've already had one."

"Abel told me. He said you'd cleaned up, too."

"Yeah."

"I'll be there in five minutes. The code's two knocks, stop, then repeat."

"Got it." I threw away the detritus from my meal and waited.

His deliberate tap-tapping came soon thereafter.

"How are you doing?" said LaSalle, handing me a brown lunch bag. In it were three miniature bottles of Glenlivet, a roll of adhesive tape, gauze, and ointment.

"I figured you could use the booze," he said. "And a new round of bandaging."

"Thank you." I set the bottles in a row on my worktable. "I didn't think you could buy alcohol on Sundays in this beautiful town."

"You can't." He pulled out a chair, straddled it. "I've had those around the house for a while, waiting for a special occasion. I figure you being alive counts."

I went to the dressing area to get a plastic cup.

"I'm thinking this isn't a social call," I said, opening the first bottle.

"It's not."

"What brings you here?" I poured while asking.

"A couple of things." LaSalle picked up the medical supplies, motioned for me to extend an appendage. "First of all, I want someone to stay here with you."

So much for healing in solitude.

"I don't think that's necessary," I said.

"I do."

"Really?"

"Yes."

"Okay." I didn't have energy to oppose him. Not tonight.

"Good. I'll call Officer Doyle in a minute," he said. "You'll like him."

The detective wrapped my left wrist then started on the right. His firm touch had a sensual quality. I blushed and then realized what he'd said.

"You want a man to stay with me?"

"I think it'd be wise."

"A man."

"He's cuter than a button," said LaSalle.

"Detective, I'm not in the mood for love here. I need sleep."

"And I need you safe." He'd moved on to my ankle, balancing my foot on his thigh.

"I need me safe, too."

"I'm glad you feel that way," he said; his tone stole an ounce of pleasure from the scotch. "Here's the situation as it stands. No one has seen Josh since last night. Mae's truck is back at her house, but that's it. No one's around." He picked up my other foot. "Same is true at Charlene's place. Travis is out of town. We knew about that. But Charlene's nowhere to be found."

"Any theories about why they've all conveniently disappeared?" I said.

"Not yet."

"Lovely."

"I don't think I told you. We found Becky Tan. She's in Singapore at her mom's." LaSalle still held my foot in his hands, though he'd finished with the Florence Nightingale routine. "After her visit with you, she started driving west. Didn't stop till she hit L.A. She told police in Singapore she couldn't stand being in the country of her husband's murder for one more minute."

"I don't blame her." I took a drink of the scotch. I liked LaSalle's hands on me.

"Apparently a Buddhist monk in California told her he would start praying for Colonel Tan and that his soul would be all right."

"At least she won't have to worry about that any more, poor woman," I said, thinking about our last talk. "Somebody ought to tell her about what happened to me."

"You won't believe it." He stroked my leg. "Actually, you probably will. When they told her you were missing, she said she knew it and that you'd be okay."

"I bet she said Colonel Tan told her where I was."

"Pretty much," he said.

"Did she say he was watching over me or something like that?"

"Not that I know of," he said.

"What about her charming brother?"

LaSalle looked down at his hands, my leg, and stopped abruptly.

I lowered my foot.

"Cho?" I said.

"We still haven't found him." The detective took a crumpled tissue from his pocket and blew his nose. "I don't think he's involved in your kidnapping. But he probably shot out Mae's windows."

"Why would he do that?"

"The man has a lousy temper. He probably decided to take things into his own hands."

"Yeah, like Roc Johnson," I said.

"We've been watching him, Sasha." LaSalle sighed. "The chief was none too pleased with the report I made." He stared at my left leg. "Bandage looks crooked on that foot. I'd better redo it."

Whatever his motivation, I assented.

"If Roc's up to something, we can't prove it yet." He unwound the gauze. "More important than us, Abel is watching him. Roc won't cross Abel."

"What do we do now?" I wanted more scotch, but not enough to disengage from LaSalle's ministrations.

"That's what I wanted to talk to you about."

I reached for the second bottle, made a show of opening it. "Lay it on me."

"Mae's coming home tomorrow. We've let it leak to one person who we think is involved. We think it'll flush out Josh, too." He was stroking my leg again and noticed it. "Ah, what the heck?" He lifted my other leg and caressed that one as well.

"Ummm," I said, eyes closing.

"Sasha, we want you to go over there tomorrow morning. Tell Mae you heard she was back and that you want to make amends. Between her release and your reappearance, chances are someone is going to panic and do something dumb."

"What happens if something goes wrong? How do I know I'm going to be safe? Are you going to storm the house?"

I moved my legs. Had he been trying to preempt my objections with tenderness?

LaSalle scooted his chair close to mine. "Listen to me," he said. "No one is going to hurt you again. Mae's place is bugged top to bottom. We'll have a full crew across the street monitoring your every breath." His eyes met mine. "Frankly, I thought you'd like to help us nail whoever did this to you."

"You must be pretty desperate, involving civilians," I said, my face hot.

"Not desperate. Impatient."

We sat there, across from each other. So close we could feel the other's breath. LaSalle reached out and gently touched my cheek.

"I don't want you to do this if you're scared," he said. "But you've got to believe me. I won't let anything happen to you."

I took his hand in mine, and whispered, "I'll do it."

"You will?"

"I will."

"Okay."

"Okay, then." I drained the second scotch, opened the third, and drank straight from the little bottle. I wiped my mouth with the back of my hand.

LaSalle rested his hand on my knee.

In a stronger voice, one filled with resolve, I said, "I'll do it."

FORTY-NINE

OFFICER DOYLE WAS Bob fifteen years before I'd met him. Handsome, full head of hair the color of hazelnut shells. His body slim and fit. A wedding band gleaming on his clean, manicured hand.

He'd settled in the cushy chair next to my worktable, a thick book in his lap. It had one of those obvious science fiction covers—aliens and sexy women. Doyle wore plaid socks on his unshod feet, which were propped up on the bed in front of him.

We didn't talk much; it was after eleven.

I winced, remembering my PR plan corrected but sitting in the computer waiting for a final printout. Sighing, I turned on the laptop and hooked it up to the printer. As it chugged away, I reproofed the pages.

Some of my recommendations might raise a few eyebrows—the chief one being the use of the old Clovis hotel to create the *Clovis UFO-Human Impact Museum* (CUHIM for short). The building would become a repository of information about how abductees and UFO witnesses had been treated by the government, their families, and friends since their experiences. We'd focus on what their lives had been like before and after their encounters. The approach would be different enough from the Roswell museum—complementary to, not competing with, its more famous cousin. The combo would create a UFO corridor for tourists, one that could draw an audience to both cities.

If it took off, we could add a "whistle blower" component. The paranoia aspect would attract the conspiracy crowd. I also had written in a method to exploit the Internet, using kids from the community college to research and disseminate information to the right sites.

And my pièce de résistance: helping develop a new field in therapeutic counseling—one that could benefit the community college and maybe Eastern New Mexico University in Portales. A fledgling program devoted to working with abductees and those who'd had close encounters.

Overall, it was a strong, professional plan with lots of opportunities to take action in a cohesive, step-by-step approach. Each of the components could exist independent of the others. If one part was too difficult to implement, it could be left until later. I was proud of my work, proud of the innovation in spite of everything that had happened since I'd gotten the assignment.

The more I thought about it, the more I wanted a consultant role. Rather than being in Clovis for months or years on end, I'd train others to do the grunt work. I'd be the brains, make the bigger money, and scare up other projects around the state.

When the last page fell from the printer, I handed the plan to Doyle.

"Can you make sure this gets to the Chamber tomorrow morning?" I said.

"Sure," he said.

Work done, I closed the laptop lid and turned off the light over my bed. Doyle turned off the lamp he'd been using and snapped on a mini one he'd attached to his book. I wondered if he would lie down in the bed once I was asleep. Silly question. His job was to guard me.

My job was to worry about the morning.

FIFTY

"EXCUSE ME, Ms. Solomon?"

I grunted out of my dream, drowsy and grumpy with too little sleep.

"What time is it?" I said.

"Nine," Doyle said. "We need to head over at ten. Would you like me to order some breakfast?"

"Sure." I sat up, more awake. "Are you coming to this?"

"I'll drive you, then get out of sight."

While he ordered food, I dressed in the bathroom.

What does someone wear to a set-up? Black pants, shirt, heels? Leather suspenders and a gun strap? I settled for jeans and a summer sweatshirt that Mae had given me a few years back.

The coded knock at the door transformed the butterflies in my stomach into rocks. Doyle motioned for me to hide in the dressing area. I peeked around the corner. Frank stood at the entrance with a bag of food in one hand and a salute in the other. He didn't come in.

For a few minutes, Doyle and I ate in silence. Greasy, fatty, salty fast food. I took a third biscuit and dipped it in coagulated gravy, making sure to get as many of the miniscule pieces of sausage as possible. Our plastic silverware met at some hash browns.

Doyle said, "Either you're nervous, or you love this stuff."

"I've never done anything like this before. You know, set up a friend."

"You're doing the right thing," he said. "Just act natural."

"Yeah, right."

"As natural as you can." He took a bite. "If you get scared, just remember we have all kinds of people across the road, ready in a second's notice."

"How can you be there without Josh catching on?" I said.

"We've got a phone company van. One of the guys will be halfway up the pole, watching." Doyle wiped his mouth with a flimsy napkin. "Two or three will be in the van, listening. A couple of men will be stationed in the ditch near the house. They've been in position since before sunrise."

"You know all this for a fact?" I said.

"This isn't my first bust. If that's what you're talking about."

"Well, that's reassuring."

"Good," he said. "You want that last biscuit?"

I shook my head.

Doyle looked at his watch, took a bite. "It's about time. Are you ready?"

"As ready as I'm going to be. But…."

"What?"

"Shouldn't I wear a tape or a mike or something?" I said.

Two knocks, stop, then another, sounded at the door. Doyle gave me the hide-and-seek signal again. I complied.

"Where's the star of the show?" said LaSalle.

"Hiding."

"Sasha? You can come out."

I did and lost color with each step toward him. I regretted eating all that food.

"How are you doing?" he said.

"Groovy."

LaSalle assessed me with a critical look.

"Really?" he said.

"I was better before you came in."

"I have that effect on women."

It worked; I smiled.

He smiled.

"No, really, I'm feeling a little nervous," I said.

"You wouldn't be human if you didn't." He lifted my hand and inspected the wrist-job he'd done the night before. "These still hurt?"

"You must be magic. They're practically healed." This felt an awful lot like flirting.

"Good." Snap. He let my hand fall and was all business again. "I'm going to be in a van across from Mae's house."

"Great."

"No one's going to let you get hurt," he said.

"I don't want to blow it."

"You won't."

"Ask him about the mike," said Doyle.

"Don't I have to wear a tape recorder or something in case someone confesses?" I said.

"We've got it covered. Every room in that house is bugged. You can't be anywhere without us hearing and recording. It'll be fine."

"Marvy."

LaSalle put his hands on my shoulders, solid and strengthening. He bent his knees until our eyes were flush.

"Sasha, focus on what they did to you and to Colonel Tan." He wouldn't let me look away. "Remember how much Mae's depending on you. That should be enough for any of your doubts."

"Mae's going to be so hurt by this," I said. "I feel like I'm betraying her."

"We don't know who betrayed her yet, but it wasn't you. You're going to save her skin." He squeezed my shoulders for emphasis. "Got it?"

I nodded.

"Okay. Come on," he said. "It's party time."

FIFTY-ONE

THE SKY WAS BLUE, the wind was blowing, and the trains escorted the beginning of a new workweek. We got to Mae's too quickly. I didn't even have a good opening line, a convincing reason for coming to her place. Doyle dropped me off behind a clump of trees at the end of the driveway. No one from the house would see the car or its departure…if anyone was even looking.

I took my time walking up the graveled path, reluctant to rush into this drama. Evidence of the violence done to Mae's windows glittered on the ground, reflecting sunlight, but the house looked as it had the day I met Travis. The new windows, still marked with their manufacturer's labels, glistened. My noisy approach set off the dogs, barking and yipping beyond the front door. I could hear Mae telling them to be quiet, restraining them.

At the door, I paused, looked around to see if I could spot the listening device. LaSalle said they'd put bugs in every room. Did that include the front porch? I rang the doorbell, set off a new round of doggie cacophony.

Mae opened the door, her face two years older than a week ago. Surprise first, then disdain sculpted her features.

"Sasha," she said, the bulge in her cheeks pumping where she bit back the anger. "You look like hell."

"Mae, we need to talk."

"I don't know what about." She stood at the entrance, blocking my way.

"About who told the police about your abductions. About how I think it ended up in the newspaper." I lowered my voice. "And I think I was abducted by the same crew who got you."

"Why should I believe you?" She spat onto the porch. "After what you put me through, I can't believe you have the gall to come to my door wanting to talk. I should let these dogs bite the crap out of you."

"No need to mince words, Mae. Say what you really feel." I gave her a half-smile.

"You're a piece of work, Sasha," she said, shaking her head. "You've got some nerve."

"Let me come in, Mae. Let's talk." I wanted to get into the house, to be sure that the guys, whoever they were, could hear every word.

"What are you doing in Clovis anyway?" she said. "I thought you'd gone home." Suspicion replaced the initial thaw.

"I've been here all along, Mae."

"Don't lie to me. Theo said you went home. Tail between your legs."

"No—" I stopped myself. Confrontation wouldn't get me into her house.

"Oh, what the hell," she said, holding the door open and pulling the dogs away from it as best she could.

The house's banal exterior didn't reflect the inside's eccentricity. Upon entering, I remembered some of the reasons I cared so deeply for Mae. Her love of learning, her eclectic world view. Books covered surfaces like scholarly dust. Casual, abundant. Modern art—paintings and sculptures—peeked through whatever open areas remained. A computer with a big-screen monitor took up an entire table in the living room. Crushed paper overflowed the wastebasket next to the desk. Reams rested on the couch in the indentations left by the dogs.

An open kitchen overlooked a living room with one

rounded partition and lots of windows. Beyond the house was the walled-in backyard, greening now. The swimming pool remained ugly with neglect. The bright batch of kids' toys had been thrown without care to one side of the area near the far wall. Kids hadn't played with them in some time.

"You working on a new project?" I pointed to the papers.

"I'm going to write my story. About being taken into protective custody and those jackasses in Albuquerque. It's going to be about the importance of family. That's something you could learn more about, Sasha. Family." She worked her lower jaw forward, back again, like she was playing with her dentures—only she didn't have any. "My daughter was with me every minute she could be. When's the last time you talked to your mom?"

"That's low, Mae."

She shrugged her shoulders, walked into the kitchen and poured herself a glass of water. "Charly told me about how you leaked my abduction story to the paper so you could get hired for the PR job here." She took a sip, dumped the rest in the sink. "She says it worked, you got it. Was it worth it, Sasha? Was it worth our friendship?"

Stunned, I sat motionless.

"Humph. That's what I thought." The satisfaction in Mae's voice jolted me into speech.

"You can't believe that," I said. "I'd never betray your trust." I joined her in the kitchen. "I don't have the job yet. I turned in the proposal this morning."

She washed dishes with sharp motions, the fury barely held in check.

"Mae, have you actually read the article in the paper? Or talked to the police about how they found out?"

"I don't need to."

"Oh, right. You've never let me lie to myself." Frustration permeated my words, making them difficult to utter. "Why are you determined to ignore the truth? Charlene's the one who got you committed. She's the one who called the police and the newspaper."

"Don't be vindictive. She did no such thing," said Mae.

"How do you know that?"

"Because of her shock when the police took me away. Because of countless things that a mother can see in her child, if their relationship is anything to speak of."

Another punch to my emotional gut. Mae knew what she was doing.

"I'm not going to fight with you about your daughter," I said. "But I swear I didn't tell anyone about the abductions until after you'd been taken away."

"Well then, who did?"

"Josh? Theo? Charlene? Isn't it possible one of your little darlings let it slip without thinking?"

"None of them knew, Sasha. None of them. You were the only person I told," she said. "I didn't even trust my own kids. I had to go trust a stranger."

"I'm hardly a stranger," I said.

She shrugged her shoulders again.

"Where's the article, Mae? You've got to read that article."

"Charlene's got it for me somewhere."

"Sure she does."

"Is that what you came to say? If it was, we're done here. I won't have you blame my children for your mistakes." Her flinty expression saddened me, her face etched with such unhappiness.

"Get real, Mae. Do you think I'd sacrifice a sixteen-year friendship for some piss-ant job? You should know me better than that."

"I thought I did."

This was getting us nowhere. My mission didn't have to do with Mae's blame. I swallowed my ego long enough to ask, "Where's Josh?"

"What does Josh have to do with anything?"

He's a kidnapper and a murderer. That's what.

"Just tell me where he is," I said.

"He's back in California. Left last week." Mae's voice exuded exasperation. "Theo said Josh took off once things got tough. He's always had a weak stomach for trouble."

Theo, the source of all erroneous information. Josh and Theo, what a team. Maybe Charlene was innocent and her brothers were the culprits. I hoped the guys who were listening realized what was going on.

"I know for a fact he was here on Saturday night," I said.

"And how do you know that?"

He gave me coffee laced with drugs and kidnapped me.

What if the police weren't the only ones listening to our conversation? Josh could be in another room, eavesdropping. What was I supposed to do? This was where the script hadn't been written yet, where LaSalle and the others hadn't given me a clue.

There was a knock at the door. The dogs' ears sprang up. The barking and yowling commenced.

"Now what?" Mae's annoyance prevented her from containing the dogs. They jumped on the door, forcing it closed even as she opened it. "What do you want?"

"Sorry to bother you, ma'am." I heard a man's voice, as sensual as a fresh fig. Frank, dressed in a phone man's uniform, motioned for Mae to come outside. He didn't acknowledge my presence. I took it for a good sign that they'd heard what was going on and had decided to intervene.

"Sasha, I'll be right back," Mae yelled, following him. The dogs went with her, leaving the house quiet.

Except for a single thump in the room right next to mine.

FIFTY-TWO

I WANTED TO SHOUT, "Hey, guys, come and get him!"

Bluster, wrath, and uncertainty vied for supremacy in my heart. Should I storm in, knowing the police would follow close behind and nab the SOB? Or should I wait for a signal? LaSalle had urged me to remember what had been done to me. I did, with an immediate clarity that reddened my face and made my pulse thud in my ears.

Caution be damned. I strode to the door, turned the knob. Then, before he could run, I hurled it open with such force it crashed into the opposite wall, surprising both my quarry and me.

"You're not Josh," I said, searching the room for an open window.

"What are *you* doing here?" the man yelled, dropping his book. I knew that voice. In a minute or two, I'd figure out how. The surprise on his face had nothing to do with the quickly opened door and everything to do with me, *Sasha,* opening it.

"I could ask the same of you." I stalled, searching my mental Rolodex to remember where we'd met. Breathing fast, I backed into the open doorway, observing him, assessing my surroundings. Big wooden desk, laden bookcases, decanters of amber liquors, maroon leather chairs with matching ottomans. Light warmed the room through a set of glass doors at the far wall. I stared at them, wondering if someone—Josh—had escaped when I'd turned the knob.

"Your question is immaterial. You've got no right to be

here, whomever you are." The man had regained his composure, spoken his words with precision. On the table next to his chair were lines of white powder, a tightly rolled dollar bill.

"Having a morning toot?" I said.

He squatted to pick up the book, grunting as if in pain, and then stopped, leaving the book where it lay on the floor. He straightened his plump form and with a voice both unctuous and filled with malevolence, came toward me, saying, "I do believe it's time for you to go, Ms. Solomon."

He knew my name!

Where had I heard his voice?

He came closer. The odor tipped me off and the way he moved confirmed it. The short alien, the male, the one who'd threatened me with the scalpel. The voice belonged to a caller who had tried to intimidate me on the phone a few days before. Theo.

"You sonofabitch!" I shoved him back from the door, wanting to ram his head into the floor; hoping the bricks had the solidity to do real brain damage.

"What are you doing? How dare you."

"Keep on talking, mister. You're digging your own grave," I whispered.

"You're supposed to be dead! Get out of here!"

I shoved him again, the rage filling me with a need to rip out his oily black hair in handfuls.

"Wait a minute. Wait a minute. Can't we can talk about this?" He'd switched into the negotiator.

It might have worked in court but I wanted blood.

"We could have talked about it before you strapped me to that gurney." I pushed him toward a corner near one of the glass display bookcases.

"You've got it all wrong. Josh and Charly planned everything."

"That's right. Keep squealing, pig."

Trapped, his back to the wall, he actually snarled at me. I thought he was preparing to bite. Theo barely topped my height. I could take him out, have him singing soprano for months. He lunged at me. Never in my life had I thrown a punch, but I did now. His belly was soft, but meaty enough to hurt my already throbbing wrist and the top of my hand. In spite of the pain, the gush of air he expelled made me want to punch him again. And he smelled awful.

I pulled my hand away for a second hit. He bulldozed me backward with his extra weight, and with a beefy fist, smashed me on the collarbone. My gasp of agony shook the windows. Distracted for only a second, I found my opportunity to retaliate and held out my leg. He tripped, but not before grabbing behind my back and pulling my braid with his entire body mass as he went down.

With a thunk, I landed on top of him, my head flexed at an awkward angle as he held onto my hair. My hands sought his wiry locks. Ah, but his hands were occupied with my braid. I reached around until I found his ears. Lifting his head, I slammed it down onto the floor. His hold on me lessened.

"Where is he? Where's Josh?" I did it again, panting.

"Let go of my head," Theo demanded. Everything about this man—his tone, his size, his stench—made me want to hurt him.

"You tell me where he is," I said.

"After you let go."

He was in no position to bargain. I suppose he needed a little reminder. I yanked his ears harder and tried to push his face into the bricks. He whimpered, relaxing for a pause, then attempted to buck me off. I bent his neck back to let him speak.

"Did you say something, pig?"

"He's in the milk house."

The choice was split-second. Stick with this bag of slime or find Josh?

No contest.

Josh had kidnapped me; the physical urge to hurt him deep and rough overwhelmed me. I let Theo's head smash to the floor, saving the rest of my ire for the real culprit.

"Don't even think of getting up," I said, my voice a hiss. "The police have the house surrounded. You're dead meat, pig. I hope you rot in hell for what you did to me and your mother."

I heard movements in the living room. A man yelling my name. I jumped up, rubbed my collarbone, and opened the glass doors leading to the backyard. Scaling the high wall, I vaulted and landed hard, my ankles screamed. Pain didn't matter. I wanted Josh for myself.

In a crouch, I ran through the alleys between corrals. My thoughts seethed, driving my legs forward. I wanted to kick his face in. Below me, a group of cows rambled in one of the tunnels on their way to being milked. I jumped into the throng, bending lower to hide amid the big, warm bodies. My face butt level, my feet squishing in fresh dung, I pushed near the front of the line, guarding my cover. Then it was up a ramp, through large garage-like metal doors and into the washing area.

Cold water hit me from every side. My mouth opened to cuss and then closed on liquid-born hay and dirt. I kept my body low. The herd followed the lead cows into either side of a room higher than the work area. Each cow meandered to her stall, guided into position by a long, mechanized metal rod. Two men in rubber boots and aprons reached up to attach suction cups to the cows' udders.

The workers began at the far end of the line, one on each side, progressing in my direction. I slipped inside the holding area away from the men's view and scurried to the cows that had already been hooked up. Watching until both men's backs were turned, I squeezed through the iron bars down onto the floor, and ran with all my might, away from them and into one of the tiled hallways.

From my tour with Travis, I knew the layout of the milk house—the location of the office, where the workers took their lunch break. What I didn't know was where Josh might be.

I shivered. Through an open door leading outside, I heard car doors slam, saw men running. A big business by New Mexico standards, the dairy farm had more than one hundred employees. I slowed my gait and tried to look like one of them. Fat chance. How many sopping wet women traipsed through the building daily? Tiptoe soft, I rounded a corner and saw a uniformed policeman show his badge to a worker. The man he spoke with shrugged and followed him out of the building. I headed down another hallway and ended up in the machine room.

Josh could be anywhere.

At one of the side entrances men milled about, flighty and nervous. Though most probably worried more about an immigration raid than a police bust, their restless energy served my needs. The more employees who were distracted, the less likely they'd be to notice anything out of the ordinary. Since I'd entered the milk house, I'd been concerned that someone might sound an alarm if he saw me. With that, my plan to squash Josh like a bug would evaporate.

I could smell the milk cooling area and moved toward it. When Travis had shown the room to me, I'd been interested in the windows atop three feet of tiles. I'd wanted to ask, *why bother?* We'd watched the two men work in the room, hip waders on, the sour stench of old milk strong even through the glass. They cleaned the milk filters, flushing them with water and disinfectant. Pale white liquid ran down a large drain in the center of the room. Lining the wall on the opposite side of the cleaning area towered seven stainless steel rounded doors with matching locks resembling giant steering wheels. If I were a kid, I'd pretend the doors were in a submarine or spaceship, designed to withstand intense pressure from the other side.

Today, a woman stood alone in the white room, her back to the glass. From the way she moved her arms and hands, I figured she was talking to herself, the monologue passionate. I strained to hear her. My skin goosebumped when I succeeded. Charlene. Her voice was the same as the one I'd feared two nights before. How could I not have known?

Perhaps she sensed me; I don't know. She turned. In the instant before I ducked, I caught a glimpse of her eyes, half-crazy with cruelty. Her long brown hair, the color of mud, hung in screwy ringlets around her oval face. Sane, she'd been pretty enough with her peach skin, pink lips, and high cheekbones. At this moment, my friend's lovely, lying, and deadly daughter had a complexion the color of tallow.

I sank farther, back to the tiles, thinking about my next move. It felt like I'd met Charlene a century ago, that the dinner at the Cotton Patch had been during another lifetime. What should I do? Should I find LaSalle and his team and tell them what I knew? Should I—?

Her scream made me flinch.

"You're going to drown, you idiot!" she said.

I peeked at her. She faced the tanks, her rail-thin body swaying to an internal rhythm. Frightening as hell.

Common sense struggled with the urge to shove Charlene's head into the lock on the milk tank. I could stuff it right through, making a steel noose for her.

No, I need a weapon.

Fit, wiry, and muscular, with at least five inches over mine, she'd be able to rout me in body-to-body fighting. I had to surprise her. Plus, the idea of a weapon—hard and dangerous—appealed to the part of me that wanted to knock the living daylights out of her.

On my hands and knees, I crawled to the next room. Travis

had pointed it out, saying the employee break area was popular with his workers. I let myself in, careful to make no noise. Vending machines filled with snacks and soda pop made money for the boss and satisfied his minions. A bag of potato chips wasn't what I had in mind; it'd hardly flatten Charlene. The table held a bowl of apples. Maybe I could stun her with a well-aimed fruit. On the counter, the coffee machine dripped with a new pot; I could throw that at her. There was a plate with nondairy creamer—funny that—and a sink. I looked for a knife in the basin, but found a heavy wrench, wet and beautiful.

I'd only have a few minutes before the police found us in this corner of the milk house. I wanted to use my time well.

Profound, body-filling breath. Armed, I walked upright, in control and suffused with the intent to hurt, to maim the woman who'd done so much harm. Yet when I saw her again, the miniscule leashes restraining my impulses vanished.

I kicked the door open and screeched, "You pathetic piece of—"

"Sasha? You're supposed to be dead!" Charly gaped. In an instant, she caught herself and charged at me.

"Don't you wish," I said, taunting her.

We slammed into each other. She backed away, breathless and bewildered.

"What did Colonel Tan ever do to you?" I said, readying for another attack.

She answered, her nonchalance sickening, "The slant? Better dead than alive."

I stopped with the atrocity of her words. Then shook my head to free it from her insanity.

"You can't be serious," I said. "That's no reason to kill anyone."

"It's the best reason of all."

"Okay, okay." I held my hands up in a fake truce. "But what

does any of this have to do with Mae? How could you turn
on your own mother?"

"You fucking idiot," she said.

The words sizzled for a split second, then she made her move.

FIFTY-THREE

SLOW-MO: CHARLENE, arms pumping, hands balling in fists, lunged. Head bent downward to propel me into a wall. I aimed the wrench low to crack her skull in two. I could taste the motion, starting with her chin, and moving up to her brain. She perceived the danger and changed her tactic midstream, stopping two feet from me. Without strain, she caught my arm, twisted it hard behind my back. I hollered in pain, my injured collarbone breaking in another dozen places, my wrist bleeding again. Too much. My ankle buckled. I took her down with me.

"My *mother?*" she whispered, her peppered breath acrid in my face. "You don't know anything." A drop of her saliva hit my upper lip. "More like daddy's little whore. He forgot everything but her little pussy." She kinked my arm with more force. "You think I'm gonna let her get away with that?"

"Let go of me, Charlene."

A sharp, short laugh emitted through her barely opened mouth. It was a victorious sound; she thought she had me.

Not yet. I seized a wad of her hair with my free hand and twisted it with all the fury that had built inside me since I'd first arrived in Clovis. Shocked, she slackened her grip. We rose in unison, a terrible ballet. I liberated my aching arm, planted my feet, and swung.

Charlene dodged the blow. Then laughed again.

"We'll take you out. Slaughter you with the cows, you filthy kike."

Whatever humanity I had, deserted me. I charged, head lowered like a bull, and aimed for her midriff. She fell but recovered her stance with amazing agility.

"That the best you've got, Jew bitch?"

The biggest breath I've ever taken. A roar that reverberated and bounced wall-to-wall. With both hands I clutched the wrench, raised it as high as I could and surged toward her.

I sensed someone behind me, but didn't care. Something grabbed at my weapon and missed. A hard shove in my back destabilized my attack. Unable to stop the momentum, I flew past Charlene and slammed the wrench into the wall beyond her. The impact created a five-inch hole in the tiles. Dust and shards hit me as I collapsed to the ground.

Oh, no.

No fall was going to stop me! On all fours, I turned and prepared for my next assault. The wrench hefted for another blow, I rose to my knees. And stopped cold.

Three uniformed policemen grappled with Charlene, all arms and legs, while she struggled to get free.

"Let go of me, you bastards!" She bellowed nonstop vitriol. "Theo will slap you with lawsuits faster than you can spit. Police brutality! I want my lawyer!"

LaSalle rolled his eyes in response and sauntered over to me. He stood by my side and tossed a bored look her way. In silence, we watched the policemen force Mae's daughter out of the room.

"Have a seat," he said, taking the wrench from my white-fingered grasp.

I sat.

"You having fun?" LaSalle joined me on the floor, legs outstretched.

"Not really."

"No, I suppose not." He smacked the wrench against his open hand, shook his head. "What were you planning to do? Kill her?"

"I don't know. I just wanted to hit her really, really hard."

"I bet." His shoulder touched mine. I didn't move, didn't want to break the connection. "You decided to take them all on your own, huh?"

"I wasn't thinking straight." I held my head up with my hands. "They were the two aliens. Charlene and Theo." I cleared my throat. "I don't know where Josh fits in."

"Neither do I." He leaned into me. "Theo's been squealing, though. He's got a pretty vivid imagination about his sibs' involvement. Somehow, he's totally innocent."

"You can't believe that."

"The two of them are guilty as sin." LaSalle smiled, his eyes more amused than I'd seen in days. "Who taught you to fight?"

I kneaded my forehead with my palms, winced at the pain flowing from foot to neck.

"Hey, it worked," I said.

Nodding again, LaSalle turned the wrench in his hands, smacked it a few more times.

"Charlene's a big girl," he said. "Looked to me like she'd overpowered you." He held up the tool. "This here? This was a clear case of self-defense." Not waiting for a response, he stood and extended his hand to help me up. "Come on. We need to talk."

I held back, surveying the room where I'd almost become a murderer. In the quiet aftermath of Charlene's departure, there was a pinging sound, not dripping water or milk. It stopped, started again, intentional, in a pattern.

LaSalle and I looked at each other.

"You don't think—" I said.

LaSalle was out the door, calling for help, before I could finish my sentence.

Alone, I searched for the sound, my gaze alighting on the milk storage tanks.

"Josh? Are you in one of these?" I said.

The sound continued, a steady pattern. I thought I heard something else. A voice perhaps. LaSalle returned with one of the dairy workers I'd seen in the room on my tour with Travis. The man listened, then pointed to a tank with the number six on it. He and LaSalle worked the wheel until the thick door opened.

"Dios mio," said the man.

LaSalle reached in and assisted a battered, oxygen-deprived Josh when he stumbled out onto the tiled floor. His face was bloodied, bruised. A purple and red mass swelled around an eye, forcing it closed.

"Get a doctor!" said LaSalle, who then left to find one himself.

"I'm fine," said Josh in a faint rasp. He sat, his back propped against the tank's open door. He saw me. "You're alive."

"I'm alive."

"They told me they'd killed you." He coughed, cringing with the pain and effort.

"Nah. They just wished they had." I moved closer to him. "Why, Josh? Why did you kidnap me?"

"I didn't want to, Sasha. When I left my California number, I hoped you'd figure out something was wrong." His gaze turned inward. "By then, they'd told me about the murder, about staging the abductions." He whispered, "I hoped you wouldn't come with me. I didn't know what to do once you accepted. Couldn't you tell something was wrong?"

"I thought you might be in trouble."

"Yeah, no kidding." Josh wiped his nose on his sleeve. "They had a gun on me when I called. And then at Denny's, they were in the parking lot with guns on us both."

"Why didn't you tell me when we were in the truck? Why didn't you take another route? Or go to the police station?"

"I was scared, Sasha. They kept me at gunpoint ever since they told me about the murder. I couldn't believe it. My own brother and sister." He coughed again, "And to do that to Mom."

LaSalle had returned while Josh was talking. He stood in the doorway, listening.

"They're absolutely crazy," said Josh.

"You didn't know what they were going to do to Sasha in that shed?" said LaSalle.

Josh shook his head.

"Steve Cummings followed us all the way there, his lights off," he said. "He had a mammoth rifle in his front seat. When we got out there, I told them all I'd had enough, that they couldn't make me hurt you." He looked at me, then away. "Steve must have hit me with the rifle butt. I don't remember a thing until I woke up in the tank." He unfolded a clenched hand. "Thank God, I had this. You might not have even known I was here." He showed us a quarter.

Two paramedics came into the room.

"I was so scared they'd fill the tank," Josh said. "They were going to kill me, too."

"Not to worry," said LaSalle.

The emergency workers tended to Josh first, testing his reflexes, looking into his eyes with a penlight, gingerly touching his face.

A minute later, they attended to me.

"You might have a broken collarbone," one said. "We need to get you to the hospital."

"No thanks," I said.

"You need an x-ray."

"If it's broken, what can you do?"

"Tape it. Help minimize the pain."

"If I don't get it taped, what's the worst that can happen?" I said.

"It could grow back crooked. And it'll hurt more."

"I'll take my chances." I'd had enough of gurneys and restraints for a lifetime.

LaSalle put a bracing arm around Josh and said, "Why don't we all take a ride down to the station?" He appraised me with a long stare. "You okay?"

"I've been better but I'll live."

"Come on. I'll buy you a cup of coffee."

We walked through the tiled hallways, past the hushed stares of aproned and plastic-bedecked workers.

Outside, the sunlight shone in the flawless sky, bluer than it should have been. LaSalle guided us to his car.

"You're in real trouble, son," the detective said to Josh. "Even worse, if Sasha here decides to press charges."

"I know it," Josh said.

"This is where you're supposed to ask me for a lawyer," said LaSalle.

"I don't want one. I've got nothing to hide."

"You going to make it difficult for this young man?" LaSalle addressed the air above my head, acting as if he didn't care about the answer.

"Way I see it, there was a gun pointed at us in the parking lot," I said. "Another on the road to the shed." I shrugged. "As far as I'm concerned, Josh probably saved my life."

"I kind of thought you'd see it that way," said the detective with a wink that ran electric right through me.

FIFTY-FOUR

I BIT OFF A NAIL. Then another. A cup of crappy coffee in my hand, I sat in LaSalle's office and waited. It had been at least an hour since we'd arrived.

Eyes and brain searching for something to do, I noticed a clear Lucite box I'd not noticed before. I got up and peered into it. On a swatch of tan velvet lay a brass plaque with the inscription: *Congratulations on your retirement, Master Sergeant Henry LaSalle.* Several medals surrounded it, along with stripes from a uniform and a little green patch.

"Like my decorations?" said LaSalle. He crossed the distance between us, choosing to stand behind me. I could feel the warmth of his body against my back.

I tensed, swallowed.

"What are they?" I said.

He moved the hair from my neck and spoke, his lips not quite touching my skin.

"I took some risks, helped some people," he said.

"In the Army?"

"More or less."

"What's that mean?" I wanted him to clear his desktop and throw me down upon it.

"I worked in intelligence for a few years," he said.

I turned, my face an inch from his. "You were a spy?"

He rubbed his cheek against mine.

I closed my eyes, ready for a kiss.

"You lovebirds ought to close the door if you need privacy," said a smooth voice. Frank grinned at us from the doorway.

The intensity of the moment popped.

"Took you a little too long, Henry. We were all kind of wondering where you'd gone off to," the lawman teased. "You always were a bit slow."

"Can it, Frank," said LaSalle.

"Ouch, that hurt, Henry," he said, in mock pain. "Ms. Solomon, we've got a few final questions. Are you up to it?"

"Let's get it over with," I said.

Agent Frenth's absence blessed the gathering. LaSalle, speaking slowly and making sure he had eye contact, asked me to tell everyone what had happened from the moment I'd rung Mae's doorbell to spying Charlene in the cleaning area. I took the hint and told my story, minus the part about the wrench.

"Why didn't you wait for the police before going to the milk house?" The bald man's neutral tone played like he already knew what I'd say.

"I don't know. I guess I went sort of crazy."

"Pretty understandable, if you ask me," said Lew Mason.

Thank God the milk house hadn't been bugged.

"Can I ask you all a couple questions?" I said.

"Fire away," said LaSalle.

"Was Charlene tapping Mae's phone?"

"Why do you ask?" the bald man said.

"Seems like every time I called Mae, I got Charlene. At least in the beginning. And since I know they don't live together—"

"Call forwarding," said Frank.

"What?" I said.

"She got call forwarding—unbeknownst to her mother—and then forwarded all Mae's calls to her own house. Made it sound like she lived in the same place."

That explained a lot. More questions to ask, though I didn't look forward to the answers.

"Charlene called Mae her father's whore. Why would she say that?" I said.

"All the King kids have different mothers," said the bald man. "They're Damon's kids. He and Mae made a practice of finding and taking in his illegitimate offspring."

"And Charlene's angry about that?" I said.

"She thinks Mae forced Damon to take her away from her real mother. Of course the mom in question has helped fuel the fire." He frowned, reached a decision. "Theo's mom died in childbirth and he was given to an aunt who couldn't have cared less. As soon as Mae found out about Theo, she insisted on bringing him to the farm and treating him as her own."

"Damon was a smart man in everything but his own bed," said Frank. "Apparently he couldn't keep it in his pants."

"That was uncalled for," said LaSalle.

"Henry, you know it's true." Frank turned to me. "Theo, Charlene, Josh—they're the ones we know about. We think Cummings may have been a fourth, though why Damon didn't claim him is anybody's guess. In the case of Charlene, the mother was only too happy to get rid of her little baby. But Charlene must have heard a different story."

"How did Charlene find out?" I said.

"The mom contacted her," said LaSalle. "She lives in Lubbock. Had a case with Theo and put it all together."

"Oh, God. How horrible for Mae," I said.

No one spoke for a long time.

LaSalle finally broke the silence by thanking me for all I'd done. Around the table, each man did the same, told me how brave I'd been. We shook hands, nodded heads, spoke nothings I'd forget after a good night's sleep.

My car waited in the police parking lot; someone had transferred it there from the Denny's. As I drove out, Mae's pickup pulled in. I fought the urge to crawl under the dash, to hide from her and her new tragedy.

No need.

Unseeing, she tottered toward the door, a pallor to her face, a curve to her spine I feared might never straighten again.

FIFTY-FIVE

"IT'S OVER," LaSalle said, coming into my room several hours later. "The police in Lubbock found Colonel Tan's car parked in Theo's garage. There was enough blood in the back seat to condemn him for life."

"That's just plain stupid," I said. "Why would Theo keep all that stuff? He's a lawyer, for heaven's sake."

"I guess he didn't know what else to do with it. Maybe he was worried about his fingerprints being all over the car. I don't know yet." The detective shook his head, sat on one of the beds. "Charly and Theo are spending their time blaming each other. They've completely forgotten Josh."

I scrunched up next to him, curled my feet underneath me. My ankles hurt. I bumped into him as I changed position. He put his arm around me.

"In a weird way, I can understand the abduction thing. And Mae. But why kill Tan?" I said into his armpit. Amazing. He smelled of cinnamon, clove.

"I could say it was the wrong place and the wrong time, but that isn't quite accurate. Colonel Tan had two—no, three—things going against him that night. He loved looking at stars, he didn't know enough about our culture, and he was Asian." LaSalle stroked my hair. "If he'd stayed home or taken a different road, he'd be alive. If he hadn't been from a country that respects the authority of the military, and hadn't gone to see what Charly and Theo were up to, he'd be alive. If he hadn't been Asian, he'd be alive."

His lips brushed the top of my head. "His wife's story panned out."

"What's the deal with being Asian?"

"Naked bigotry." LaSalle let go of me. "Those kids suffer from one of the worst cases I've seen. Theo blames everything wrong in his life on *Chinks*. Charlene's missing out on Miss Clovis, nineteen seventy-five, was because of, have you guessed? *Chinks*. And Steve Cummings, he lost all his money in lousy investments. Who's to blame? *Chinks*. It makes me sick."

"It's still kind of weird they fixated on Asians, isn't it? There're what, like, five, in this whole town? It'd make more sense to be angry at Hispanics," I said.

"Well, Damon was pretty bitter about his World War II experiences. He probably passed that on to his kids."

"That's right. I remember Mae said something about the Bataan Death March."

LaSalle nodded.

"And Josh?" I said.

"Seems he escaped the hatred."

"Speaking of hatred, what about Cho? Did you ever find out why he came to the hotel that night?"

"No. But we haven't tried that hard." LaSalle sighed. "He'll turn up in Singapore in a few days—after his contact at the embassy in Arizona tells him about Charly and Theo. Frankly, I'm glad to have him out of my hair."

"What about Roc and Bud Johnson?"

"Abel's taking care of it."

"They bugged my room. And the hotel manager, was he in on it, too?" I began pacing.

"We're not going pursue it. Not unless you insist." LaSalle held my gaze. "In the grand scheme of things it didn't do any harm."

Sure, in the grand scheme it was a non-issue. In the little scheme of my life, of my privacy, it was a great big deal.

He watched me.

"Sasha, the case is solved. No one is going to bother you again," he said. "Whatever lousy judgment Roc and the others showed, it was related to the Base's safety—not you."

I leaned against the dresser, next to the TV. LaSalle got off the bed and stood in front of me, surrounded my legs with his own and held me tight.

"No one's going to bother you," he said. "You've got my personal guarantee."

"No one?"

"No one but me."

FIFTY-SIX

THE TROUBLE WITH religious people is they're not loose. That's all I'll say about Henry.

On second thought, I'll tell you this much. We slept together, fully clothed. I wanted more. He did, too.

I'd better get the job in Clovis.

I needed the money. I needed to figure out how I really felt about Bob. And I wanted to find out what could happen with Henry.

Before I left town the next morning, I called Mae's house. Josh answered.

"How are you doing?" I felt awkward, as if I'd caused all their family dysfunction.

"Not great," he said. "Marguerite's coming out for a few days."

"That's good." Pause. "How's Mae?"

"Bad. She's given up, Sasha. She says all her work, all her love was for nothing."

"God, I wish I could help her."

"I don't think she's ready for you yet."

"I don't imagine so." I let it hang until I was sure he meant it. "What about Travis? How's he taking it?"

"He got back last night. He's been over at the house, talking with Mom, helping her understand. He's a good man, Sasha," he said. "He's telling Mom not to blame you."

"Would you tell her I called? If it seems all right?" I said, my voice mousy.

"Sure, I will," he said. "And, Sasha?"

"Yes?"

"Thank you," Josh said. "I think one of us ought to say that to you." His breathing caught for a moment. "Thank you for forcing the truth to come out."

Good thing he couldn't see the tears in my eyes.

On the road a few minutes later, my head hurt with the pressure of unreleased emotion. There's a lot of beauty between Clovis and home, but I didn't notice a spot of it. My thoughts hung riveted on families, on mothers and daughters, on anger and resentment.

I hit Tramway Boulevard, the easternmost entrance to Albuquerque, a couple of hours past lunchtime. On an impulse, I took it, leaving the freeway to wind my way slowly to St. Kate's, nestled in a residential area near Presbyterian Kaseman Hospital.

Mom lay in her bed, sleeping fitfully. I kissed her brow.

Her eyes opened. "Sasha?"

"Hi, Mom."

"My love." She beamed at me, suffused with happiness. "Oh, how beautiful you are."

I hurt with the shock of her love.

She took my hand, kissed it, then closed her eyes, the smile still on her face. Without another word, she descended into calmer sleep. I waited until her breathing steadied.

"I love you, too," I murmured, then left.

Minutes later, I headed up the familiar dirt driveway to my little house. After getting out of the car, I sat on the hood for a minute, grateful to be home. One of the reasons I loved my place so much was its feel of wild privacy. Not rural like Clovis with its dairy farms and alfalfa fields. My refuge dwelled in the middle of untamed trees, interloping salt cedar, and volunteer grasses that seeded and reseeded themselves in sneeze-causing glory.

I slid off the hood and unlocked the door, expecting Leo with a snarky comment or two. Then remembered that I hadn't hallucinated under absolutely terrible stress. Perhaps the visions were finally cured. The thought stopped me midstep and I remembered how Mae had looked at the police station, the deadness to her once-spirited eyes. If I could have taken away her despair or lived with my worst visions, I'd have done it in a minute.

Josie, my landlord, had left a note about Leo on the kitchen table. *The cat's been moping since you left,* she'd written. *Won't eat much of his food.*

The house smelled stale. I walked into the bedroom and found my cat stretched across two pillows. He raised his head at my entry, then let it fall as if it were too heavy to hold up. I prepared myself for a "well, what took you so long?" or "finally remembered me, huh?"

Instead, he said nothing. His thick fur had lost its healthy sheen. He seemed sluggish, too quiescent. I went to him, worried. Patted his head and petted his back.

"What's the matter, boy? Are you sick?" I said.

He licked a paw with alarming listlessness. His weak purr stopped and started at random. I continued petting him, looking here and there for signs of kitty leukemia or AIDS. He nuzzled against my hand, purred with more enthusiasm.

From any other cat, this would be normal behavior. From Leo, it was a death knell.

I got up, ready to take him to the emergency clinic.

"What's the matter, Leo? You want me to call the vet?"

I couldn't bear this, not after all that had happened. I needed this cat, his warmth, his friendship, his dependable crustiness and independence. I threw myself on the bed and closed my eyes. Warm tears fell into my ears. I cried for Mae, for the Tans, for me.

Leo licked my cheek with his rough tongue, his old fishy

breath a welcome perfume. Opening my eyes, I looked into his yellow ones.

"Are you okay, kitty? Do you need a doctor?"

He stared right at me, blinked as if savoring the moment. And then in a gruff voice said, "Gotcha."

HARLEQUIN®
INTRIGUE®

WE'LL LEAVE YOU BREATHLESS!

If you've been looking for thrilling tales of
contemporary passion and sensuous love stories
with taut, edge-of-the-seat suspense—then
you'll love Harlequin Intrigue!

Every month, you'll meet six new heroes
who are guaranteed to make your spine tingle
and your pulse pound. With them you'll enter
into the exciting world of Harlequin Intrigue—
where your life is on the line
and so is your heart!

THAT'S INTRIGUE—
ROMANTIC SUSPENSE
AT ITS BEST!

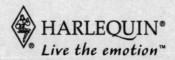

HARLEQUIN®
Live the emotion™

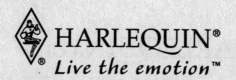

HARLEQUIN®
Live the emotion™

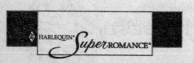